Disappearing Home

Disappearing Home

Deborah Morgan

Tindal
Street
Press

First published in 2012
by Tindal Street Press Ltd
217 The Custard Factory, Gibb Street,
Birmingham, B9 4AA
www.tindalstreet.co.uk

A CIP catalogue reference for this book is available
from the British Library

ISBN: 978 1 906994 32 7

Typeset by Tetragon
Printed and bound by CPI Group
(UK) Ltd, Croydon, CR0 4YY

For John, with love

I

When they first sent me out to steal I was ten years old. The bag bothered me most. It was dirty on the outside as well as the inside. With brown leather handles that were frayed down to white wire. They burned your skin if held for too long. Later, they told me I held it too high, like a bloody shield, and too far away from me when I walked with it. They said I held it like it was a disease. It's only soil. A bit of soil can be easily washed away. I was making it obvious. That was the last thing you did, make it obvious. That was stupid cos that's how you get caught and if you get caught you're on your own, you stupid bitch.

Coffee and salmon, I am to take nothing else. Two large jars of coffee and three tins of salmon. Boneless salmon. Tinned salmon doesn't take up much room. Get four tins if it's easy. I have money for a packet of malted milk biscuits.

When I get to the till I am to make sure the bag is zipped all the way along. The zip has teeth missing halfway and sometimes it refuses to slide any further. I take one jar of coffee, drop it into the bag. And two tins of salmon. The zip glides easily to the end and I let out a breath.

The lady at the till smiles. 'Aren't you a good girl, doing your mum's messages?' I smile back and step outside into the cold, where they are waiting.

The second time, instead of holding the bag up high, I am to leave it on the ground. Instead of simply dropping the goods into the bag, I am to kneel, pretending to fasten my lace. That way the items can be easily slotted between the open teeth of the bag. Bend, kneel, slot. Say it: Bend, kneel, slot. I wanted to say they forgot 'take'. There was little use for bend, kneel, slot without take. I'd be slotting in thin air. I remember it like this: TBKS.

I remind them my new shoes are slip-on. They say it doesn't matter. It does to me. Balling up a wad of toilet paper, I push as much of it as I can into the breast pocket of my gingham dress. A couple of stitches snap, which leaves a hole that my little finger can wriggle through. A quick glance in the mirror reveals one gobstopper breast. I start again, folding the tissue into a flat rectangle. Instead of using my shoe, I plan a pretend sneeze, dropping then picking up the tissue instead of tying laces I don't have. They said my attempt was okay last time, given that it was my first.

This time they expect me to get two large jars of coffee and four tins of boneless salmon. If you're going to do it, do it properly.

They don't hand me the bag until we are near the shop. I see Angela, a girl I sit behind in school, walk in ahead of me with her mother. 'Hi, Robyn,' she says, waving. I smile and wave back. She is swinging a red vanity case, with a gold lock; she has gold buckles on her shoes.

I have seen shiny red fabric on the inside of the case. She opens it up sometimes at break time. Tiny loops of thick black elastic have been sewn along the top in a straight line, to hold things high up. A toy red lipstick and nail varnish, a matching pink comb, brush and hand mirror. Everything slots in place, held firm, like Jesus on the cross. Felt-tipped pens, pencils and rubbers can fit inside too. They rest on the bottom of the case, like a crowd. You'd never fit a jar of coffee inside.

Angela looks over. She lets go of her mother's hand and walks towards me. 'Want to come to mine to play?' Her voice is sweet, like lemon bonbons.

'Don't know.' I fidget.

'I've got skates.'

'Oh.'

I catch her looking and hide the bag behind my back.

'Wait here. I'll go and ask.' She pulls her mother by the hand and walks back over to me. 'Hello, Robyn, Angela wants you to come over to play this afternoon. Is your mum around so I can ask her?'

'No . . . She'll let me though.'

'You're not here alone, are you?'

'No. My mum's meeting me by the chippy.'

'Do you know where we live?' Angela asks.

'Yes, next door to Mangum's shop. I only live round the corner, in the Gardens.'

'See you at four then. Stay for tea till six?'

'Okay.'

They walk away.

Dizzy at the thought of spending two hours with the vanity case, I finish my task without using the toilet paper. I check what I've taken: two large jars of coffee and four tins of salmon. I zip up the bag. It closes easily. All that's left is to buy the biscuits. I bend down and take the coins from my shoe.

There is a different lady on the till. She has thick lines between her brows that bunch together when she speaks. 'That's a big bag for such a small packet of biscuits.'

'It's got spuds in it. They're my mum's.' I don't wait for the change.

'Did you get it all?'

'Yes.' I lift the bag up towards them but they don't take it.

'You were quick. That's it. Quick means not getting caught, quick and quiet.' As they speak, my heart beats faster and our pace quickens all the way home.

Inside, they take the bag. The contents are carefully lined up on the floor. As they say a name, they tap each item.

'Coffee for old Alf, he'll buy a jar after a kiss from me,' Mum says. 'And Mag, we bought that clapped out record player off her.' She smiles. 'We can go out tonight now.'

Dad's eyes flash. 'Tom'll be up to his eyes in Guinness when we get there. He'll take two tins of salmon. I'll rev Joan up a bit, she'll take a tin. We'll sell them, ask Eve for a stay behind.'

I ask to play out. They don't look up when they say yes.

It is a sunny Saturday, but the sun isn't a warm sun. I skip all the way to Angela's house, feet rubbing inside new shoes I got for Christmas. I know they won't be back from the shops yet, so I sit on the pavement across the road and wait. A bedroom window is open and I can hear a song being played. *You better beware if you've got long black hair.*

My hair is dark brown, cut just below my chin. I have a few freckles around my nose that I don't like, but the ones on my arms are like squashed chocolate drops. My ankles are so skinny I can span them with my hand. I take off my new shoes. My toes are nasty. Long and thin. The second toe is longer than the big toe and, when we do PE, some of the kids laugh and say it means I will kiss girls when I grow up, on the lips. When I show my toes to my nan she says take no notice. It means you're going to be a ballet dancer.

I rub my cold feet in my palms. Finally, Angela turns the corner with her mother. I slip my socks and shoes back on and walk over. 'You're early,' her mum says with a smile. 'Hold this for me while I find my keys.'

Peeping inside the bag, I see candles, Nulon hand cream, coffee and massive bandages like my mother has. Angela takes me up to her room. She has a picture of a man on the wall above her bed. He looks kind around the eyes. He is wearing a cream suit with a red flower in his lapel. She tells me his name is David Cassidy. Her big sister Kate doesn't like him any more, as she likes Donny Osmond now, so she gave her the poster. Angela tells me Donny Osmond is nowhere near as cute as David. He can't even sing. She tells me she's going to marry a pop star when she grows up.

We play outside on the step with her dolls. They have a back yard, but her mum says we have to play in the front because the bin men are on strike and it stinks in the yard. Angela says she saw a rat inside one of the rubbish boxes. She gets her skates out and I have a try with one for a long time. She does the same with the other. Up and down the street with the same skate until our legs ache.

Angela's mum comes to check on us. 'One of your legs will grow longer than the other doing that.' She laughs.

When she walks back inside I try with two skates. I fall and cut my knee. Angela shouts her mum. She cleans the blood away and puts a plaster on it so I can't bend my knee when I walk. I'm glad she didn't see me fall.

Angela's dad looks like David Cassidy. He has dark hair with long sideburns. He gets out of his car and locks the door. There are no other cars in the street. 'Hiya, gorgeous.' He tickles her under the chin then turns to me. 'Who's this?'

'It's Robyn, my friend.' He fluffs up my hair.

'This is my dad, he's a 'lectrician,' she says proudly.

I don't know what my dad is, so I say nothing.

We play until it's time to eat. Angela says I can play with the vanity case after tea. We have mashed potato and minced meat in gravy, with tinned peaches and conny-onny milk for dessert. At the table her parents sit close to each other and laugh out loud.

'I got the candles for tonight's blackout, love,' her mum says.

'No need. I'll string up the car headlight bulbs, one in the living room and one in the kitchen. Keep them for the bedroom, for later, eh love?' He winks.

'You're so clever.'

She leans over and they kiss, right there in front of me and Angela.

After we help clear away the dishes, it's time to go back outside to play with the vanity case. No sooner have I sat on the step and flipped open the lock than I hear my name being shouted. I close the case, put it on the step and stand.

Angela stands up too and looks where I'm looking.

'What's the matter?'

At the end of the street my mum's face thin and pale against her pillar-box lips. 'Where the fuck have you been? We thought you were lost. Your father's searched all over, across to the big square and everything. Get here now. We're waiting to go out.'

Avoiding Angela's stare, I run down the street. I'm thinking, why can't I have a better life than this?

2

There are five squares altogether in Sir Thomas White Gardens, or Tommy Whites as we call it. The big square is right in the middle, with four smaller squares branching off at its corners. Our square faces St Domingo Road, behind the church of Our Lady Immaculate. The priest's house is on the other side of the road, right opposite the church. We can see cars and buses crawling by from our front door because there are no flats opposite to block the view.

Two squares sit on the right of the big square, two on the left. We live with Nan in a two-bedroom flat on the second floor.

The ground-floor flats come with front yards. When the weather is warm, grown-ups fold their arms and lean over the landings to smoke, flicking grey ash down into a neighbour's front yard. Older boys sniff up hard, drop thick balls of snot to the backs of their throats, edging them to the tip of their tongues, ready to gob down. If you're unlucky and live in a ground-floor flat, ash and green gooey spit can end up in your hair.

On every landing there is a chute where we empty rubbish. It all drops down into a massive bin on the ground floor. The door of the chute is made from heavy iron, with bits of every-one's rubbish stuck to the inside of it. A visit to the chute after five o'clock will reveal what was for tea that night. Eggshells, potato peelings, beans, soggy bread crusts, tea bags and plenty of brown cigarette ends that remind me of unwashed teeth. For something so heavy, the chute door only makes a slight thudding noise when it closes against the dark furry stuff that grows around the edges.

I hate going to the chute. It stinks. I hold my nose and close my eyes. Sometimes I open my eyes and find half the rubbish on the landing floor, like now. Only I've missed it completely. I leave the mess there. Close the front door before anybody spots me. Nan answers the door when Mrs Naylor knocks to tell. Her bottom lip drops when she speaks, revealing too much gum. She has thick lines either side of the crotch part on her cream trousers; they match the lines under her eyes. There are red stains down the front of her blouse. She catches me looking at them, tuts, tries to rub them away.

'You want to watch that granddaughter of yours, got the divil in her.'

I have to kneel down and pick it all up with her on the step as she tuts and shakes her head. She always sticks her head in and out of her doorway waiting for the thud of the chute door, she'll spy the shadow of a body passing her window. Mrs Frost comes out with her daughter, Anne, each carrying a bag full of rubbish. Mrs Naylor pats Anne's head. 'There are nice kids that live on our block.' She points a twiggy finger at me. 'See what I caught this little divil doing? I was after her like a bullet. No respect.' She looks down at me with eyes the colour of smoke. 'And don't be giving me them black looks, cheeky cow. It wasn't me that created this mess.'

We should wear special chute clothes, like beekeepers, with long gloves, a mask and everything. That way she'll never find out who drops what. Pile it all on her step until it blocks up the doorway and she'll never get out. Let her feed off the scraps, grope with two thin fingers through her letterbox, scratch away at the stinking heap, until she shuffles something through the gap and it drops onto the floor, and she'll squeal because she believes she has hit the jackpot.

When I've finished, I sit on the settee. Nan opens the living-room door. She is holding a cup in one hand, a pinny in the other. Her legs are half-past five on a clock. You notice it most when she stands up straight, against her stick. She blames the doctors.

'All done?'

'Yes.'

'Are they still in bed?'

'Yes.'

'I'll make a quick cuppa. Wash this pinny through in the sink while I'm at it. Want anything to eat?'

'Not yet.' She closes the kitchen door.

Nan washes every day in the sink.

Mum does a weekly wash in the bath. She puts the clothes in first, fills up the bath with hot water, adds a little cold then sprinkles OMO washing powder all over the top for a *Bright Fresh Cleanness*. The bathroom smells chalky sweet. Kneeling down, she swooshes the water to make the suds bubble up. She's brisk. She pushes one item at a time up and down in the water, rubs away stains until she's satisfied it's as clean as it's going to be. Then she rinses it in cold water. She wrings it out with her hands, squeezing out every last drop of water, until it sits, like a fat twisted snake, on the side of the bath.

After the clothes are rinsed, her hands are red and wrinkled. The mangle is used to wring the clothes out even more. No matter how much she rinses in the cold water, the mangle still squeezes out a line of white soapy bubbles. The twisted snakes come out of the rollers like the skin on the top of Nan's bad leg. I hear my dad's shirt buttons crack as they roll through. Then it's time to peg out. That's my job, now I'm taller.

The washing line is an adult's arm's length away, over the landing. I can't quite reach, so I have to lean forward on my tiptoes, belly on the landing wall, reaching outwards for the rope, my middle finger pointing to the sky.

In my nightmares, I see Mrs Naylor creep up behind me. She bellows down my ear, 'Boo!' I'm falling over the landing in a panic, yelling for help, trying to grip onto the washing line, Mrs Naylor's grey curly mop visible above the line; I fall down, pick up speed as I go, hurtling towards the ground.

Now, as I reach for the washing line, the pile of wet washing slung over my shoulder drags me nearer to the ground than I want to go.

My finger hooks the line. I pull it towards me and begin my task. I can hang five items on the line using just six pegs, leave the knickers till last. Tell Mum there's no room left.

Most of the pegs are clipped onto my clothes with one clamped firmly between my teeth to start me off. I don't want to lose the line and have to lean out again. I overlap corners to share one peg. Towels and jeans are the worst; the fabric is too thick to overlap. Pegs give up under the strain and catapult down into front yards to join the casserole of ash and spit.

Sometimes, if I lose concentration, our clothes end up there too, and I have to leg it down the stairs and get them. Rub snot and ash off Dad's faded Levi's. Then hang them out, like it never happened. Nan says you should check pockets for holes in case pennies fall out and are lost. If you push your hands inside wet pockets the fabric is thin and crumpled like it's not meant to last. It's hard to get your hand back out of wet pockets.

Now I follow Nan out onto the landing and sit while she pegs out her pinny. We have a small front step that is cool to sit on in the summer. It has brown square tiles, with an eight-inch concrete border on the edge, painted black by my dad. Nan mops it every day with pine bleach. I watch the light patches spread across the dark patches as it dries. Mrs Naylor walks along the landing. She's changed her clothes. She looks down at me.

'Taking in lodgers now, May?' she says. 'Council know?'

Nan does not turn from the washing line.

I spit on the tip of my finger and dab two dark eyes and a smiley mouth in the middle of a tile. The spit runs out before I finish. Mrs Naylor turns her eyes towards me. I dip my finger onto my tongue for more spit and shudder at the sour taste. She smirks, satisfied; then walks away, the back of her skirt sucked too far up her chocolate brown tights. Before she goes inside her flat she looks back at me like I remind her of something.

Once our front door is open, you step straight into the lobby. It takes two cartwheels from here to get to the living room. It takes half a cartwheel to get from one side of the kitchen to the other. You have to finish the cartwheel with the soles of your feet facing the ceiling, then bring them straight back down to the position they started in, so it's not really even half a cartwheel. It's probably more like a handstand. The cooker is the only thing in the kitchen that's not cupboards or a sink. It has four grey electric rings that swirl round like licked liquorice.

The living room is big enough to fit a dining table and sideboard. The dining table is pushed right up against the wall so that only three sides are used. It is covered with a white tablecloth that has holes in the weave. Once the table is set, the sugar bowl, salt, vinegar and plates cover the holes up.

Beside the table is Nan's dresser. It annoys her that she can't see into the mirror to comb her hair, or open the drawers, because our settee is pushed up tight against it. My dad moves the settee for himself, looks in the mirror for ages, glides the comb backwards across his black hair until he gets the quiff sitting just right.

'All done.' Nan smiles, drying her hands on the hem of her skirt. She rubs her bad leg. 'It's going to rain,' she says. Nan can feel how the weather's going to be in her bones. She spoons sugar into her tea, dips the warm spoon back into the bowl. I pick it up and suck the sugar clumps off the spoon to take away the sour taste on my tongue.

She takes her sweet, milky tea back into the bedroom. I wait a few minutes then knock. 'Come in.' Her room is my favourite. Her bed is new, a divan, with a gold, quilted headboard. Her radio is on a small table next to her bed. She turns it on for the news, nothing else. A small dressing table without a mirror has a photograph of a boy wearing a flat cap, a knee-length tweed coat and long grey socks that stretch all the way up to his short trousers. He is looking away from the camera, leaning against a low wall. There are tall trees in the distance.

'Is that the little boy who lives down the lane?' I ask.

Nan laughs. 'No, he belonged to a couple . . . I used to clean for them. Paul, I think his name was.'

'Can I go with you next time?'

'That place is long gone.' She picks up the photograph. 'He died in the war, just a lad, terrible, so young. He was ready to go even before he was called up, wanting to be like everybody else.'

She places it back on the dresser. 'Does no good thinking too much about it. No good at all.' She drinks her tea then puts on her cream camel coat.

'Are you going out?'

'On a message to the housing.'

'What for?'

'To hurry them up with a place of my own now Christmas is out of the way. Three weeks your mother said you'd be here. It's been four months. It pays to pester sometimes. You've seen how bad I am trying to climb the stairs on this block. Last time I was at the housing they said they had a flat for me, Scotland Road, ground floor.'

'Not the ground floor, with a front yard?'

'No. Inside a block with lots of other people, with one back yard for us all. They're brand new.'

'Where's Scotland Road?'

Her light blue eyes look into mine and she smiles.

'Not far. You could gallop there with your strong legs if you wanted to visit.'

'I want to,' I say.

'Then as soon as I've got the keys you can come and see it.'

'Can't I live with you?'

'It only has one bedroom.' She tilts her head towards their room. 'Besides, *they* won't let you.'

'But if you don't tell them where you live, how will they find me?'

'They can go to the council and get my new address.'

She pats the space beside her on the bed and I sit down. Her arms wrap around me for a few minutes before she speaks.

'Don't for one minute think you're like them, you're not. You're cut from a different piece of cloth altogether. Don't forget that, promise?'

'I promise.'

She picks up her brown scarf from the dresser and folds it into a triangle, lowering it over her head. She ties both ends into a knot under her chin. Only her white fringe is visible. She holds the scarf in place, pushes her fringe over to the side.

'Can't I go with you?'

'You can't. I'll meet you back here later. Tell you all about it. Okay?'

I nod.

She cups my face between her hands.

'We all have to grow up some time, Robyn. You're going to have to do it sooner than others. I know it's tough. Better times will come. You'll see.'

She picks up her bag, drops in the keys, then leaves. When Nan goes out, the air feels different on my skin, like shoes on the wrong feet. I pick up the photograph and cover myself with her warm blankets, the smell of Nan right up under my chin. The lazy tick of her clock fills the room. And I think about what she said about me being different, but all I want is to be like everybody else. I look down at the photograph of the boy, who wanted to be like everybody else. He is staring into the distance, with no expression on his face. I'd like to whisper a thought into his ear. Somehow make it possible for him not to go to the war. But if he can do that, then I shouldn't be scared of going to the chute and pegging out washing.

3

In school, it's not the same between me and Angela. She tells Anthony Greenbank, who sits next to me, that I ran off with my mum and never gave her mum a thank you or nothing for my tea, or for letting me come over. Angela says, 'That's cheeky, that. Isn't that cheeky, Anthony?'

Anthony nods.

She speaks across me but doesn't look. 'My mum said manners don't cost a penny. She won't get invited again. Lesley never leaves mine without saying thanks.'

She's always been friends with Lesley. For a while, that day I played at her house, I thought it might become the three of us.

Before play, Angela drops her pencil. 'Where's that pencil gone?' She says this to Anthony. As I hold it up she turns away as if it's my fault. I feel the turn of her body like a pin prick. Anthony watches with sideways glances, like he's used to it. He takes the pencil and places it on Angela's desk. Sits back down, all smiles, and waits.

At playtime, while we play *catch the girls, kiss the girls*, Angela and Lesley kneel on their coats, faces towards the wall, playing with the vanity case. The bottom of Angela's braids curl up either side of her neck, like a pair of brackets.

Lesley wears a red Alice band in her black hair, a red that perfectly matches the vanity case. They catch me watching, then look away. And I think how kneeling like that must hurt your knees after a while. If I had my pillow with me they'd let me play. I'd push it against the wall so we could all kneel on it. I watch them putting on lipstick in the hand mirror, then braiding and unbraiding each other's hair.

My hair is too thick and too short to braid. I tried it once, using the wide elastic bands my parents wrap around their Embassy coupons. The braids felt heavy and stiff and wrong.

I carry on looking. I don't mind being ignored. I mind that I can't ask her why. Being ignored has no words, nothing. Once words are involved there's no going back. That's why I don't ask her why. Instead, I use my own distractions like the itch in my scalp, or the false turn of a heel that makes me fall. I can hear them laugh.

'Ugly mug fell over,' Angela shouts. Then I remember the game. That's how I get caught.

Gavin Rossiter plants his soggy lips directly onto mine. 'I've got one,' he shouts to the other boys, who ignore him, still zigzagging across the playground after a random pair of lips. Nobody else has been caught.

'Eee!' Angela squeals. 'Gavin kissed ugly mug.'

By the time Gavin turns back round I am on my feet. Hands balled into fists. I lunge at him, pounding into his chest until he crashes backwards against the toilet wall. He starts to wail, one hand on his chest, the other on his back, holding himself up. I run across the playground and lock myself in the girls' toilet until I hear the bell.

Inside the classroom Gavin's red eyes glare at me. From behind his times-table card he mouths, *Stupid skinny cow.*

Gonna get you.

The lesson starts and we begin chanting:

One six is six, two sixes are twelve, three . . .

Our teacher is called Mr Thorpe. His hair is light brown. He has a moustache that he strokes. He has two deep number eleven lines at the top of his nose. When he gets angry, they join together at the bottom and make a V.

We turn our cards face down for the test. He points a long stick around the room, firing questions.

'Two times six?'

Gavin flips his eyes to the ceiling, head tilted to the side. 'Erm . . .'

'Too slow.' Mr Thorpe points the ruler at me. 'Seven sixes?'

'Forty-two,' I answer immediately. He smiles, before striding over to the other side of the room. I catch Gavin looking. He mouths *Swot*, then turns away.

Nan says if you're asked a question and you know the answer it's bad manners to keep it to yourself. There's something about knowing the right answer to a question that makes kids like Anthony Greenbank nearly burst with wanting to tell it. I never shout out answers or put my hand up. I wait until I'm asked. I'm good at waiting.

At dinner time we line up in pairs, hand in hand. Mrs Black, the dinner lady, pokes us into a perfect train. It's a ten-minute walk to the canteen, a couple of blocks down from Father O'Malley's house. She checks her watch. Looks down the line at Gavin, one shoe slipped off. 'Come on, Cinderella, we're going to be late for the ball.'

Everyone laughs. Everyone calls her Blackbeard because of the dark hairs on her chin.

We file inside a corrugated-iron hut filled with tables and chairs. A gold jug of water and six small glasses are in the centre of each table. It's only gold on the outside; inside it's black.

I join the long queue for dinner. Steak and kidney pie, mashed potato, peas, carrots and gravy. I carry my plate carefully, intending to eat every last scrap. Before I pick up the knife and fork, Gavin is at my ear.

'Stupid skinny cow,' he whispers, pulling the jug across the table towards me. It glides, as if on ice, hitting my plate with a crash. The cold water tips, into my dinner, then seeps inside my knickers. I stand up sobbing. I can feel it run down my leg, soaking my socks.

Gavin sings, 'Robyn's wet her knickers.'

Blackbeard grabs my wrist and marches me across the canteen towards the kitchen. My shoes squelch as I walk. Everybody stops and laughs.

'Clumsy cow,' Blackbeard tells the cook. 'Only gone and soaked herself, hold us all up now.'

I don't speak.

The ladies who served us dinner don't speak either.

Once she goes back into the canteen, they all help me to dry off. One of them smiles then touches my arm.

'You ate anything, love?'

I shake my head, not feeling hungry any more. 'I'll save you something back.' She walks to the other side of the kitchen, her Dr Scholl's flip-flopping against the soles of her feet. The cook hands me a towel and tells me to dry my legs. I take off my socks and she rolls them about in a dry towel.

'Is your underwear wet?'

'No,' I lie, pushing the towel deep down into my shoes. She hands back my socks. 'There, that's the best I can do.'

'Thanks,' I say, feeling better.

The lady wearing the Dr Scholl's returns with a plate of food. One scoop of mashed potato sits in the middle of the plate. It has two peas for eyes, two small carrots for horns and straight fork tracks make a wide mouth. Dark gravy has been poured over the top for hair.

'Remind you of anybody?'

'Don't know,' I say.

She takes a pair of scissors from the drawer and cuts off tiny ends of her dark hair. She takes a few then pushes them into the potato head, just below the mouth. 'Remind you of anyone now?'

I nod, smiling.

Before taking the plate away, she uses the wrong side of a spoon to squash the head down flat.

'Better get rid of the evidence, eh?'

We laugh together.

She returns with a plate of apple crumble and custard. 'Finish putting your shoes on, then tuck in.'

During afternoon play I find Lesley alone with the vanity case. 'Where's Angela?' I ask.

'Inside, reading with our sir. Will you mind this while I go to the toilet?' She hands me the vanity case.

'Me?' I reply, trying not to sound too excited.

The contents of the case are lined up neatly on the playground floor, ready for a game. I sit down, cross-legged on the cold concrete, and stare. Unsure where to begin, I take too long thinking and the bell rings.

When we get back to class we are given handwriting practice. We are not allowed to talk. I don't look at Lesley or Angela. I grip the case between my ankles.

The final bell rings and I grab my duffel coat then leg it to the main gate. I don't cross with the lollipop man. I head towards a quiet spot further up. For a second I think about going back. Tell

Angela I forgot the case was in my hand. Say sorry. Then I realize she won't believe me because I don't believe myself.

Once I am home I check Nan's room. She's not in. Up on her bed, the case in my lap, I lay each item out side by side. The white bristles on the brush look glossy and soft. I trace my fingers around its edges. Let the tip of one finger sail across the top, only half-touching, like a whisper. Slide slowly deeper and deeper inside the bristles, easing them back towards the handle, feel them slip forwards. In circular movements on my palm, round and round they swirl. I close my eyes, sink inside Nan's covers.

From the tip of my scalp I brush, in long strokes, to the ends of my hair, over and over. Shoulders drop, legs stretch. Lips smile. I purr like a cat. Let slide-away thoughts melt to nothing.

The light from the hand mirror is a dragon's tongue licking the ceiling, the walls. It finds tiny tears in the candyfloss wallpaper.

A sticky patch on the lipstick twisted away in the sheet. Gazing in the hand mirror, I run the cold, pink hardness across my lips, expecting something to happen. Nothing does. The sound of a knock on the front door makes me drop the mirror. When I pick it up it has a small crack at the top.

My mum opens the door.

Angela stands on our step with her mother.

'Robyn, Angela would like her case back.' She looks at me, lips pulled tightly together.

I hand the case to Angela.

'You shouldn't take things that don't belong to you. That's stealing,' Angela's mum shouts.

Mrs Naylor walks past going the wrong way.

I shout back. 'Angela shouldn't say things . . .'

'What things?'

'She said I could play with it.'

'Did you say that?'

Angela shakes her head.

'Liar, you did, when I was at yours. Anyway, I was only minding it till tomorrow.'

Mum nods. 'Course she was. Making a big deal out of nothing,' she says, pushing her face towards them, 'aren't you?'

They turn to leave. Mum bolts down the stairs shouting after them. 'Thinks she's too good for everyone, that Pamela Jennings; stuck-up cow.'

Mrs Naylor walks back along the landing. She points at me and Mum. 'It's the likes of you lot that gets this area a bad name.'

'Fuck off. Mind your own business.' Mum slams the door in Mrs Naylor's face.

The creak from the letterbox makes us both jump.

'For your information, it is my business. You don't know who you're dealing with. Just you wait,' she shouts through the letterbox.

Mum grabs my arm and closes the living-room door. She catches her breath. '*She* doesn't know who the fuck *she's* dealing with.' She grabs my arms tighter. 'You keep away from that lot. You hear?'

I nod, head into the kitchen to help set the table.

4

They take me into town on the number 17C bus. The seats are comfy and I get to sit by the window. My mum takes out a box of Players No.6 and lights one. When it's lit, she puts another one in her mouth and lights it from the already burning tip, sucking like a baby with a dummy. She hands one to my dad. He has LOVE tattooed on the knuckles of his left hand and HATE tattooed on the knuckles of his right. He takes the cigarette with his LOVE hand. Mum crumples up the empty box, throws it on the floor. Dad blows smoke into Mum's short brown curls. 'That's the last of our fags. We'll be gasping later.'

We stop at St George's church. Mum glares over my shoulder, out of the window. There's a group of people standing outside the church, hair lifted by the wind. Some have orange sashes draped from their shoulders. Women pushing prams; one licking her thumb and stooping to rub away at a mucky face, purse falling from her pocket. Coins roll across the pavement, bounce off a huge drum balanced against the church wall. Children squeal, scoop them all up in a race and push each other out of the way. Then hand them back. Men huddle, heads together, lighting their cigarettes. The driver beeps his horn and waves across the other side of the road at somebody who waves back, before he pulls away, past the graveyard.

My dad speaks without taking his eyes from his reflection in the glass. His sideburns are thick and black; they stick out like they're trying to grow away from him. He turns his face to the side, wets a fingertip and presses one of them back down. He does the same with the other one then looks out of the window. 'Proddy bastards, getting ready to march.' He puts two fingers up at a man wearing a sash. The man sends two fingers back. Dad turns to Mum. 'Tell her what she's got to do.'

She stands up and sits next to me, her voice low in my ear. 'Joan's new baby grandson is getting christened soon and Joan's got no money for the suit.' She takes a big suck on her cigarette. 'She's seen one in town, but it's too dear. I told her we'd help.' Clouds of smoke escape from her mouth as she talks. 'I'll show you the one she wants when we get there.'

Once we get into town we make our way to a shop called Blacklers. Mum says, 'If anyone's looking, don't bag it. Wait.' She hands me the bag.

'Can we get a new bag?' I ask.

'Not today, Robyn. Pay attention.'

A line of children wait to ride a black and white rocking horse. There's something fantastic about this high-up indoor horse. How it creaks under a shiny body and black eyes. Once the boy that's riding is finished his voice trembles when he asks for another go. His nan runs him to the back of the queue.

I follow them further into the children's department, towards a rail full of white clothes.

'How are you going to find it in this lot?' I ask.

Mum bends her knees a little to see the sizes better. Her fingers walk across the hangers, like Mr Thorpe finding my next reading book.

'This is the one.' She grins. 'Three pearl buttons up the front and a sailor collar. This one's nought to three months. We need to find six to twelve.'

Dad joins in the search along the rail while I stand and watch. The handles on the bag burn my skin.

'Got it. Now watch carefully, Robyn, I'm putting it right at the very back of the rail. That way you can go straight to it. Remember, the very back.'

'But it'll get all dirty in this bag.'

'No, it won't. Your dad's lined it with paper. Make sure you put it on the paper.'

A lady with tangerine lips and a green floaty scarf smiles beside Mum. 'Darling, aren't they? Who's being christened?'

Dad walks away.

Mum's face flushes red. 'We're just looking.'

The lady looks disappointed. 'If you need anything, I'm over here,' she calls over her shoulder as she walks away.

'Watch her, nosy cow.'

Mum takes my hand. We follow Dad down the stairs.

'What did she say?' he asks when we catch up with him.

'Nosy, that's all. Best waiting for a bit, till it gets busier.'

We walk around town looking in shop windows. The sun burns down on my head. I unbutton my duffel coat.

'Can I have a drink, please?' I ask.

'There's no money. If you get the suit for Joan, we'll buy you a Thirsty Pack,' Mum says, holding the bag for me.

'Dandelion and burdock?'

'Whatever flavour you like and a bar of chocolate. We'll head off to Dolly's shop, eh? You'll like that.'

'Yes.'

'Let's go back to Blacklers; with any luck that cow'll be on her break.'

It doesn't take us long to get to Blacklers. Once we're outside, they hand me back the bag.

'Now, what floor are you going to?'

'Second.'

'Where's the suit?'

'Right at the back of the rail.'

'What size?'

This is stupid. She's already put the suit where I can find it. I want to scream. 'Six to twelve months.'

'Good. Don't bag it if anyone's looking. Try to get it as quick as you can, on the paper.'

Upstairs, I head straight to the christening rail. The bag is unzipped. I take a look around. The shop is much busier than before and tangerine lips is nowhere to be seen. I find the suit exactly where we left it, check the size; slip it inside the bag. One of the pearl buttons gets stuck in the zip and I try to pull it out. I free it, but the button hangs by a thin thread like a wobbly tooth.

When I look up there's a lady staring at me, eyes wide. What amazes me is that I see her looking but still shove the suit inside the bag like I think she can't really see me or something. She looks at me, mouth open. I hurry away from her as fast as I can, bump into another lady with a pram.

'Watch it!' she shouts after me.

'Stop, thief!' a woman's voice behind me shouts. 'That kid's got something in her bag.'

I look nowhere but straight ahead. On the third stair down I feel a tug on the hood of my coat. I get yanked back one, two stairs then fall down on my bum. I stand up and hurl the bag down the stairs. Nothing falls out, another tug at my hood. I wriggle out of my coat sleeves, take the stairs two at a time, scoop the bag up on my way. At the bottom, a quick look behind, tangerine lips on the stairs, a duffel coat held high in her hands. I head for the door, bump into children queuing for the rocking horse.

'Watch it, you!' a man's voice shouts after me. Everyone looks. My heart feels like it's grown a new thud.

Once I am outside I hear Mum's voice.

'Robyn. Over here!' I spot them on the other side of the road. The bones in my legs feel like they're dissolving. 'Run,' I scream. They bolt away across the road. I'm behind them, running as fast as I can, holding the bag tight against my chest. I don't look back.

We knock at Joan's house and she opens the door with a huge smile on her face. 'Come in. Wasn't expecting company. Have to excuse the mess and the smell, but with so many lads. It's their feet.'

They tell me to sit down on the settee while they talk in the kitchen. Mum takes the bag with her. Up on her walls there are pictures of the Virgin Mary and Jesus. Mary's red heart is on the outside of her clothes, decorated with a row of flowers. She has red lips and blue, gazing eyes. Flames leap from her heart and she looks so sad. On the bottom of the picture it says, Bless This House.

Knots of laughter drift in from the kitchen. My shoulders ride up towards my ears, hands together between skinny knees.

Finally, they come out.

'Who's a clever girl then?' Joan beams holding the christening suit up high. 'He'll look like an angel in it. A few stitches and we'll have that button on good as new. Thanks, love,' she says, patting my knee. 'You did good.'

Mum hands money to my dad. He pushes it into his pocket.

'Well, got to get going, get this one a drink.'

Joan hooks the christening suit over the frame of the Virgin Mary. It covers her face. She sees us to the door.

I look back at Joan and she smiles. 'You did good,' she says. It doesn't feel good stealing things. Good to me is sitting for a whole day with Nan telling me stories, or getting all of the washing to fit on the line with just a few pegs. This is the kind of good I want back.

After tea I fall asleep on the chair. When I wake up I hear Dad talking about me, so I don't open my eyes.

'She nearly messed up on us today. More trouble than she's worth. She was too interested in that fucking rocking horse,' he says. 'She wasn't concentrating.'

'I don't like town,' Mum says. 'It was lucky they only got her coat.'

'Fucking rocking horse; at her age an' all.'

'That coat still had loads of room in it. Some of them assistants think the shop belongs to them the way they follow you around.'

I hear a creak from the living-room door; Nan's stick bangs against it, her cup and saucer rattle.

'What does she want?' Dad says.

'She's only getting a drink.'

Nan is angry. 'I can hear you, you know.'

'This is every fucking night now. Tell her to close that door, there's a draught on my back.'

'Close the door, Mam.'

'That's my coal fire warming your feet.'

Mum's voice. 'So you've said.'

I hear Nan banging around the kitchen, rattling cutlery. The sound of the kettle being filled. After a few minutes I hear her stick bang against the kitchen door.

'Turn that telly up,' Dad says.

'Robyn's asleep.'

'I said turn it up.'

'Move that paper, Babs, while I sit down,' Nan says.

Dad says, 'For fuck's sake, there's no privacy here. Why can't she drink that in her room?'

I can hear Nan slurp her tea extra loud. I know that she's tipped it onto her saucer to take the heat away.

'Tell her, will you. Like being in the fucking zoo.'

'Mam?'

More slurps.

'Oh, for fuck's sake. I'm not sitting here listening to that. I'm going to bed. Turn everything off before you come in.'

'I'll be in now.'

'Hurry up.'

The living-room door slams shut.

'He treats you like a child,' Nan says.

'Can't you be happy for me?'

'He'll never work for you.'

'Leave it, Mam.'

'Lazy good-for-nothing.'

'Here we go.'

'You gonna take that, day in day out?'

'I said leave it.'

'You threw better away.'

'You mean better ran away.'

'He came back.'

'Yeah, when it was too late.'

'And what about Robyn?'

'What about Robyn?'

'She's asked to live with me.'

Silence.

'And what did you say?'

'What do you think I said?'

'If she asks me, I'll say no. Anyway, of course she wants to live with you, you spoil her rotten.'

'That's not the reason and you know it.'

Dad's voice shouts in from the lobby. 'You comin' in or what?'

'Better do as you're told.'

'I'll go when I'm ready, not when I'm told.'

'Not finishing your cider?'

'No. I'm not. I'm going to bed. You made sure at the housing we're down as living here, didn't you?'

'Course I did. Wouldn't see my own family out on the street.'

'No. You're all heart, aren't you?'

'There's still half a bottle left in this cider. That's a waste.'

'You take it, you're taking everything else. The sooner you move out the better.'

Dad's voice louder this time. 'Babs?'

'Your father will be turning in his grave.'

No answer from Mum.

'I said . . .'

'I know what you said. Let him turn fucking somersaults for all I care.'

The living-room door slams shut; Nan's cup and saucer rattle. She covers me with a coat, turns off the light; shuts the door.

I open my eyes, look out of the window. Mum will have a cob on with me now for wanting to live with Nan. She'll think I love Nan more than her. I love them both, but it's wrong to want to leave Mum. I'm being selfish. Mum would miss me if I left. Outside, the light in the window opposite goes out.

5

Mum and Dad haven't come to bed yet so I get up. Earlier on, about an hour after tea, Nan went to the pub to meet Nellie and her husband, Chris. She had to ask Nellie a favour.

Nan hasn't said anything for a couple of days about moving out. Mum says the people at the housing were probably lying about having a place for Nan, to get rid of her. I hope that's true.

The telly is on but the living room is empty. I call out to them, heading for the kitchen. 'Anyone in? Mum, Dad?' I check the clock. Ten past nine. I look out of the back window; it's dark outside. I can see two shapes I know lit up under a streetlight. Mum and Dad hurrying towards the Stanley. I tell myself they've only gone for the last hour, that's all; they'll be back soon.

The glass is cold on my nose. There's not a soul in the big square, not even a dog or a cat. It's creepy. On the television a beautiful woman lies in bed. Her windows are open wide and a man with a powdery white face appears. He wears a black cape with red shiny lining. His black hair is brushed back.

He strokes the woman's cheek with the back of his hand. The camera zooms in on her face as she wakes up. She sees him and screams. He hisses and I can see two long, white teeth. He flips the cape to the side of his face, stoops low. When he has finished, drops of blood trickle down the sides of his lips. The camera swings back to her neck and there are two tiny red marks. He flaps his cape. It turns him into a black bird and he flies out of the window along with whatever she could have done to save herself.

I grab the brush from the cupboard and use the end of the pole to push in the OFF button on the television. Once it's off, I go back into the bedroom, sit on the side of my bed. My legs shake. The more I tremble the more I'm terrified he'll come through the window. After a while I tell myself I am being silly. People can't come out of the television and if they did they'd only be as big as a hand. Mum and Dad must have gone out and left me in before; nothing bad's ever happened. So why should it now? I distract myself by rummaging around in Mum's wardrobe. I love trying on her clothes.

She has a skirt with tiny houses, cottages I think, printed along the hem. I asked Mum if she'd save it for me for when I'm older and she said she would. There's no harm in trying it on now.

I drag out Mum's clothes, all the while listening for the scrape of a key in the lock. I sort them on her bed; skirts, tops and trousers. She has four skirts but the new one's not there. I choose a black flared one with huge pink and green flowers printed all over. My mum did a twirl in it once, the hem ended up around her shoulders. I try it on, bunching up one side of the waistband and wrapping it tight with an elastic band. I match it up with a black polo neck sweater and black patent leather slingbacks. A safety pin holds strap to buckle to finish off the look. I pretend I'm getting ready to go to the Stanley.

Her make-up bag is in the bathroom cabinet. Panstick, powder puff, ruby red lipstick, pressed powder and a peach blusher, all nearly empty. I've looked before, but never used any of it. This lippy isn't like the one in the vanity case, it's softer to touch. I have to push the tip of my finger right down to the bottom of the tube. Most of it ends up inside my fingernail. I dab it onto my lips, press powder all over my face.

Nan tells Nellie things she doesn't want me to hear, she sends me from the room with her eyes. She told Nellie Mum's let herself go. She said Mum was always smart when she worked in the Odeon, before she met him, never wanted for nothing. Then Nellie tells Nan that Chris is on his way out, coughing up blood. He's promised to pack up the fags but won't see Doc Atwood.

I watch my red lips move in the mirror. I try out a new word I heard our headmaster, Mr Merryville, say to Mr Thorpe: *'As most of the building repairs are complete, there is a possibility that the trip to Colomendy will go ahead after all.'*

Po-ssi-bil-it-y. I count the beats on my hand. The picture that comes into my head is of a five domino. I say the word out loud, five times. Try it out as the fifth word in a sentence. *I think there's a possibility it could rain rabbits.* Ha!

Back inside the cabinet, neatly folded, is one of my mum's big bandages. I open it up, there are two thin loops either end. I place it on my head, where my fringe starts, then curl the loops around my ears. I twirl and twirl, start to sing:

'*On the mountain stands a lady, who she is I do not know . . .*'

I don't hear the front door closing. I can't smell the ale on them yet. Don't see their eyes deciding whether or not to tell me off.

'Well, well, look at you. Aren't you the belle of the ball?'

I scream, holding my chest. When I turn around my face burns. 'Don't tell my mum.'

They look at each other. Burst out laughing.

'What is that on your head, Robyn?' Nellie asks.

'A hairband; I made it.'

'Of course it is. Come over here.' My nose is squashed against Nan's shaking chest as she unhooks it. 'Take no notice of us, we're way behind with the mysteries of fashion. Get washed now and back into your pyjamas. I've just seen your mam and him in the Stanley. They'll be back soon.'

Nellie fishes about in her pockets and shakes her head at me. 'You're a peculiar one all right,' she says. 'Here, take this slummy and buy yourself a real hairband.'

I don't take her money. She says she'll leave it on the mantelpiece for me.

'Where are the boxes, May?'

'What boxes?' I say.

'You'd better hurry and get changed. They'll be back any minute.'

I get changed fast; wash my face in the bathroom sink. Tidy all Mum's stuff before they get back.

Chris knocks, asking for the door key off Nellie. I let him in, watch him pick up Granddad Jack's photograph. 'We had a time of it me and you,' he says. Chris's face is red. He sways like he's on a boat, calls me in from the doorway with his head. He talks at the picture.

'Worked together me and Jack, blacksmiths.' He flops down in the chair, coins jingling inside pockets. I sit on the couch; Nan and Nellie are laughing in the kitchen. I hear the crick crackles of the chip pan heating up.

He shakes his head. 'Still can't believe he's gone.' He puts up his fists and punches the air. 'One of the best, his dad, his name, it'll come. Trained him in a barn in Crosby . . . trained him with the little bit he knew. If Jack Crown punched you, it felt like, like Thor's hammer had landed.'

He hiccups, pulls out a cigarette from behind his ear, lights it, throws the match into the dead fire.

'Did you see him fight?'

'Only missed one; Nellie went into labour with our Mary. Sammy Garrison he fought.'

He takes a long pull on his cigarette, index finger smudged yellow like his hair.

'I saw him in his best fight. Hundreds had tickets but got locked out.' He smiles into the other side of his eyes. Punches air. Ash drops into the shiny turn-up on his trousers. 'Come on, Jack, finish him, that's it give him a taste of Thor's hammer.'

I want to turn his eyes inside out. See what he sees.

'Tell me what you see.'

He opens his eyes. 'Eh?'

'What can you see? Tell me.'

He stands. 'Remember, Jack was a welterweight, but quick, quick, like this.' He sniffs. Fists tucked under his chin. Weaves his head from side to side, up and down, like a window cleaner's rag.

The kitchen door opens. Nan brings us a plate of chips and two slices of buttered bread each.

Chris tears off the end of his cigarette, throws it in the fire; hides the other half behind his ear. Nan shakes her head at Chris, puts the plate on his knee, gives me a smile. 'Make yourselves a chip butty before they get cold.'

Nellie brings out the same for her and Nan to share.

Once we've finished Chris stands up, swaying, taps one side of his nose at me.

Nellie takes the empty plates into the kitchen. 'You still want me to help you, May?'

'Robyn can help me now she's awake. Chris looks tired; you two get yourselves off home.'

After they've gone Nan calls me into her room. I can see two cardboard boxes: one is already full. 'You can give me a hand for a few minutes if you want.'

'Did you get the keys?'

'I'm getting them tomorrow. So I believe. If it happens, you can come down as soon as I'm settled.'

Nan believes whatever life throws at you, you just have to deal with it the best way you can. She believes that television is a curse, and, once a week, lemon curd sandwiches can be eaten for tea. She hands me a white paper bag then snatches it back before I grab hold. I know her game, played it a hundred times over, but I don't feel like playing. Not tonight. 'Go on, guess.' Something in her voice changes my mind. She hides the bag behind her back.

'Pear drops?'

'No.'

'Bull's eyes?'

'No.'

'Chocolate éclairs?'

'No. Think nappies.'

'Jelly babies?'

'Yes.'

'Which hand?'

I choose left.

She hands me the bag.

'You'll get a room of your own, when I'm gone.'

While we chew, she shows me how to start wrapping with the cup in the corner of the newspaper then roll. Tuck what's left over inside. When she's sure I know what I'm doing, we take a pair of matching cups and saucers. She tells me this is all that's left from a full tea set, a wedding gift from her mother. 'In Belfast my mam and her mam would solve the world's problems over a cup of tea.'

She shows me a white shirt she's kept that belonged to Jack. 'This was the last one I remember him wearing, before he went back to war. Look, nearly every button cracked when I rolled it through the mangle, me worrying about replacing them before he came home.'

'What war?'

'The last war.'

She lifts it up to her nose and smells. 'Not so far away.'

I find a bunch of letters, tied with an elastic band. Flick through them. They haven't been opened. She takes them from me, holds them up in both hands, looks at them, name and address upside-down. It makes me think.

'Do you want me to read them for you?'

'I don't need to hear them, the words. I just like to hold them.'

'Where did you meet Jack?'

'I'd just finished work, when I met him, waiting in a tram stop outside the Adelphi. I checked the time: I wanted to wash my hair before bed and the tram was late. When I looked up, there he was grinning like a lunatic in front of me.'

'"Got time for a walk?" he said.

'I couldn't help smiling. "You're a fast worker."

'"That's me. I'm a fast one all right."

'Held out his arm to me and that was that.

'On the way home, we walked through Stanley Park. It was a warm June night. I let myself do things with Jack that I hadn't done in years, sat down next to him on the grass, rolled my stockings off. Let grass tickle my bare legs.

'Let him push me, one hand behind his back on a swing. His warm hand against my corset.

'I can remember everything about that night, an entire lifetime down to those few hours, like a slice of perfectly cut cake. I had found something that mattered, something real.'

She looks around the room. 'Is there anything you'd like?'

There is a photograph, of her as a young woman. She sits side-on, a crucifix hanging from a thin chain. Her fringe creased into a wave. I pick it up.

'That was taken in Jerome's on London Road. I was working at the Adelphi, silver service, my day off. Vanity, I thought afterwards, when I heard about Jack in the war.'

And she tells me what Jack had told her, and how he got used to the screams, and the sound of guns.

'Can I write on the back of the photo in case I forget?'

I go into the living room and get a pen. I write: *My nan. Jerome's London Road.* Nan finds a frame for it and I stand it on the mantelpiece in the living room. She turns off the light.

'Why did everything have to get dark?'

'You mean the power cuts? That's a good dark, love. Nothing to be scared of; it's the poor people teaching the rich people a lesson. Sometimes you have to fight for things to be fair.'

'Like you pestering the housing?'

'That's right. Lie down and say nothing, people will forget all about you. There are good fights and bad fights. Come on now, into bed before they get home.'

I say goodnight and try to get some sleep. But Nan turns on the radio in her room too loud. I can hear it through the wall. A bomb has exploded on a coach. Twelve people have died, two of them are children. *God forgive them,* Nan says, *killing innocent children.*

I'll miss the way Nan barges into her own living room, late at night, refusing to be a visitor; tells both of them, who are resting their feet on her lino, to turn that contraption down. They look at her like she's something they don't need to see; unflushed pee in a pan. She looks right back at them like they are itchy sores. I try to find that look in my own eyes, so I can throw it at Angela.

My dreams are of Jack surrounded by the deafening sound of gunfire, men either side of him wounded, or worse. Writing letters home that would never be read. I see the words:

My Darling May,
There is a possibility I'll be home next month. We'll go to Southport on the train . . .

Possibility. The b stands to attention like Jack, when he first joined the army.

6

Stephen Foley has been chosen to take me to the headmaster's office. In the corridor he grips my wrist with both hands. I snatch it away. 'Get off me. I know where the office is.'

Stephen looks hurt, like he's just trying to make the best of the job he's been given. I don't care. I won't let him touch me.

Blackbeard comes out of the office with the dinner register. 'What've you been up to?' she asks.

'Nothing,' I say.

When she walks away Stephen says, 'I reckon you'll get six of the best for nicking Angela's vanity case. Sean Holmes got six of the worst for nicking fags out of Mrs Heraty's bag. She's a teacher, though.'

When I tell him I don't know what he's talking about, he explains that six of the best means palms and lower fingers, while six of the worst means fingertips.

He knocks at the office door. Mr Merryville is sitting with both shoes up on the desk, ankles crossed, swinging backwards on the legs of his chair. There are no windows in the room, just walls lined with important-looking books and files. In the corner by the door he has a tall filing cabinet. Right in the middle of each drawer there's a card with three letters of the alphabet on it. Except for the bottom one, that has Y and Z. There are no kids in my class (or the whole school) that I can think of, whose second names begin with Y or Z. It's probably empty.

Mr Merryville's eyes rest on Stephen.

'Name?'

'Foley, sir. Stephen Foley. Mr Thorpe sent me down with Robyn, sir.' Stephen turns to me. 'Please, sir, here she is, sir, can I go back to class, sir?'

I glance at quick-lipped Stephen and suck away a smile. Mr Merryville catches me and makes his eyes small. 'Close the door properly, Foley, on your way out.'

Once Stephen has gone, Mr Merryville turns to me. 'So, you think stealing another's property is funny, do you, Robyn?'

I do not speak.

He opens the drawer of his desk and takes out a thin wooden cane. I have read about it and him on the toilet walls.

MERRYVILLE'S CANE TICKLES

MERRYVILLE'S CANE IS MADE OF LIQUORICE

MERRYVILLE IS A SAD SLAG

MERRYVILLE GROWS SNOT IN HIS GOB

Mr Merryville stands up, drapes his jacket across the back of a wooden chair. He wears a white shirt and a blue tie, printed with tiny, darker blue triangles. When he opens his mouth to speak, both corners of his lips are thick with spit. Green spit. He does not lick it away.

'Hands.'

I hold out my left hand.

'Both of them.'

'I've had stitches in the other one, sir.'

'Still in?'

'No, sir. Taken out last week.'

'Hands.'

I hold out both hands.

Pacing up and down in front of me, he taps the cane into his palm. I can taste his breath in the musty air. He wears a gold signet ring on his little finger.

Mr Dolly had a gold signet ring on his left middle finger. I noticed it during our drive to the hospital. He used the ring to tap out a rhythm on the wheel; it had four quick beats and one more, slightly further away. I was carrying an empty lemonade bottle around to Dolly's shop. Mum had asked me to buy her a loosie and a match, with the money I got back. On the pavement outside the shop, I fell and dropped the bottle. My right palm slammed down into a chunk of glass.

Behind the counter, Dolly was weighing cola cubes for a boy I'd seen around. The contents of the silver scale shushed into a white paper bag. Both corners of the bag were twisted out like ears. When she handed him the sweets she saw the blood all over her floor. On her tiptoes, she nosed over the counter.

'Sorry. I fell over, there's loads of glass outside as well.'

She felt for the little bell under the counter and shook it wildly. Her husband came lolloping down the stairs, his dark beard curly, like the king of clubs. 'Whoa there, Dolly, where's the fire?' he said.

When he saw my hand he ran back upstairs to get a towel. He wrapped it around my hand while Dolly fetched his car keys. Dolly wrote down my address and sent the boy with the cola cubes to tell my mum.

It was brilliant, sitting up front, totally different from riding on a bus. You could see everything. Stretched across the back seat was a long bag, with sticks poking out of the top.

Inside the car it was warm. Mr Dolly's glasses slipped further and further down his nose. At the lights, he pushed them back up again with his first finger. He looked in my direction now and then, asked me about my teacher, my friends. By accident, he turned on the windscreen wipers when we were taking a left turn, then explained the car was new, he'd only taken it out once before. I didn't speak again, just in case he crashed.

When we got to the hospital, my hand was throbbing and spots of blood had seeped through the towel. I didn't want to get out of the car. I felt like Lady Penelope out of *Thunderbirds*, Mr Dolly my Parker.

A doctor and a nurse looked at my hand. 'You're a brave girl,' the nurse said. 'I've seen kids with smaller scrapes than this take off the roof with their screams. Let's get that glass out, then a few stitches; we'll have you out of here quick as a flash.'

Mr Merryville is quick as a flash. He beats the cane down again and again on my hands. Six of the best, my head lighter than it should be. Under my skin, I can feel the heat of a blazing fire. I can hear the cane whoop through the air as he speaks.

'You are a perfect example of the evils of greed. A calculated act, without as much as a second thought for the person you were stealing from. There are places for people like you.'

As he talks, the spit spreads, as if it's trying to fasten itself across his mouth, both ends meeting in the middle, so all sound stops. 'When you get back to class write out one hundred times, *I shall not steal*. Bring it to me at the end of the day. Tell your mother I want to see her.'

One tear zigzags down my face, as if it's unsure where it's meant to be. I reach for the round brass door handle with a ringing in my ears, my fingers a spray of hammering wispy bulges. I can taste the fear of others who never got out. I try again, my fingers still won't curl. I imagine him behind me smiling to himself. *Close the door properly, Foley.*

I can't think. How did the others get out? Perhaps some lay flat on the floor and used the soles of their shoes to twist the handle. They could have waited a whole morning for the feeling in their hands to return, Merryville grinning behind them. Did they use their dry lips to twist the brass handle? The accidental tap of teeth on metal unbearable, they could still be here, behind the shelves, inside walls, whispering their desperate stories of how they tried to escape.

My eyes are drawn back to the bottom drawer of the filing cabinet, Y and Z. *Young Zombies*: the names of all of the kids that did something bad. All the kids still trapped somewhere in this room, names scribbled on bits of yellow card. If I don't think of something fast, my name, Robyn Mason, will join them.

Just as I run out of ideas, Stephen Foley opens the office door. 'It's Mr Thorpe, sir. He's waiting to start the test, sir, maths, says he needs Robyn if you're done, sir.'

Once we are outside I kiss Stephen Foley on the cheek.

His face goes red. He nods at my hands. 'Let's see?'

I hold out my palms and he screws up his face.

'He wants to see my mum.'

'I wouldn't tell my mum, she would kill me. And your dad?'

I would never tell my dad. He's bad enough even if you make too much noise moving around the flat. I'm scared to flush the toilet too loud. He gets a cob on for nothing, especially when he's skint. I'd rather get the cane all over again than tell him I've been in trouble.

'My mum would wrap the cane around his neck,' I say.

Stephen's eyes grow big and he flashes me a smile.

When Mum finally arrived at the hospital she went mad. 'He didn't lay a hand on you, did he? Dirty bastard.' Her words pinched me. I shook my head. She said I should never get into a car with a stranger. With a shove in my back, she marched me towards the exit barging past Mr Dolly. She threw him a cool glance.

I couldn't help but look back and give him a smile. Palms up, he sent me a wriggly finger wave. When we reached the end of the corridor I looked again, and saw him flop down on a bench, sitting on his hands.

A couple of weeks later, the scar looked like those waves we make between the lines, before our real handwriting practice starts. It edged my fingers like a frill.

Carol sits down next to me on the stone steps of our block. Carol's got a bike so when she plays out she usually rides off with the other kids who have bikes. I've played skipping with her once before, ages ago. She's nice.

I'm just home from school, but there's nobody in. She's been to the first landing to give Mrs Frost an envelope from her mum.

'Locked out?' she says. 'Come over to ours to play.'

We want six pence to buy two balls. Carol's mum sits in a dark wooden chair on her landing. She wears Baby Bonnet pink on her toenails. Her bare feet grip the concrete. She has beautiful toes that slant downwards, like the edge of a roof. She eyes Carol twirling her red plaits round and round her first fingers. Carol looks defeated before she opens her mouth. 'Can I –?'

'If it's money, there is none.'

Carol turns on her heels and I follow her down the steps.

'I hate her,' she says. 'If our Colette was asking though it'd be different; she gets anything she wants, spoilt cow. She has got money: I shook her purse this morning and it rattled.'

Carol says she needs to think. Singing helps her think. I laugh at the way she's not afraid to sing out loud.

> *I asked my love, to take a walk.*
> *To take a walk, just a little walk.*
> *Down beside, where the waters flow.*
> *Down by the banks, of the Ohio.*

'Do you have any secrets?' she asks.

I think about the shopping bag with the frayed handles and the vanity case. My face feels hot. 'No.'

'Giz your hand,' she says.

'What?'

'I'll read your fortune, giz it.'

I give her my left palm, curl my fingers around the scar on my right hand. I look at the pink line of scalp that parts her hair. We are the same age, but when she looks up, her forehead only reaches my neck.

'This is your lifeline.' She strokes a long curvy line that ends at my wrist. 'You're going to live a long life. But there's a break here. That means a big change will happen. Look, I've got one, but mine's broken well after yours. Now, squeeze your thumb up towards your first finger. See those lines, you have four. That means you're going to have four kids, two girls and two boys.'

I am amazed. 'How do you know that?'

She laughs. 'My nanna Rose showed me. There's your travel line. It's deep. You'll go on a plane, no, lots and lots of planes.'

'Did she show you any more lines?'

'No. Nanna Rose says if you know too much about what life has in store, you'll never get up in the morning.' Carol looks up to the second landing. A lady is pegging out her washing. 'I've got it.' Carol claps.

Mrs Cliff is a tall lady with tiny silver hoops in her ears that match her tiny silver curls. She answers the door with a fistful of pegs that she stuffs into the pocket of a flowery pinny. 'Do you want anything from the shop, Mrs Cliff?' Carol asks.

'You must have been reading my mind. I could use a five packet of Woodbines, and a box of matches from Dolly's.' She walks down the lobby to fetch the money. Carol whispers in my ear. 'Last time I got her a fish from the chippy she gave me five pence.'

Mrs Cliff hands her the money. 'Let your mam know where you're going,' she tells us.

When we get to the bottom of the block I hear Mum shouting my name. I tell Carol to knock up for me when she gets back. 'Time me,' she says. 'Count like this, so it's fair. One, piddle piddle, two, piddle piddle.' I join in and we both laugh.

'Be careful, it makes you want to wet yourself,' Carol shouts, running across the big square towards Dolly's shop. 'We should end up on the same number when I get back. So don't cheat.'

I think about playing two balls with Carol, maybe going to the park to play on the swings. Be best mates like Angela and Lesley. I picture Angela seeing me and Carol together, telling Lesley all about us.

On the way home I look up at Carol's landing. Angela's mum is talking to Carol's mum. When they see me Angela's mum shouts,

'Talk of the devil, there she is, look.' She points a finger at me and shouts louder. 'Robbing little cow.' I put my head down and run past the block as fast as I can.

On a pay day, the air changes in our flat. Dad gets out the record player and his LPs, turns up the volume. Elvis, Johnny Cash, Jim Reeves, Dean Martin. All singing about bad times, wine, love, and how they just can't help most of the things they do. He's singing extra loud. He's just got it back from the pawn shop. Everything's okay.

Dad drinks anything. Mum drinks cider. When he's nice-drunk, like he is now, his face grows kinder the way it once started out. He jumps in with the words before the singer, pointing and laughing at the speakers like they can see him, making it a competition he always wins. Then, the needle gets stuck. The same word is sung over and over again, like it's in an argument and not being heard. Just for a moment, his face is back to the way it was.

I race to the record player, lift the arm and flip it up, like a dog's paw. You can blow on the needle, to clean it. I like to pinch away the soft Brillo pad of fluff. The scratch of the needle, as I ease it onto the record followed by the smooth, smoochy voice, makes everything okay again. I've jumped the arm too far ahead and words are missing. He doesn't notice. He's not interested any more.

He pulls Mum up close to dance. She rests her head on his shoulder, eyes closed. He tries to lift her at a high point in the song. She laughs a forced, dusty laugh that blows itself out before it gets warm.

Mostly, I steal glances. When they get drunk I can look for longer. Sometimes when they are really drunk, they fall. End up with cut heads and black eyes. Drink takes away their tongues. I feel older than they are. Carol doesn't knock for me.

Next morning they get up late. Holding their heads like wounded soldiers, looking out through empty-barrelled eyes. When you don't say much, you learn to listen better, to read the sounds other people make without words. Mum can make you feel bad without saying a word, without looking at you. I haven't set the table yet. She tuts and walks away into the kitchen. Dad gets edgy when there's no money left. He shifts in the chair onto his other hip, crosses one leg over; rattles the newspaper until it nearly rips.

Dad turns on the telly. It's the news. A little girl has gone missing somewhere near Liverpool. Dad turns to Mum. 'I bet I know who murdered that little girl.'

Mum shushes him. With a toss of her head, I'm sent out of the room. I close the living-room door and listen through the gap.

'It'll be that prick,' Dad says.

'Who?'

'Whatsaname, talks funny, Dolly's fella with the beard. Somebody in the pub told me he came here from Manchester. I've seen him with the kids, all smiles and fucking free sweets.'

'Oh yes. I forgot about him, dirty bastard. She might not be dead.'

'She's dead all right.'

'What makes you so sure?'

'Gone all night, no word? Use your brain.'

'If that's true, someone should burn that bastard.'

'Now you're talking.'

The kitchen door opens. The heavy sound of a kettle being filled, the crackle of a match against the side of a box. The smell of fresh smoke, Dad's voice slow and clear.

'Someone needs to torch that shop, with him in it.'

Mum catches her breath. 'What about poor Dolly?'

Dad sneers. 'Poor Dolly? She'll be in on it.'

Without me even touching the door it creaks. He's there in a flash, cigarette clamped to the side of his mouth, dragging me into the room by my ear.

'Look what I found listening at the door. What have you heard?'

'Nothing, I only wanted a drink.'

'Little girls with big ears shouldn't listen at doors. If I find out . . .'

Mum interrupts. 'Leave her. Back to your room now.' Her voice is panicked. 'She hasn't heard anything.'

7

Mr Wainwright is standing at the office door. He tells me he's a social worker and all he wants is a little chat. He turns; walks with rounded shoulders that make the back of his jacket swing too far up. He sits in Mr Merryville's chair and I sit opposite him.

He unzips his black leather bag and takes out a pad, pushes a small bottle of lemonade out of the way, careful not to let me see. Behind his round glasses, two slits for eyes. He doesn't have many lines on his face but he has smoky, old man's hair.

I look at his pen. It got here in its own black box. It is dark blue, with a gold belt around its middle and a gold clip to grip onto a pocket. He twists off the lid, flips open his writing pad. The part of the pen you write with looks more like a dagger than a pen. He begins to write, a giant blob of blue ink appears on the page. He rips that page out, balls it up and throws it into the bin, starts again.

'So, Robyn, do you like school?'

I do not speak.

He fills my silence with the crisp sound of his pen gliding across the page. Taking a deep breath in, he smiles. It is a small smile I have seen before. Mr Thorpe saves that smile for Gavin Rossiter when he has shown him for the fifth time how to add without using his fingers. Mr Thorpe looks to the classroom ceiling and says, *Jesus tonight,* sends Gavin to tidy the books in the library for the rest of the morning. After dinner Mr Thorpe is nice again. He nods at the cupboard for Gavin to get out the toy cars. Tells him to pass the biscuit tin over and hands Gavin a Rich Tea. Inside the tin is where he finds the note: *Dolly's shop will go on fire.*

Mr Wainwright shuffles his bottom all the way back into the chair and leans forward. 'Would you say you liked school, Robyn?'

I nod.

He writes.

'What do you like best about it?'

'The dinners.'

He writes.

I think he writes *greedy cow,* and I smile.

'So, you like school dinners. What's your favourite?'

'Everything.'

He writes.

I scratch my head.

He writes.

I think he writes *Robyn has nits,* and I smile.

'Who are your friends in school?'

I shrug.

He writes.

I shiver. Somebody's walking over your grave, Nan says.

'Is there anything you're scared of in school or at home?'

Burning water fills up my eyes. I blink it away, looking down. I think: I'm scared to wake up in the mornings, scared to breathe too loud, scared to be left in with my dad on my own. But I can't say it. I could never say it out loud, to anybody, or he'd kill me.

When I look back up, Mr Wainwright's face is all white, like he's going to drop down dead. He has sweat on his forehead. On the telly, when anyone takes a funny turn, people give them a drink. I grab his black bag and search inside for the lemonade. It's not there. Then I see the zip on the other side.

Mr Merryville walks in the room and catches me, elbow-deep in the bag.

'Robyn Mason, what are you doing?'

I ignore him, panicking to get the zip open.

It's there. I twist off the top and tilt it up to Mr Wainwright's lips. He makes a good noise in his throat, all the red coming back into his face. Mr Merryville stands by the open door stiff as the statue of Mary.

Mr Wainwright loosens his tie.

'What do you think you're doing, Mason?' Mr Merryville shouts. 'Rummaging around in an adult's bag?'

'Sir, I . . .'

'Don't deny it. I saw you with my own eyes.'

Mr Wainwright says, 'It's okay, really, she helped.'

'Get back to class. I'll come and deal with you later.'

For the rest of the day I can't concentrate on my work. Every time the door handle squeaks my belly does a handstand. Just before home time Mr Merryville calls me out of class. On the way to the door I spit on my palms and rub them together thinking maybe the cane won't hurt as much. Outside, Mr Merryville smiles at me. 'Robyn, I didn't understand what you were doing before. Mr Wainwright explained and he sends his thanks.' Then he walks away. Easy as that. No telling off and no cane. I realize I've worried all day for nothing.

*

A couple of days later, when Dad's not home, I tell Mum about Mr Wainwright. 'That's not all you've got to worry about,' she says. 'The headmaster sent a letter, wants to see me. Good job I opened it and not your father.'

Mum says I'm to stop taking things from school, otherwise they'll be knocking on the door next and, if that happens (she whispers, nodding at Dad's empty chair), he'll go mad.

8

I haven't seen Nan for ages. It is Chris who hands me a piece of paper with her address written on it.

17 VESCOCK STREET (OFF SCOTLAND ROAD)

LIVERPOOL 5

(OPPOSITE ST SYLVESTER'S CLUB)

I read the address over and over again. Chris laughs, says I'll read the words right off the page if I'm not careful.

'She wants to see you Saturday.' February is my favourite month of the year. Saturday is my eleventh birthday.

'How do I get there?'

'You walk fifteen, twenty minutes away. Round the back of St George's church, to the grass hills, down them, all the way to Netherfield Road, cross that, down to Great Homer Street, then on to Scotland Road.' Chris can't stop coughing, his face bright red. 'Ask anyone on Scottie where St Sylvester's Club is. You'll find it.'

As he walks down the steps I can hear his wheezy chest.

I follow Chris's directions, and once I'm on Scotland Road I show a girl a bit older than me the address. After that, Nan's block is easy to find. I knock at the door, half thinking a stranger will answer. But it is May, my nan. Blue-eyed May, stick swinging over her arm, legs half-past five on a clock.

'Look at you, happy birthday.' She hugs me around the waist. 'Still as thin as a straw. Come in, I'll show you around.'

I love the place. The feel of smooth new walls painted clean, like mint imperials. The kitchen is double the size of the one in Tommy Whites. Brand new cupboards, cream, brown wooden handles and a baby blue worktop. Even room for a small table and two chairs in the corner.

Her bedroom is lovely. She has a cream furry rug by her bed to step out on when she gets up. Above her bed, Jesus lies, arms open wide, on a wooden cross. Nan's special prayer: *Goodnight all the Angels in Heaven. God keep me safe till morning.*

Without asking, I take my shoes and socks off, sit on the bed and wriggle my toes in the furriness.

Nan laughs. 'You look like an escaped lunatic.'

The toilet and bath are brand new, her mangle slotted in the corner.

I don't like the smell. It's a dry, gassy smell that Nan says is caused by the blow-out central heating. She points to a grid low down on the wall. I notice them in every room. 'I'm not using it. I'd rather throw my coat on if I feel cold. Save on the bills. Save on the dust as well.'

Just across from her front door she takes me up a narrow staircase to the first floor, two front doors opposite each other. Then we climb more steps to the second floor where Lily and her husband, Frank, live. Lily opens the door, looking too young to be a pensioner. She has long nails and short words.

'May?'

'Just the key, Lily, to show my granddaughter the back yard.'

'A minute.' She disappears down her lobby. 'Here we are. Pass it back through the letterbox soon as.' With a quick smile, she closes the door.

There's not much to see. An empty washing line, a square of concrete with a couple of trees planted around the edges. Beyond the back fence there is a playground attached to a school. 'We're going to get benches out here, Lily says. So we can sit. There are better places to sit.'

Nan locks the back door and I run upstairs to give the key back to Lily. It's her husband Frank who opens the door with no shirt on. He takes the key from my hand. 'Just getting a shave,' he says, pressing his neck too close to my face. 'Smell?' I don't move. He kisses my cheek. I run away, take the stairs two at a time. I hear him laughing behind me. Downstairs, Nan has the radio on. 'I might put a little bet on, Robyn. I've had a tip. Your face is as pink as a tongue.'

She switches the radio off, and puts on her coat and scarf, ready to go out. Folds a handkerchief around a piece of red cheese, another around a knife, pushes them into a black shopping bag. 'Coming?' she asks.

I nod.

After Nan puts her bet on, we head off to Soho Street. On a Saturday, down on Soho Street, Sayers the bakers sell day-old cakes and bread at less than half price. There's a queue that stretches all the way down the street; people don't seem to mind waiting.

Mrs Naylor comes out of the shop carrying a pile of white cake boxes stacked on top of one another, tied together with red ribbon. She parades them along the queue. The lady in front of us shouts to Mrs Naylor.

'Feeding the five thousand, love? I hope you left something in there for us.'

Mrs Naylor nods in her direction. 'These are a special treat for my grandchildren.' She throws a nasty look right at my nan.

I turn to Nan. 'What's the matter with her?'

'She knows the game's up with me.'

'What does that mean?'

'I know what she's up to. I can read between the lines.'

'What does that mean?'

'It means nobody can pull the wool over my eyes.'

'How do you read between the lines?'

'You need to think about why people do what they do.'

'Oh.'

'And what's in it for them.'

I watch Mrs Naylor walk away. 'Will she give all those cakes to her grandkids?'

'Have you ever seen her grandkids visit?'

'No, never.'

'She might eat a couple herself. But most of them will stay in their boxes and rot. I caught her the other week, tipping loads of cakes down the chute. As far as I know she fell out with her son years ago. Her grandkids don't even know she exists.'

'Why did she buy them and say they were for her grandkids?'

'Why do you think she bought them?'

'Because they're cheap?'

'People make up games all the time, Robyn. She's made up a little game to amuse herself. This one is to fire up the envy in people.'

'But it doesn't make sense. Why would she want people to hate her?'

'Not hate her, remember her. Nobody around here looked twice at Mrs Naylor before she started buying that many cakes.'

Inside the shop, the shelves are nearly empty. The ladies serving behind the counter wear white overalls, with an orange Sayers badge on the pocket. Nan buys four egg custards and two Vienna loaves, one loaf for us and one for the birds.

We head off down to the Pier Head to watch the boats come in. It's busy when we get there. Two men coughing up their guts shuffle along on a bench to let us sit down. They stamp out cigarette stumps. There's nothing much left of their shoes but holes.

It's breezy by the river and Nan asks me where my coat is. I can't tell her I haven't got one, so I tell her I forgot it. I surprise myself at how easily I am learning to lie. 'We won't stay long,' she says. 'You'll catch your death.'

This is my favourite part of Liverpool. The Liver Building sits on the edge of the Mersey like a palace. A palace guarded by two magnificent birds. I like the idea of being watched over by something that has wings. Something that can pick itself up and leave if it feels like it, and doesn't have to tell nobody where it's going.

Nan looks towards the water. 'I got off the boat in this very place from Ireland with no shoes on my feet. I couldn't have been much more than three years of age.' She turns to me. 'Hungry?'

I nod, shivering. The wind blows drops of salty water to my lips.

She unbuttons her coat and tells me to put it on. Cuts open the Vienna loaf and cheese on a tea towel, her body curved into the wind. She has a pink cardigan with rows of little holes down the front. A slice of white fringe blows out from her scarf, flapping like a wing. She flicks it out of her eye with her knuckles.

The bread and cheese taste chewy and creamy and delicious. I huddle inside the coat, watching the pigeons flock around us, let the *eeeee*ing of the seagulls above us take my sad thoughts away. I watch the water foam up against itself.

Taking a bite out of her butty, Nan picks off bits from the other loaf for the birds. She throws the bread out towards the railings, as far away from us as she can.

One of the men next to us frowns. 'That's good bread you're throwing, lady.'

'Would a custard pie stop your moaning?'

He smiles and nudges the man next to him.

Nan hands the box over like a prize.

'Is it all right to give me mate one?'

Nan nods at him, mouth full.

They take one custard each and hand the box back.

When we have finished eating, both of us share the coat, one sleeve each. With the empty cake box, we shuffle over to the bin, laughing, rolled tightly together, like a Twix. Three women push babies in prams backwards against the wind. Behind them, little boys pull off sweaters and twirl them above their heads, long strands of springy navy wool flying from their cuffs.

Cupping her face in her hands to warm it, Nan says she'd love a cup of tea. We head off for the number 3 bus. On the bus it's warm. Nan asks me if I want to stay on until the last stop then get back on again. I say yes. It's a free ride all the way with a bus pass, one penny for me.

We take the front two seats downstairs. I have the window seat so I can see everything. Nan takes her scarf off and smooths down her hair. We ride across the city. Nan points churches out to me, tells me their names. St Anthony's, St John's, I can't remember all the names. And pubs she used to go to with Jack when she was younger, and washing lines. You can tell a lot about a person from their washing line, she says.

The bus stops at a block of flats like ours. Nan points to a flat on the first floor. A pair of men's blue jeans and a pair of knickers hang on the line.

'Newly married woman, no children yet.'

'How do you know?'

She shakes her head. 'The jeans will never dry.'

'Why?'

'She's pegged them out by the waistband. And lace frillies? It's their first six months of marriage, I'd say.'

With two fingers, she taps out a tune on my arm, sings it out loud.

> *What's the time? Half past nine.*
> *Hang your knickers on the line.*
> *When they're dry, bring them in.*
> *Iron them with a rolling pin.*

'It's like being a detective.'

Nan nods. 'Okay, Robyn, you have a go.'

Squishing my nose against the window, I look across at a line that has too many clothes on it.

'Second floor, third door on the left: too many clothes on it. A family of six, maybe? Four kids, man and wife?'

Nan shakes her head. The bus starts to pull away.

'It takes practice. Two kids, man and wife. Everything looks brand new. Maybe her man's had a big win on the horses and she's showing off.'

Nan points to a line full of towels. 'The woman who pegged that lot out has got terrible worries. Look how each towel is folded again and again before it's been pegged. They'll never dry. Mind somewhere else, I'll bet.'

The bus pulls away. Nan closes her eyes and drifts off until the last stop. We get off, board another bus and begin our journey home. On a wall behind the bus stop there's a small black and white poster advertising a boxing match. Nan sees it, smiles to herself. I say, 'Nan, tell me more about Granddad Jack.'

Nan rubs her leg, scrunches her face up with the pain.

'Jack couldn't sleep the night before a fight. He'd walk from Crosby to Liverpool town centre and back again. That's what he was doing the night I met him. He said walking helped to clear his head.

'Jack's passion was boxing. His father, Mick, trained him in a barn during the night while Rosie was asleep. They had to train in secret because Rosie didn't want Jack to fight. She'd lost her brother, John. He died after being in the ring. The referee didn't stop the fight in time. Rosie was there. She saw everything and she never got over it.

'One night, Rosie followed them to the barn and saw them both with their gloves on. She was furious; went at Mick with a pitchfork. Jack said she wouldn't speak to either of them for months. When he saw how much he'd upset his mam, Jack made her a promise he'd pack in boxing.'

'For ever?'

'For ever.'

'That's so sad.'

'Jack was never the same man once he gave up his passion. At first, he told me his promise to Rosie was more like an interruption to his career. He said give it a year or so, Rosie will come around. But that's not how things worked out. I lost three boys before I had your mam; I couldn't carry them. When she was born she only weighed two pounds. We didn't think she'd survive. Jack spoiled her rotten. Took her everywhere, gave her anything she wanted.

People said she was spoiled. And she was. I had murder with Jack over it; your mum ended up a spoilt madam. And maybe she got what she deserved with that lazy good-for-nothing.'

When we get off the bus on Scotland Road, I ask Nan if I can come back to her flat. I think about her two-seater settee, me fast asleep on it, my legs dangling over the side.

'It's getting late, Robyn. Off home now before it gets dark. Come down and see me whenever you like. Wear your coat next time.' Nan starts to walk away.

'Just for half an hour?'

She stops. 'Is everything all right?'

'Yes.' I panic. 'It is late. I'll come down next Saturday.'

'Something on your mind?'

I shake my head, turn away and start to run home. 'Nah, see you Saturday.'

'C'mon now, don't make me wring it out of you.'

'It's nothing, honest. See you Saturday.'

In bed, covering myself up, I think about my nan with her lovely new flat. I think about having a place I can go and visit whenever I like. A place I can go and not have to think about stuff.

Nan still thinks I'm the old Robyn, the Robyn who tries her very best to be good. If she finds out what I'm really like now, she'll probably tell me to stay away. If I talk about stuff to Nan, I know it will spoil everything. Talking about stuff, like my stealing, would be the same as pegging out dirty nappies beside clean white towels.

On the morning of my birthday, Mum said my present hadn't arrived. She said I'd have to wait until Monday. After school, I race home and find a Raleigh Chopper in the hall. It is bright yellow, with a black L-shaped seat that smells like sunshine. The handle bars are high, with yellow and red tassels at the edge. Dad says he'll carry it downstairs for me into the square. I'm so excited I take the stairs three at a time.

Once I'm on it a group of kids surrounds me. One of them pats the back bit of seat behind me. 'Giz a takey?' she says.

I look up to the second landing where Dad and Mum watch.

'Can't, I'm not allowed.'

The kid looks up too and backs away.

I ride off into the big square. The bike doesn't feel like it's mine. I try to ride it the way I've seen the other kids ride. I get off and walk it around in a circle. Push it straight, faster and faster, jumping on bum-first while it rushes away from me. I ride standing up on the pedals until my legs ache, the seat a soft place to rest.

I ride through an old puddle with the front tyre, draw an S over and over, until there's a chain of them the length of the square. Lift the handlebars up, ride with just the back wheel on the ground, until it slams down like a horse refusing a fence. Pedal backwards round and round again and again in a complete circle, until I'm dizzy.

Use the tip of my sole to spin down one pedal fast, listen to the *whirr* and watch the edges blur. Make it go fast without using the pedals. Bum off the seat, run it down a hill, jump back on, legs out to the side screaming *wheeee wheeee*. Trace the way thick rubber zigzags across the tyres.

When I get back, I lift the Chopper up the stairs, careful not to bash it against the walls when I turn a corner. I get to our door all out of puff. Before I can knock, the door is flung open. He grabs the bike into the lobby and turns on the light. Slams the front door shut. Gets down on his knees, feels the tyres, spins the wheels around and checks the yellow paintwork. Licks the tip of his finger, rubs away dark splashes. Spins the pedals forwards and backwards, pulling the brakes hard.

He looks up at me, his dark eyes small. 'You've hammered this, you ungrateful bastard.'

I look down at the floor. He stands, pushes his face too close to mine. I can smell beer and smoke on his breath and it makes me feel sick. 'You don't deserve to have it. It isn't even paid for yet. Get to bed now.'

In the last year of junior school, we get to go on a trip away from home, for a whole week in May, to a place called Colomendy. Mr Thorpe gives us all a letter to take home, saying a small deposit is needed as soon as possible. We will be given a payment card and we can pay whatever we like off the trip, as long as it is all paid two weeks before we go. The classroom buzzes with the news. Outside, letters are waved high at the gate.

When I get home Dad puts my letter on the mantelpiece. 'What have you been up to?'

'Nothing.'

'What's all this then?'

'Don't know,' I lie.

Mum takes the thick glossy catalogue off her knee and puts it on the floor. 'I'll open it,' she says.

She tells him it's about a trip away for a week.

'How much?'

She tells him and he says bloody schools and their bloody money. 'If she carries on wrecking that bike the way she has been doing, she's got no chance.'

Mum shouts at Dad. 'Don't dictate to me what Robyn can and can't do. She is going, and I'll make sure of it.' I'm going away soon, I'll be able to tell Nan. A tiny balloon painted rainbow colours swirls in my chest. It fills me, from my toes right up to my head. I rub my hands together and feel it inside them. This, I think, is what happy feels like.

The next time I take the bike out I ride it through to a square I have never been in before. This square is darker than ours, calmer, with less wind. It smells stuffy, like a slept in bedroom. I sit on the seat and look up at the early morning washing lines. A couple of shirts wave their arms at me; a skirt flips up a whoops-a-daisy hem.

On the top landing, last door on the right, heavy jeans in three different sizes with their pockets hanging open touching the wind. Cream sweaters, with three brown stars on the front and knitted collars. Three lads I'd say: a toddler, one a bit younger than me and a bigger one.

Going into this new square is like entering a different country. Heads above the landings are familiar but different. Reading the washing lines makes me feel like I am visiting a relative. I don't have any aunties or uncles. The only homes I have ever been in, apart from our flat, is Joan's house, Angela's house and Nan's new flat. It is a perfect way for me to find out about other people's lives, without them knowing anything at all about me.

I ride the bike back into our square. Dad watches over the landing. He tosses his head towards the stairs for me to come up. I stand up, try to get off the bike, but the pedals dig into the backs of my legs, trapping me. He carries on watching. The tip of the seat pushes into my back like a gun.

9

Before the end of morning assembly, Mr Merryville asks us to put our hands together. We are to say an Eternal Rest, for Arthur Raynard who died last weekend. When we have finished, Mr Merryville's shoes squeak, squeak across the polished floor, like there's an army of mice inside. They stop at Angela. He tells everyone how Angela, a valued member of our school, and her mother, are to be commended for being of great comfort to Mrs Raynard during her time of need. He pats Angela's head. Angela's red face disappears behind her hands.

Later that morning when we are in the middle of doing collective nouns, Mr Merryville comes into our classroom. Mr Thorpe's face brightens. He picks a brand new stick of chalk from the box. 'Ah, you're just in time to witness how well the class is doing with their collective nouns.' He turns to the board.

Mr Merryville scans the room. 'Yes, yes, wonderful I'll bet. I'm here to borrow Angela. Ah, there you are.' He's managed to get a man from the local paper, to interview Angela and her mother. They're in his office right now. 'Exciting stuff,' he says, mainly to himself, rubbing his hands together like he's trying to start a fire.

Mr Thorpe says nothing. The chalk drops to his side. He watches Mr Merryville leave the room, pat, patting Angela's head. When the door closes, Mr Thorpe snaps the chalk in half and throws it on the floor. Rubbing his hands together to remove the chalk, he looks around the room. This happens sometimes, when Mr Merryville has interrupted the lesson. He will stand up, walk around the room trying to find things, things that didn't bother him before. The number eleven at the top of his nose has changed into a V.

'Tommy Taylor, have you had breakfast?'

'Yes, sir.'

'Then why are you eating your cuff? Maureen Clarke?'

Maureen looks astonished. 'Yes, sir?'

'Stop chewing your hair. You'll drown the nits.'

Her face flushes pink. 'Sorry, sir.'

He spies the lid off the biscuit tin. 'Who has been at the tin?'

Faces drop under Mr Thorpe's eyes.

'Anybody?'

Silence.

He looks inside the tin. 'They must have eaten themselves then.' His head shakes. He lifts the tin up, bends his knees and tilts his head to look underneath. Like a magician, he taps the side of the tin with a ruler. Shakes his head again, tips the tin upside-down. A few crumbs and an empty packet of Rich Tea spill to the floor.

'I placed a packet of biscuits in here yesterday. A full packet. Now they've gone. We must have a mouse. Don't you think?'

No answer.

'Cat got your tongues?'

Silence.

Mr Thorpe picks up the empty packet, walks over to Tommy Taylor and scrunches it under his nose.

He found a fistful of broken biscuits once, in Tommy's pocket. Tommy blinks his eyes away inside his head. When he opens them again, Mr Thorpe digs him in the ribs with the ruler. Tommy knows what's coming so he rolls to the floor with a thud. Mr Thorpe walks back to the tin.

'No more biscuit money out of my pockets for greedy mice.' He picks the tin up and drops it *clang* into the bin under his desk.

Tommy starts to get up.

'Stay where you are.'

Trisha Fisher raises her hand.

Mr Thorpe ignores her.

He walks back over to Tommy. 'Open your mouth.'

Tommy opens his mouth and Mr Thorpe pokes his nose too close inside and sniffs. I imagine Tommy sinking his teeth deep into the nose, while we all pile in and thump Mr Thorpe until he drops to the floor, staring up at something that looks like his nose sticking out of Tommy Taylor's teeth. He grasps at the place on his face where it once was. We watch him watch Tommy swallow it down whole.

Mr Thorpe starts to shake Tommy's sleeves. Up and down they go, like a scarecrow in a windy field.

'Maybe they're up his sleeve, crumbs hidden inside his ripped cuffs? Is that why you nibble them?'

He bends down, drags the jumper up over Tommy's head. His ears get stuck in the neck and he lets out a moan. Mr Thorpe pulls harder; they spring pinky-red back into view. Once the jumper is off, Mr Thorpe shakes it, throws it to the floor.

Trisha Fisher puts up her hand again.

'What, girl?'

'I need the toilet, sir.'

He checks the clock on the wall. 'You can wait until break.'

Trisha Fisher leans forward ready to pounce at the clock.

'A scabby little mouse has poked its greedy nose into my biscuit tin and ate the lot. What's to be done?'

Gavin Rossiter puts his hand up.

'What is it, Rossiter?'

'You could lock them away, sir, so scabby little mice can't get them.'

'Lock them away? What do you think they are, prisoners of war?'

Trisha Fisher's hand goes up again. Her wide scribbly mouth is closed tight. Her mum's been up to the school before; she told Mr Merryville Trisha's got to go to the toilet whenever she needs to cos she's got a weak bladder.

Mr Thorpe looks at her, his voice has risen to a scream. 'I said wait.'

He walks back over to Tommy. 'I know who to lock away in a cupboard. Dirty little thieves who steal things that don't belong to them.'

My face burns.

Somebody squeaks pissy wissy at Trisha Fisher.

She bursts into tears.

Mr Thorpe walks back to his desk and leans against it, like it's an old friend.

I look across at Stephen Foley; he's got his palms over his ears. The sound of the bell makes us all look at the clock.

Tommy Taylor jumps up, wearing just his vest. Slips back into his seat. He stoops, not taking his eyes off Mr Thorpe, paws around the floor for his jumper, finds it, holds it to his chest. The bell rings again. Breathless, we wait to be dismissed. With a careless hand, Mr Thorpe waves us away. Tommy legs it across the room, wriggling back inside his jumper. Trisha Fisher, cupping the middle of her skirt, knees locked, takes baby steps towards the door.

Once we are on the playground, I hear Anthony Greenbank talking to Gavin about Mr Thorpe. 'He's a loony.'

'I know,' Gavin says. 'All over a crummy biscuit.' They don't laugh. It's too soon to pretend it was funny.

Anthony tells Gavin about Arthur Raynard. 'He used to let me off if I never had enough money. Once, these big kids robbed my dad's paper money off me. When I told him what had happened, he gave me the *Echo* for free. Dolly would never let you off like that.'

I turn to Kevin and whisper. 'Who was Arthur Raynard?'

He shakes his head. 'Dolly's husband, you nit.'

I can hear Dad's shiny cherry blossom shoes *clit-clat* down the stairs. Stop halfway. He taps his pockets but the matches aren't there, so he turns around, shoes *shish shish* back up the stairs.

The scrape of the key in the lock then his voice from the hall: 'Get my matches off the mantelpiece.'

And Mum, handing them to me out of her pocket.

In the hall, holding open the front door, see him shake them to his ear. 'They're not mine. Off the mantelpiece, I said.'

Back into the living room, Mum's already got them open. Takes out a pinchful, tucks them, goodnight God bless, inside the box I hold.

When he's gone, I walk into the kitchen. Mum is rolling the tip of her cigarette across the electric ring. Little sparks of fire fall to the floor, burn themselves out halfway down. She draws on the tip, blows out a mouthful of smoke that fills the tiny room. 'Bastard,' she says in a quiet voice.

He's just flung his tea all up the wall. Said he didn't like liver and onions, she should know that by now.

She told him to fuck off. He sprang up out of the chair. Got the shoe polish and brush from his all-dolled-up box under the sink, said he'd do just that.

On the playground, freezing winds blow up from the Mersey, rattling the open windows. The sound of his name, Arthur Raynard, blown inside classrooms like dead leaves. Something bad has happened to Mr Dolly and I didn't catch it in time.

Trisha Fisher skips around the playground, her face unscrewed. Tommy Taylor sits on the ground, back against the wall, eyes everywhere, as if something of his has been stolen. There's a crowd around Angela. I stand right at the back where she can't see me. Since the vanity case thing happened, there's a part of me that thinks if she doesn't see me, she'll forget all about me, and what I did.

Angela tells everybody, like she's on the telly: she was in Dolly's shop with her mum when the police came. Dolly was standing on her little ladder, reaching to the top shelf to weigh two ounces of jelly babies.

Tipping them into the scale, she said she might take a nap, in about half an hour, when Arthur got back.

Dolly split open a box of Galaxy Counters, stood them to attention behind each other inside the glass counter.

And the police officers who walked in, saying her name like a question. *Dolly Raynard?* Asked her if there was somewhere private. Somewhere they could talk?

Handing over the jelly babies to Angela's mum, Dolly said she couldn't leave the shop, so they could say what they had to say right there.

They told her there had been an accident. Mr Raynard.

Angela's mum handed the coins over, took the white paper bag. Asked Dolly if there was anything she could do.

Dolly twisted the lid back on the jar, left it on the side; lifted the end bit of the counter up in her hand so they could pass through to the other side.

At the shop door, Mrs Leary, *ooeee*ing to Dolly that she'd meet her at seven o'clock, outside the bingo.

Dolly handed Angela's mum the keys, told her to lock the door. Just for a little while.

Angela and her mum guarded the shop on their own, while Dolly took the officers upstairs.

People banged on the door. Her mum said *clear off* under her breath and wrote on a ripped paper bag BACK IN TEN MINUTES then taped it to the front door.

When the police had gone, Dolly sat on the brown stool in the corner, picked the bobbles off her cream Arran cardigan.

I turn to the girl beside me on the playground, who is in the year below me. Her mouth open wide. 'Has she said how he died?'

The girl shrugs.

'Will you ask her? Go over and say, how did he die?'

The girl pushes to the front and taps Angela on the arm.

'On his way home from playing golf in Crosby, Arthur Raynard died in a car crash.'

That afternoon, Mr Thorpe is a pale ghost of his morning self. He calls the register with a voice that sounds like it doesn't believe itself. He says Mr Merryville wants us in the hall, for a special presentation.

Mr Merryville holds a small silver trophy. He reads out what's written on it, *Special Pupil Award*. He shakes Angela's hand, gives her the shiny cup. She stands in front of the whole school, holds the cup up to her chest and grins.

10

Mum is peeling potatoes with a long knife. It has a brown handle with silver studs. She can take the skin off a whole potato without stopping. It looks easy. An old sheet of newspaper is laid out on the draining board; the peelings coil around each other like dark snakes. There's a pan of salty water ready on the worktop. In the living room Dad watches horse racing on the telly. She hands me the knife. 'It's time you knew how to peel spuds.'

I hold the knife in one hand, the potato in the other. The potato feels gritty and rough. Bits of soil cling to my nails. I pierce the skin on the potato, but I can't get the knife to budge.

'You've gone too deep,' Mum says. 'Just lightly take off the top, or there'll be nothing of any good left.'

I try again. This time, the bit that drops onto the paper looks more like Mum's peelings, only shorter.

'That's it. Now.' She points at a small black lump. 'Make sure you cut all the eyes out, all the bad bits. See if you can peel the lot by the time I get back from Dolly's. I need a packet of fags and fancy the walk.'

It takes me ages to peel one. The knife keeps slipping off the side bit of the spud. I cut deep then shallow bits out. Try to get the eyes and get the roundness back but it gets smaller and smaller. In the end, the shape it started out as has disappeared. It's all corners and triangles now. It would fit neatly on a teaspoon.

I pick up another one and try again. I start it okay. It's the roundness that's hard to hold. I cut it in half. Then lay it flat, like an upside-down cup without a handle. I slice away like I've seen Nan do, when she cuts a Vienna loaf. It's easier to take the skin off in thin slices. I speed up. Cut more and more potatoes. It's fun hearing them plop into the pan of icy water; they leave a trail of white mist behind them.

Dad comes into the kitchen behind me. He dips his hand into the pan and pulls out a handful of potatoes. 'What's this?'

I don't answer.

'I said what the fuck's this?'

'I've peeled the spuds.'

'Call these crumbs spuds? We're having a roast, you stupid bitch. That's good money you've wasted.'

I'm not sure at first what the burning is in my ear. I hit my head on the way down, legs sprawled, ears ringing. I think I've slipped. I cup my ear in the palm of my hand and it's soaking wet. So is my hair. I see his raised hand above my head, water dripping. When I look up again he's gone back into the living room.

I stare at cupboards I think could have jumped up without moving. He's back in the kitchen, standing over me.

We hear the front door slam. Mum is in the kitchen.

'She slipped,' Dad says. 'Must be water on the floor.'

I stare at his navy blue slippers with their thin yellow stripe and the knife on the floor next to them.

He catches me looking then stoops to pick up the knife.

Mum throws her cigarettes on the worktop, gives me a hand up, my other hand still on my ear.

'Let's see,' Mum says.

Dad takes a cigarette out of the box and strikes a match.

I take my hand away and Mum says it's all red.

Mum grabs a tea towel and wets it under the cold tap. 'Here, press that on it. You must have banged it on the cupboard.' She looks at Dad lighting his cigarette. 'For fuck's sake get out, there's no room in here as it is. Standing there gawping.'

Dad gives Mum a bad look.

'She's just being a baby,' Dad says.

'I told you to get out.'

He stays exactly where he is. Smoke curls around his mouth.

I go to my room and lie on my good ear. My good ear. I say it like it's something I need to take better care of. Like Nan's Sunday tablecloth.

I feel safe in my room, just my bed and me, the pillow a soft place to think. I toss around what happened. I didn't see him hit me. I must have slipped. But I felt the sting before I fell. The sting was what made me fall. But I might have slipped, I'm not sure. The story changes so many times in my head until I don't really see it myself any more. To stop thinking so much I walk my fingers across the candy-striped sheets; I count thirty stripes across. The drumming in my ear won't stop and I want to scream at it.

Mum's head is at the door. 'All right?'

I nod.

She checks my ear. 'Hungry?'

'No, tired.'

'I'll let you sleep then.'

You shouldn't have gone the shop and left me with him, I want to say. The door closes and burning water fills my eyes. 'Mum,' I say out loud. 'Mum.' But she doesn't hear. I should have told her then. But what could she do? He wouldn't even leave the kitchen when she asked him to and she had a look in her eyes I've never seen before.

The flush of the toilet, then Dad's face at the door, his voice low. 'Be very careful what you say. Kids with big mouths get taken away, where nobody can find them.'

I turn away onto my bad ear and it hurts. 'Fuck off,' I say in my head. The door closes. I turn back around to check he's gone.

Next morning, Mum checks my ear. 'You'll live,' she says.

I nod.

'How did you manage to do that?'

'I tried to lift the pan. Water tipped out. I slipped.'

She walks away. Takes out a cigarette and lights it.

I I

I am sitting on the step. There are noises in our square, shouting. I look over the landing and see nine stars. I've seen them
before, somewhere. I think of my bike, the new square with no
wind. That's it, the washing line, last house on the right. Three
boys, with mops of wild curly hair shout. *Rubbish. Rubbish taken.
Any rubbish?*

They push an old Silver Cross pram that has bags of rubbish
inside. The smallest boy is pulling a toddler along by a dirty rope
attached to a go-kart. I run downstairs to take a closer look. The
toddler has an old bicycle wheel between his hands which he uses
as a pretend steering wheel. Two lines of bright green snot hang
from his nose, propped up by his thick upper lip. The tip of his
tongue curls up to take a lick.

Rubbish. Rubbish taken. Any rubbish?

Mrs Kinsella, who has a front yard, comes out carrying two bags.
'Here you go, lads.' She swings the bags onto the pram, hands a
coin to the tallest kid. 'Here's a penny for your trouble, Bernie lad.'

She walks over to the toddler in the go-kart, lifts the hem of her
pinny to his nose, pulls the green number eleven away. 'There.

That's better, Johnny.' She walks away, the hem of her pinny pressed into a pinch. Bernie drops the coin inside a black sock and tucks it back in his trouser pocket.

Dad comes out of the block. 'What're you up to?' he asks.

'Nothing,' I say.

He twists my bad ear between his fingers. 'Don't move out of the square. Remember what I said.' When he lets go, it starts to throb all over again.

Behind a cloud of smoke Mr Sanderson wheezes down over the third landing. 'Hold on there, lads, giz a minute.'

The boys shuffle the bags around on the pram to make more room.

Dad walks away through the arch towards the Stanley.

From her step, Mrs Kinsella pulls a face. 'You'll get nothing off that tight sod. Sanderson wouldn't part with daylight.'

Bernie passes me as he races up the stairs to give Mr Sanderson a hand. They load three more bags onto the pram and Bernie says to the oldest lad, 'Come on, Ged, we're done.'

Mrs Kinsella watches Mr Sanderson walk away without giving the boys a coin.

She calls over to him. 'Ahh, eh, Billy lad. Give the lads a penny, for their trouble.'

'Look, love,' he says. 'If I had a penny I'd give it.' He turns to the brothers. 'The lads know I'll see them all right when I get my dole.'

She puts a hand in her pinny pocket. 'I've a penny to lend you.'

He shakes his head. 'I don't lend trouble.'

Before she closes the door, she whispers across to Bernie. 'Told you. Wouldn't part with his own shite.' Her voice sounds pleased.

I follow them up St Domingo Road, past the wash house behind St George's church to a piece of wasteland. They pile the rubbish in the middle of the ground, brown paper coal bags tipped upside down then laid flat. From Ged's pockets, tiny pieces of coal are sprinkled on top. Bernie takes a box of matches out of his pocket.

'Move our Johnny further back, Ged,' Bernie tells his brother, before striking the match. He bends, moving the flame from side to side until a piece of paper catches light. He looks over to the wall where I'm hiding. I jump back. Hope he hasn't seen me.

'You can come and watch if you like,' Bernie calls.

I walk over towards the fire. Yellow, red, blue and orange flames nudge against each other. The smoky smell of burning: the wind carries it away, changes its mind, blows it back against my cheek like a kiss.

Heat burns through my trousers and warms my bones. Johnny's hands reach out to me; squishy fingers wriggle for my attention.

Bernie laughs. 'He wants you to pick him up.'

I hold him in my arms, not too close to the fire. He points, face lit up, leaning forward, like all of us, wanting to touch it. He grips my bad ear and I cry out. He laughs, tries to do it again, but I pull my head right back. He's heavy, like a bag of wet washing, thumb inside his mouth, fingernails no bigger than a tear. His everywhere eyes are green and he takes in everything. He stinks to high heaven.

Bernie notices my face change.

He holds out his hands. 'Pass him.'

I try to hand him over but he won't go. He presses his head into my shoulder and it feels good that he doesn't want to let go.

'He likes you,' Bernie says, pulling him away.

Bernie throws Johnny up in the air and catches him. Puts Johnny's back into his belly, clasps him around the waist and twirls around and around. Johnny squeals in bubbles, catching his breath again out of the wind. Still holding Johnny tight, Bernie opens his legs and swings him through them singing, *What's the time, Mr Wolf?* *One o'clock, two o'clock.*

Ged stands in front of the baby, sticks out his bum, the baby kicks it. *Three o'clock, four o'clock.*

Bernie looks at the clock on top of St George's church.

'Find more sticks, Ged. Let's build the fire up a bit before we go.'

Ged doesn't move.

'Go on,' Bernie says.

Ged finds a few sticks and throws them on the fire.

Bernie puts Johnny back in the cart. Takes a few steps back and runs towards the fire. He leaps over it; flames lick the soles of his shoes. On the other side of the fire he rolls to the ground, rips off his shoes and swears. I walk over and see the sides of his shoes wrinkled up from the flames. Ged gets hold of the rope and starts to pull the baby away.

'Your turn,' Bernie shouts over to him.

'Piss off,' Ged shouts. 'Stupid loony. One of these days you won't make it to the other side.'

Bernie looks at me. 'How about you?'

Ged stops pulling the kart, shakes his head. 'Leave it, Bernie.'

'No way,' I say.

'A couple of scaredy cats, Johnny lad, that's what they are.'

'Am not,' I say.

Johnny starts to cry.

'Go on then, no dodging to the side, right over the middle.'

'Time to get him home for a nappy,' Ged says.

I take a few steps back, run up to the fire as quick as I can and leap. I clear it, roll onto my back at the other side.

'Another stupid loony, Johnny lad.'

Bernie looks at the burning fire then back at me and grins.

Ged is shouting now. 'Come on, time to go.'

But we don't move. We stay and watch the fire burn itself out until there's only ashes. We watch their dark feathery shapes flicker and melt to nothing. Johnny screams inside the kart, green number eleven drawn on again. Bernie hands him the wheel, the tip of Johnny's tongue takes a lick of green, using the tyre to wipe the rest away. Finally they head off home.

Bernie limps away, looks back at me. 'Coming?' He grins.

Bernie's mum sits, legs tucked to the side, waiting on the step, dark red hair, half-empty jar at her feet. Johnny's squishy fingers reach out. 'Come on, gorgeous lad.' She rocks him in her arms. Face right up to his, touches his cheek, beetroot-stained finger rests on the dimple in his chin. She sings to him.

> *Nebuchadnezzar, king of the Jews*
> *sold his wife for a pair of shoes.*
> *When the shoes began to pinch*
> *Nebuchadnezzar began to flinch.*
> *When the shoes began to wear*
> *Nebuchadnezzar began to swear.*
> *When the shoes began to leak*
> *Nebuchadnezzar began to squeak.*
> *When the shoes began to crack*
> *Nebuchadnezzar said 'Take them back.'*

On 'back' she lets Johnny's head fall back in her arms, chases his giggles into the lobby. Ged barges past them, goes inside. I move closer. Bernie smells musty like his lobby. Bernie's mum pulls a face.

'Who stinks then? Who's pooh-poohed then? Come on, stinky pants, in you come.' She holds her nose.

'Jesus, I'll never get used to the smell.' She looks at the empty pram. 'How did you do?'

Bernie takes the sock out of his pocket. 'I haven't had a chance to count it. Not as many bags, though. Things are getting back to normal again.'

'Never mind. At least you've got something.' She notices me. 'Who's your friend?'

I realize they don't know my name. 'Robyn. I live in the front square.'

'The one by the church?'

'Yes.'

'I don't know a soul in that square.' She smiles, takes Johnny inside. 'Nice to meet you, Robyn from the front square.'

Bernie counts out the pennies on the step and piles them up into stacks of ten. I remember Dad told me to stay in our square.

'I'll have to go,' I say.

He picks up a penny. 'Want one?'

I think about taking it, could leave it on the mantelpiece for Dad so he'll stay in the pub longer.

'No thanks,' I say.

'What number do you live in?'

'33B.'

'I'll knock up. Later.'

'Later,' I say, and head off home, a thought hot inside my head. It makes me want to scream the words out loud so I can hear my own voice saying them. *I jumped over a real fire.*

12

Packages are being delivered to our flat, huge packages and tiny packages in brown cardboard boxes. Record players, radios, watches and rings. None of the stuff is for us. No sooner has it been unwrapped than it's sold. People knocking all the time, searching through the glossy-paged catalogue, asking can you get me this or that. Mum has a list on the mantelpiece and money in her purse.

She tells me it's time I had some new clothes, hands me the Colomendy deposit in a white envelope. It's March now; Trisha Fisher paid her deposit last month, but loads of kids still haven't paid. I can't wait for Monday when Mr Thorpe gets the payment book out. I'll be one of the first to pay mine. We get a taxi to Great Homer Street Market. I have never been in a taxi before. I have never been to a market before. The seats in the taxi are ripped; it smells of cigarette smoke and sick. Mum winds her window all the way down.

When we get out, Mum pays the driver.

'You need to get your smell sorted,' she says. 'It fucking reeks back there. You're lucky I'm in a good mood.'

The driver says nothing.

I look away.

There's so much to see. Stall after stall, selling bags, shoes, thick leather coats to the floor, with flap pockets and flyaway collars. Men in white hats selling fish, bacon, eggs. Their stall smells of the river.

A lady pouring tea from a flask, cream cardigans all laid out on a table. Some have tiny balls all over them, as if they've caught a disease.

It's great. I've never seen so many people in the one place. I can't wait to go up and down the aisles, see what else people are selling.

We stop at a sweet stall. Bags of dolly mixtures, rhubarb and custards, black jacks, fruit salads, shoelaces, sherbet dabs, drumstick lollipops. My eyes stop at the fruit salads, they're my favourite.

'Want some?' Mum says.

'Silly question to ask a kid,' the man behind the counter jokes.

'Just hand them over, smart arse.'

He laughs, takes her money.

We edge against walls to let prams pass. There's shouting: *Come on now, get your bananas, ten pence a bag.* There's a man selling burgers and hot dogs. People are buying them for breakfast. The smell of onions makes me hungry. It's not even ten o'clock and people are eating bags of chips from the chippy. On a Saturday, in Great Homer Street, rules don't seem to matter. You could stay here all day and still not see everything there is to see.

Two tiny monkeys sit on a skinny man's shoulders. They are tied to his wrist by a chain. They wear waistcoats and hats decorated with gold thread. The man is dressed the same. I watch as he lifts them onto people's shoulders and takes a photograph. He has a denim pinny tied around his waist to keep the money in.

'Want a picture?' Mum asks.

I shake my head. I'm scared of their long nails digging into me.

'Might as well, now we're here.' She calls the man over.

'All right, love?' he says, pushing one of his shoulders towards her. The monkey on it opens its mouth and yawns in her face.

Mum pulls her head back. 'Not me, you daft fucker, her.'

'Which one do you want?'

I shrug.

'No need to be scared. They don't bite. I've filed their teeth down.'

'Get a move on. Which one?' Mum says.

'Any,' I say.

I look into the monkey's eyes and they are sad. Like they want to cry but can't. If you don't laugh you'll cry, Nan says. But the monkeys don't laugh either. The man has dropped one onto my shoulder and I can feel its tail swishing from side to side down my back. It smells like my coat when it's wet.

Mum shakes her head at me. 'Oh, for fuck's sake, straighten the face, will you?'

When it is over I take a quick glance at the picture before Mum puts it in her bag.

'Like it?'

Look at me. Bushy hair, eyes all scrunched up, shoulders too near my ears. I want to feed the picture to a monkey or drop it down the grid and watch the look on Mum's face as it disappears.

'Yes,' I lie.

She lights a cigarette. Takes in a breathful of smoke, shakes the match dead and throws it to the floor. She looks at the photograph again. 'Ugly bastards, monkeys. Stink as well.'

Mum takes a good look around before she decides what to buy. I try on a cream pair of trousers with six buttons on the waistband. They have two enormous pockets at the side of the leg. 'They're all the go, them,' she says. 'Birmingham bags.'

Mum chooses a sky blue, capped-sleeve T-shirt to go with them. It has a picture of three mice on the front and underneath in curly letters it says: *Three Blind Mice*. She buys herself underwear and fluffy pink slippers with a heel on; a kitten heel, she says.

We meet a woman pushing twins in a pram. Two other kids hold onto the handles at each side. 'All right, Margy?' Mum says.

Margy yawns; she has nice teeth. 'Shattered, Babs, been up since six. You see much of Eileen?'

'No, you?'

'Heard she's got a new job, working in St Michael's Market.' Margy looks at me. 'This your daughter?'

'Yeah, this is Robyn.'

Mum looks at her pram. 'It's chocca here today, don't know how you're getting through with that. Got your hands full there all right; you need to get yourself done.'

When we walk away Mum tells me she used to go to school with Margy, and Eileen. 'But all the lads were after Margy. Me and Eileen used to be dead jealous.' She looks back, shakes her head. 'Margy's fucking destroyed now.'

Margy doesn't look destroyed to me. She just looks worn out.

I don't want to go home. I love it here, especially the being outside bit; people eating from trays in the street. I suppose it would be different in bad weather. I can't wait to tell Nan about Greaty Market. Before we go I get to choose burger or chips. I order chips with fruity curry sauce on top. Mum gets the same. We finish them off in another taxi home.

At home, Dad sits in his chair. HATE fingers fast-tapping on the wooden arm. On my skin I feel something's going to happen, like Nan feels the rain coming in her bad leg.

He stands. 'Where the fuck have you two been?'

Mum laughs. 'Only to Greaty for a few bits. You were still asleep.'

He looks at the bags. 'Spent up, have you?'

'Like I said, I got a few bits, that's all. What's it to you?'

'Been fed?'

'Yes, we had chips.'

'I've had fuck all.'

'You should've got off your arse then and made something.'

He's at her throat, got her pinned up against the wall. LOVE HATE fingers close together like hot and cold taps.

The bags fall to the floor.

'Don't speak to me like I'm some snot-nosed kid.'

Her legs kick out at him.

He squeezes her neck tighter.

I scream at him to stop.

Somebody next door bangs on the wall.

Mum can't speak. Her face gets redder and redder.

I run at him with both hands flat, push them into his back. He lets go. Mum falls to the floor, gasping for breath. He turns to me. Grabs my hair and twists it round his fingers. I cry out with the pain; he throws me towards the door.

'Get to your room,' Mum whispers.

I don't shut my door. I can hear his raised voice shouting he's the boss around here and she'd better get used to it. And Mum, who always has something to say, says nothing.

The next morning, Mum stands in front of a slanty mirror to watch herself smoke. Over the sink, she lets the ash grow into a long grey finger and says, 'Look at that,' like she's grown something new. When it falls, she whooshes it away with a blast from the tap. Mum usually opens the kitchen window, but somebody walking past slid a hand in and nicked our bleach off the sill. Mum ran after them but they disappeared inside one of the flats. Dad has nailed the front window shut so nobody can get in or out.

'Here, I bought you two balls,' she says, tightening the red scarf around her neck. Not wanting to show the marks on her skin that I have already seen. 'He only gets a cob on when he's skint. He's all right, really,' she says. 'I wish you could see him in the pub, Robyn. He's a real joker, gets me up to dance, we have a laugh. There's a different side to him you haven't seen. He's been here for us since you were little. I remember he used to take you to the park and everywhere with him. He got angry because he wanted to try and make the catalogue money last, that's all. You know what I'm like with money.'

I don't remember him taking me to the park, and I don't care about the stinking catalogue money, so I say nothing.

And then she smiles, but it is not a real smile, it's a drawn-on one. When I don't answer or smile back she says, 'Play out for a bit, if you like.'

I play two balls on the wall opposite Carol's house. After a while I hear her calling me in a whisper from her landing. 'Robyn, this is for you.' She throws something down and I walk over to pick it up. It is a comic with *Bunty* written on the front. 'Take it,' she says. 'I've read it.'

'I've got a bike now.'

'Oh.'

'Coming out?'

'Not allowed.'

'Why?'

Carol shrugs. 'Mum says.' A quick glance behind. 'When she goes to work later I'll sneak out and tell you properly.'

When I get home Dad answers the door. He looks at my hand. 'What's that?'

'A comic; Carol gave me it.'

He holds out his hand. 'Give it.'

I pass it to him and he flicks through the pages, tosses it to the floor.

'Rubbish. Throw it down the chute.'

'But . . .'

'Don't back chat me. Chute. It'll be fucking books next.'

I pick it up and walk along the landing to the chute, glance behind me to make sure he's not looking. I fold it in half and slide it down my waistband. Back in my bedroom I stuff it inside the pillow case.

Monday, after school, Carol sneaks out. We play two balls against the wall until our fingers are numb. *A portion of chips, a portion of peas, and don't forget the vinegar please.* I have my own spot on the wall, a favourite brick to aim for. I slap the balls again and again against it, trying to chip bits away. The smoothness of the rubber in my palm smells sweet. I think of this tall, dark, beautiful wall as mine; that before I noticed it, nobody knew it was there.

Once you drop the ball you're out. I get out on purpose when I see Carol looking up at the sky, afraid she might make up an excuse to go in. Carol doesn't play on my spot. She takes a couple of steps to the left, finds a brand new place. She stays away from uneven bricks, chooses a couple of smoothed-out ones next to each other that she pounds the rubber against.

I sit on the floor, cross-legged, and stare at the wall. You can learn a lot from walls. Dogs pee up them, rain pelts them, winds blast them, birds bomb them. In warm weather, after a game of football, boys cool their backs on them, find gaps in the cement for fingers to dig into. Pretend they have climbed this wall or that wall; show the gaps where their shoes have been to prove they're not lying.

At night, under the glow of an orange street lamp, I have seen boys press girls against walls by the lips. Women are kept against walls with fists or words. When it's all over in Tommy Whites, walls stand, the same as they always have, solid and strong. Carol drops the ball. I run and get it. I bounce it back to her.

'Thanks.'

'Why do you have to sneak out?' I ask.

'Mum says I'm not allowed to play with you. She thinks you're a troublemaker.' My idea of being like everyone else folds itself away like Nan's headscarf.

'I still want to. It's just, she can't know about it and you can't knock up at mine.'

After tea I sneak *Bunty* out under my jumper and play two balls on the wall for ages, but Carol doesn't come out. I run all the way down to Nan's flat. Two thousand, piddle, piddle, seven hundred, piddle, piddle, and fifty-five seconds. She's on her way out when I get there, off to buy a few bits. I tell her I'll wait in the flat and have a read. Nan says that's okay. 'I've got my key. Don't answer the door to anyone, even if it's the devil himself.'

I take off my shoes, put my feet up on her two-seater couch and open the first page. 'The Four Marys,' who all sleep in a school that looks like a castle. There's plenty of gosh, golly, splendid. In a blizzard, they make stilts out of planks of wood to rescue a group of stranded actors in an overturned bus. The story makes me laugh.

When Nan gets back she makes something to eat. I watch her rub Stork all over a roasting dish then sprinkle it with sugar. She cracks three eggs in a white bowl with a thick blue stripe around it, shows me how to beat them with a wooden spoon. She butters half a loaf of bread and cuts each slice in half, arranging them on top of one another in the dish. She pours over the eggs and sprinkles two handfuls of sultanas across the top, puts it all in the oven to bake.

She asks me about the comic and I tell her about the Four Marys and their adventures.

'Would you say it was easy to learn how to read?' she asks.

'Dead easy. Why?'

'Nothing,' she says.

'Tell me.'

'You'll laugh.'

'I won't laugh.'

'Promise?'

'Promise.'

'I've decided to learn. I've got a teacher coming this afternoon. Lily got her from the community centre.'

'Good for you, Nan.'

'You don't think it's stupid?'

'No. I think it's great.'

The smell from her kitchen makes me feel hungry. Nan brings in the piping hot pudding on two plates, and puts them on the table. She smiles. 'Dig in. Tell me what you think.'

I don't need to say a word. In a few minutes, the plate is scraped clean. After the dishes are washed, Nan has her visitor. The teacher is a lady. She sits up at the table, a black case by her side. She tells Nan her name is Mrs Womack. 'This is my granddaughter, Robyn,' Nan says.

Mrs Womack nods at me, pushes her cat glasses up high so her eyebrows disappear.

I walk over to the table and see a pile of Janet and John books. Mrs Womack tells Nan to sit next to her and opens a book at the first page. She shows Nan how to sound out the words. 'C-a-t, cat. Point to the word and say it after me: c-a-t, cat.'

Nan looks over to where I'm sitting, sends me away with her eyes. I pick up my *Bunty* and go to her room. After what seems like ages, I hear raised voices then the front door slams. Nan comes into her bedroom.

'She'll never get in here again. I won't be called stupid in my own home. All I could see was *c*, a half-sucked Polo mint, *a*, a head with hair flicked out at the neck, and *t*, an upside-down walking stick. I'm too old for all this.'

'Do you want me to teach you, Nan?'

'No thanks, love. I've been put off the idea altogether. From now on, I'll listen to you read stories.'

Nan goes into her kitchen to make a cup of tea. I can't see her face, but I can hear her banging doors and rattling drawers. 'I never liked teacher-types,' she says. 'Sticking their noses in where they don't belong. They get angry too easy, wanting you to get it right first time.' She's back in the living room.

'Can't you give her another chance, Nan? Or ask for somebody else?'

'You only get one chance to insult me, then that's your lot. Saying I was making mistakes. The only mistake I made was letting her in. And the stuff she brought me, some skinny cow called Janet. I can't see Janet and John having a barney over what time he got in from the pub, or what she threw at him as he came through the door. She couldn't throw a dirty look without her eyeballs rolling out. If that's what they're getting kids to read in school, you can keep it. When I was a kid, education took place in your own back yard. Knowing how to wash, cook, clean, have children and die.'

Back in the kitchen, she bangs stuff around. Finally she comes into the living room carrying her tea, and sits down. 'If I had my time over again, I'd do what Molly Tobin did. If you lived your life ten times over, you'd never find a kinder woman than Molly Tobin. She had sense enough to start a new life, across the water in the Isle of Man.'

She points her stick at me. 'That's what you'll do if you've got any sense. There's nothing here for a young girl. As long as you keep away from men, you'll have choices. Don't make the mistake your mother made.'

On the other side of her front door I breathe out, look back in through the letterbox. She's swearing now. Nan never swears. She won't learn how to read now and all because Mrs Womack was nasty. I shouldn't have said it was easy to learn to read. It's only easy if you get a good teacher.

13

The talk in school is all about Colomendy. Gavin Rossiter said his big brother went last year and it's haunted. Angela says if she's put on the bottom bunk under Trisha Fisher, she'll die, because Trisha Fisher pees the bed.

Before home time, we have an assembly to say thank you to God for our day. The whole school sits in silence, waiting for the squeak, squeak of Mr Merryville's shoes. Today, he's wearing a brown suit that shines when he walks in the light. He wears a brown tie, a yellow shirt and brown shoes. The spit that coats his lips has spread until it covers almost his entire mouth. I can't look. I rest my eyes on the statue of Our Lady Immaculate.

Mr Thorpe and the other teachers are positioned at the side of us, there to police any foolish fidgets.

We put our hands together and make the sign of the cross: *In the name of the Father, and of the Son and of the Holy Spirit. Amen.*

There is a commotion at the back of the hall and everybody turns around. A man is standing there, swaying backwards and forwards, eyes half-shut. I kneel up to get a better look and see that it is my dad. I hear somebody say, *That's Robyn Mason's dad*. I sit back down, wanting to flatten my body inside the grain on the polished floor.

Dad shouts across the hall to Mr Merryville.

'Eh, fucking Merrylegs, get over here.'

Everybody falls about laughing.

My hands start to shake.

I turn around and catch Dad grinning at his audience. He has a dark patch in the centre of his faded Levi's.

Mr Merryville and the teachers stare, mouths open.

Dad tries again. 'Eh, Merrylegs.'

Everyone laughs.

'You fuckin' deaf or what?'

Mr Merryville marches to the back of the hall and frogmarches my dad into his office. All the kids fall about laughing.

Mr Thorpe takes over the prayers; they end fast, with everyone being ushered safely back to class.

In my classroom, I sink low into the chair, eyes in line with the desk. Angela whispers to Kevin, *Ugly mug's dad's an alky who pisses his kecks*.

I don't look up until the bell rings. Mr Merryville comes into the room and speaks to Mr Thorpe.

'Right, time to get your coats.'

I stand.

Mr Thorpe says, 'Robyn, a word.'

I wait by his desk until the room is empty.

'Was that man your father?'

'Yes, sir.'

'I'm sorry, Robyn, you won't be coming to Colomendy after all. Your father just took the deposit back off Mr Merryville.'

The way he looks at me makes me feel small, like a part of me has fallen away and been scattered around the whole school. Now Mr Thorpe knows I'm different to the other kids and so does everybody else.

I get home and Mum says she didn't know anything about him going up to the school to get the money back. 'He's probably pissing it up the wall in the Stanley.'

Dad gets home late. He's too drunk to stand up. He falls over the couch and bangs his head on the fireplace. Mum tells me to leave him there. We close the door and go to bed.

I was pleased when I told her about him coming to the school and she made her eyes small. She was on my side and I didn't want that to change. He'd embarrassed me in school and I wanted her to punish him so he'd never do that again.

Next morning when I get up, I find Dad asleep on the living-room floor. I knock at Mum's bedroom door. No answer. I open the door, but she's not there. I open her wardrobe and her clothes are gone. I don't go to school; instead I leg it down to my nan's.

She has her coat and scarf on when I get there, ready to go out. 'No school?'

'No,' I lie. 'We're off today.'

Nan is going to the shops. She tells me I can come with her if I want. Nan orders loads of stuff. Eggs, bread, milk, cheese, ginger biscuits, sugar. She puts a two pence coin on the counter. The man behind the counter says, '*Not e-nuff, not e-nuff.*'

'Robbing sods, these Pakistans,' Nan says. 'This decimal business means they can charge whatever they like.'

A long queue forms behind Nan.

I try to figure out what to do next. If I tell Nan about Mum she'll worry. If I don't tell Nan, I'll worry. If I go home and she's not back I'll be stuck with Dad. The safest bet is to stay here and say nothing.

Nan throws more coins on the counter.

Somebody shouts from behind. 'Let the woman off, you robbing Paki bastard. She's a fucking pensioner.'

Then somebody else shouts, 'Yeah, isn't it enough that you've taken our jobs?'

The man behind the counter says nothing.

Nan turns around. 'I'm no charity case. I can pay for my own messages, thanks very much.' She bags her shopping and storms out of the shop.

When we get back, I can hear the kids in the playground behind her back wall. I miss school. The lining up, the milk, the dinners, running around on the windy playground. It's the only place I know what's going to happen next. Dad coming in messed that up. But there's no more money in school. No reason that I can think of for him to come up again.

At twelve o'clock Nan gets changed into her best cream blouse. She pins a cameo brooch to her collar, brushes her hair, puts on her camel coat. 'I'm going to the club for a bit of dinner.'

'The club?'

'The League of Welldoers around the corner.'

'I didn't know you had a club.'

'Twelve until two. I've made you a jam sandwich, it's in the kitchen.'

I follow her into the hall.

'Lock this after me. Don't let anyone in, even if it's the devil himself. I'll shout through the letterbox so you'll know it's me.'

I lean over the kitchen sink and eat my sandwich waiting for Nan. The flat seems creepy without her and I can hear all sorts of strange noises. A delivery van pulls up opposite, at St Sylvester's Club. Two men get out wearing brown leathery aprons. They sit down on the kerb and have a smoke and a chat. After a few minutes, the rumble and clink of crates and barrels carted and rolled into the cellar. When they've finished, the back doors of the van are locked and they drive off.

I spot him as he turns the corner. He's wearing the same faded blue jeans and black polo neck that he wore this morning. He's smoking a cigarette. I run from the kitchen and close all of the doors. I sit on the settee, pull my knees up under my chin. The block door bangs.

He uses the knocker first.

Polite little tap, tap, taps.

Silence.

Then his fist.

The letterbox squeaks. 'Open the door, Babs. I know you're in there.'

Fists again.

The block door slams.

I stay where I am in case he's looking in through the kitchen window. I remember: he can't look through the back window. Lily upstairs has the key.

Much later, I hear a gentle knock. Nan's voice through the letterbox. 'Robyn, it's me love. Open the door.'

I race to the door. Nan steps in and I slam it shut behind her. Fasten the chain, lock, bolt.

Nan looks shocked. 'Now then, what's all this? That teacher hasn't been trying to get back in, has she?'

I tell her everything. About Dad coming to the school for the money, about him coming in drunk and about Mum gone, but I don't tell her about him hitting Mum.

'He had no right to go up to the school and take that money. No right at all, that conniving lazy good-for-nothing.' She picks up her purse. 'How much was the deposit?'

'No. Nan, I don't want to go, honest.'

'You sure? That's no problem. I'll give it. I won a bit on the horses.'

'I'm sure. I was dreading it, to be honest.'

'Don't you worry about your mother, she'll be back.'

'How do you know?'

'Mark my words; she'll be back all right. You want to stay here tonight?'

'Dunno. What if Mum's back? She won't know where I am.'

'Go to Tommy Whites and see. If she's not in, you're welcome to stay here tonight.'

'Thanks, Nan. I will.'

'If I don't see you later, I'll know she's home.'

'But how has he found out where you live?'

'I'm not bothered about that. There's only one way he'll get in here, over my dead body.'

When I get to my wall, a group of kids kneel down facing it. I walk over to take a look. They poke at something with a long thin stick, toss it up in the air, it lands in the gutter. It is a mouse. A stiff, brown, long-tailed mouse; it has pretty ears, round and curvy. So small, I think it's a girl mouse. It moves like a stone when they poke it, flies play leap frog on it. Bits of fur are missing and it's all scabbed up. The kids take turns to flick it against the wall, to see who can get it the highest.

When I get in Mr Wainwright is sitting on our settee. At first I think he's told my dad I haven't been to school. There is no sign of my mum. Dad sits in his chair, reading the paper. Sleeves rolled up past his elbows.

Mr Wainwright nods at me then leans in towards Dad. His mouth is open, but he doesn't say anything for a while. Dad acts like Mr Wainwright isn't there, newspaper up over his face.

Finally Mr Wainwright says in a low voice, 'Can I talk with Robyn, please?'

Dad rattles the paper. 'There she is,' he answers, without looking up.

Mr Wainwright pulls away; the back of his head touches the wall. 'Yes, of course, exactly, there she is.'

Then silence again. Mr Wainwright looks at the floor, rubs a thumb knuckle across his bottom teeth.

Dad turns the page, gives him a bad look, shakes his head.

I hear the squashed sound of voices from next door's telly coming through the wall.

Mr Wainwright coughs, picks up his case, tries to open the zip but it won't budge. He puts it back down on the floor, pinches the crease line down the front of his trousers. He opens his mouth; words fly through the still air like peas coming out of a shooter. 'No, I mean talk to her somewhere private.'

Dad puts the paper down and fixes his eyes on Mr Wainwright. 'Are you telling me to get out of my own living room?'

'No, no. I'm not. Can I speak with Robyn in another room is, I suppose, what I'm saying.'

Dad looks at me and nods.

I walk towards my bedroom. Mr Wainwright follows.

'You've got five minutes,' Dad shouts after him.

I walk over to the window and open it as wide as I can.

'How are you, Robyn?'

I look at his hands. No pen.

'Fine.'

'Look, before we start, I'd like to say thanks for . . .'

'That's okay.'

'Are you all right?'

'Fine.'

'Look, if there's anything you need to tell me, I'll listen.'

No answer.

'Is there anything?'

I sit down on the bed. I want to tell him everything. To tell some stranger all about how my dad hates me because I am not like the other kids. I am a clumsy, lanky always-in-the-way cow. And how I'm so thick, I don't even know what it is I've done. All I know is that it makes him hit me. I make him hit me.

'Robyn?'

There's a creak outside my room door.

Mr Wainwright looks at the door then back at me. The moment has gone.

'So, Robyn, what is your favourite subject in school?'

'I like all subjects, probably reading stories best.'

'Can I use the bathroom please?'

I get up. 'I'll show you where it is.'

Mr Wainwright opens the door fast but there's nobody there.

He comes back from the bathroom and whispers, 'Robyn, Mr Merryville rang me. He wanted me to make sure you're all right. I'm here to make sure you're okay. Does your father ever lose his temper with you?'

'No,' I say, disgusted with myself.

'Has he ever hit you?'

'I just told you. No.'

'Has he hit your mum?'

My throat cracks. 'No.'

'Never?'

'Never.'

'Is there anything else you're scared of?'

For a minute I say nothing.

'I used to be scared . . . of faces I saw in the wallpaper.'

'Used to be?'

I nod.

'And now?'

'Now I think if they were going to get me they'd have done it by now.'

It's Mr Wainwright's turn to go quiet. I want to scream at him to leave me alone. There's nothing he can do to help me. In the end he says, 'Where's your mum?'

'Gone on a message for a few bits; she'll be back soon.'

'Right.' His eyes behind the glasses are two bits of stone.

'If you need to talk, tell Mr Merryville and he'll contact me. I'm on your side, you know. I can help.'

Once he's gone Dad calls me into the living room.

'You did good telling that prick nothing. Tell them too much and they'll turn it against you. Take you away. Into a home, God knows where, Scotland, or some other miserable hole. You'll never see your mum or your nan again.' He presses a finger to his lip. 'So make sure you keep that shut.' He stands, pokes a finger into my cheek. 'You hear me?'

'Yes,' I say. 'I hear you.'

'You seen your mother?'

'No.'

'She'll be back,' he says to himself, then sits back down in the chair with his paper.

'Can I play out?' I ask.

He doesn't answer.

'Can I play out for a bit?'

'Don't move out of the square.'

14

B ernie is walking through our square.
'All right?'
'Yeah.'
'Cool bike, Robyn. Mad colour though. Giz a takey through to our square?'

I look up at our landing. Dad's not there. He must be still reading the paper. I push my belly right up to the front of the bike. 'Get on.' I have never given a takey before and I'm surprised by the added weight. When I try to pedal away the bike wobbles all over the place and Bernie starts laughing his head off.

'Can't you give takeys?' he says.
'What does it look like?'
'Like you can't.'
'So?'
'So, get to the back of the seat and I'll show you.'
'In a minute,' I say.

I stand up and walk the bike through to the big square. Bernie follows me. When we are far enough away, I get back on, Bernie grips the handlebars. He makes it seem so easy. I tuck my feet up on the bar, knees out to the side, holding onto the backrest behind. It's brilliant. I lean in when Bernie does, lean out again, unable to see what's ahead. Racing across the big square, the middle of Bernie's neck hidden under the greasy feathers of his hair, the wind wipes away his lobby smell. 'You okay?' he shouts.

'Yes,' I shout back, trying to keep the excitement out of my voice. We're in his square in no time. He gets off the bike, hands it back to me.

'See, easy. It was like I was riding it on my own. You must have hollow bones,' he says. 'Try again.'

'You're heavier than me, though.'

'That doesn't matter. It's about skill.' He gets on the bike behind me.

I try to pedal away, but the bike tilts sideways.

'It does matter. A heavy person is harder to pull.'

He jumps off, stamps one foot in front, pretends to run at me.

'Are you trying to say I'm fat?'

I laugh at his bony frame.

'Are yer? Cos if yer are, you'd better run.'

Bernie's mum shouts him from over the landing.

'Coming?' he asks.

He lifts my bike all the way up the stairs. He's out of breath by the time we get to the top landing, four flights up. Bernie's mum is waiting on the step. She smiles at me.

'Hiya, Robyn from the front square.'

I smile.

Bernie's face is red and blotchy.

'Jesus, Bernie, get yourself a drink of water before you die.'

Bernie disappears inside the flat.

'I hear you know Joan, a friend of mine.'

I shake my head.

'It is you, who got her grandson that lovely suit he wore for his christening, isn't it?'

I can feel my face redden.

'It's Johnny's shoes. They've only gone too small. Do you know that shop around by Dolly's that sells kids' stuff? The little wool shop?'

I nod.

'There's some in there. He's a little size ten. Would you run around and see what's what? I'll pay you.'

Bernie comes back on the landing.

'Bernie, check on Johnny for me.'

When he's gone back in she starts to talk again. 'I have all lads. They won't look twice at a girl. Here.' She shoves five pence in my hand. 'Buy him a pair of socks. I'll mind your bike.'

'Can I lend a coat?' I say.

She passes me a green anorak that fits fine. 'Go on now, be careful.'

When I get around to the wool shop I look through the window. There are no customers inside. I wait for a while, until a couple of women go in together. I walk in behind them and see the little shoes in a box on the counter. The size is printed in blue ink on the side of each box. Inside the size ten box there is a pair of navy blue sandals with a silver buckle and tiny little pin holes that make a half-moon across the front.

The woman behind the counter turns her back to find wool for one of the women. I don't listen to what they say, I'm only checking in which direction they are looking. My hand reaches inside the box, I grab one shoe, stuff it in the side pocket of the anorak. I wait for her to turn again, my hand ready to pounce. The other lady orders some blue wool and the woman behind the counter turns again. I'm fast. I have both shoes in my pockets and I'm not stopping to buy any socks. The lady behind the counter smiles at me. 'I'll be with you now.'

'It's okay.' I turn towards the door.

One of the women says, 'She's probably forgotten the message.'

'Kids,' the woman behind the counter says. 'Who'd have 'em?' They all laugh.

When I get back to Bernie's, his mum is waiting. 'How did you do?'

I pull the two shoes from my pockets at the same time, like a magician.

'Clever girl, Robyn.' She strokes their bubbly cream soles.

'I didn't need to get the socks.' I hand the five pence back.

'Oh, you're an angel. Keep that for sweets. Do you want to come in for some bread and jam?'

I want to say yes but I remember I'm supposed to stay in my square, and I want to see if Mum's back. 'No thanks. I'll have to go. Tell Bernie I'll see him later.'

'See you later then. I'm going to try these on Johnny. He'll love them.'

And I love doing something that helps Bernie's mum, Sylvia, out.

A white van is in our square. Gangs of kids surround it. On tiptoes, they peer in its windows, try handles, pinch tyres, lift up windscreen wipers like arms, wave goodbye with them. On my landing, two men are edging their way out of our door, carrying the television. Everyone is out looking down over their landings. I take the stairs two at a time to find out what's happening.

Mum is back. I wrap my arms around her, the smell of smoke in her hair. Dad is shouting at the men. Mum smiles at me. 'I only went to my mate Eileen's house for the night, give that bastard a scare. Let him know what side his bread's buttered on.' She winks. 'It seems to have worked. And, anyway, I can be a pain in the neck myself at times, no wonder he gets a cob on. He won't lay a finger on me again, Robyn. I mean it. If he does, I've told him, I'm walking.'

'I don't like it when you go without telling me.'

'I should've told you.'

'Next time, if you go . . .'

'There won't be a next time. Had to sleep on an ancient settee that was bust in the middle; done my back in.'

'But if you do?'

'I'll take you with me.'

The two men come back upstairs, pick up my Chopper bike, take the radio from Mum's room, and leave. We watch out of the kitchen window as they lift the bike into the van. I can't help feeling pleased when they lock it away in the back of the van for ever. It never felt like it was mine. Most of the time when I took it out, I was scared of breaking it or getting a puncture. The engine starts and three lads sit on the back bumper; they hold onto the handle of the van, trying to sneak a takey. The men get back out of the van and chase them off. Once the van begins to move they jump back on again and the crowd roars. Mum hands me a glossy catalogue. 'Throw that down the chute.'

We sit in the living room together. Without the noise from the television everything can be heard. The sound of a newspaper page being turned, the shish of Mum's American Tan tights as she crosses her legs, an ice cream van in the big square playing *London Bridge Is Falling Down*. The silence thickens and grows like a giant boil that can't be burst with a pin. Something on the inside needs to give.

'What're we gonna do now for money?' Dad says.

'I've got a job,' Mum announces.

Dad looks up from the newspaper but says nothing.

'In St Michael's Market.'

He folds the newspaper away, pushes it under the cushion of his chair.

'Doing what?' he asks.

'Serving, on a counter.'

'What counter?'

'The Nut Centre.'

'The fucking nut centre? That'll suit you down to the ground, you cracked cow.'

'Eileen, my mate from school, knows the boss and she put in a word. I start on Monday.'

Mum has been there for about a week when Dad takes me into town to see her. We take the bus without speaking. There are lots of steps to climb up to St Michael's Market. Inside, it's full of glass windows and shop doors on either side of us, selling clothes, food, jewellery and furniture. The part where Mum works is inside a set of double doors. The stalls are like square boxes, with a gap to walk in, they are close together. I can smell coffee and bacon cooking. It's early in the morning and not many people are around.

We find the Nut Centre. Piles of different types of nuts behind a long glass counter. Mum is behind the counter. She wears a lemon overall with *Nut Centre* written on her top pocket. She sings, *Yes, please?* to the customers.

Dad pulls me away, puts a coin in my hand. 'Go over and buy two ounces of salted peanuts. Don't call her Mum. Wait for the change. You hear?'

Mum's eyes flash when she sees me at the counter. 'Yes, please?' she says.

'Two ounces of salted peanuts, please,' I say to my mum, who shines, being somebody else.

With a big smile, she hands me the bag.

I hand her the coins and wait.

Behind me a man waits to be served.

A lady walks past pushing a pram, the baby drops out his teddy and bursts into tears. I bend down to pick it up.

'Here's your change.' Mum smiles at me above the counter.

I turn back round, hold out my hand.

She counts it out. 'That's one pound, four notes make five. Thank you.'

I close my fingers around the pile of money and turn to walk away.

'That'd be safer in a paper bag,' the man behind me says. 'Sending a kid out with money like that for nuts, it's asking for trouble.'

Mum's face reddens. She holds her hand out and takes the money back.

'Who are you with?' he asks me.

'My dad; he's over there waiting for me. I'm okay.'

Mum hands me the money back in a paper bag. 'Be careful,' she says then turns to the man. 'Yes, please?'

Dad is waiting for me around the corner. He takes the money and takes me home on the bus without saying another word.

Once we are home I watch him take out his old shoebox from the cupboard under the kitchen sink. Usually he plugs in the record player, puts on his favourite song, *Hey, Good Lookin'*. But the men took the record player away in the van, so he whistles the tune. Inside the shoebox he keeps shoe polish, an old grey towel full of holes, a polish brush, a razor blade, soap, a jar of Brylcreem and a bottle of Old Spice. I call it his Saturday all-dolled-up box; that's when he uses it. He gets a clean shirt from his bedroom and irons it on a towel in the kitchen, hangs it up on a wire hanger on the kitchen door.

At the sink he'll wet his chin first, soap it all the way up to his black sideburns, then slice through it with the razor blade. If he cuts his skin he'll say, *bastard,* patch it up with a bit of toilet paper. Hair next; he'll scoop out the Brylcreem with his fingers, rub it into his palms and flick his quiff into place, smooth the sides back with what's left on his palm. His shoes are polished and buffed before he goes near the shirt. Trousers on, shoes on, shirt tucked in, belt tightened, there's only one thing left to do: tap the Old Spice onto his chin.

He's at the living-room door, jiggling into his jacket. From the mantelpiece, key, cigarettes, matches into the jacket pocket, money from the paper bag pushed into his trouser pocket. He leaves the paper bag on the mantelpiece. Checks the time on the clock, rubs his hands together and heads for the front door. 'Don't open the door to anyone, especially that Wainwright prick.'

I don't tell him that Mr Wainwright came to see me in school. He told me he's taking time out from being a social worker to travel on a boat with his brother. Somebody else will be taking over, he said. In the meantime Mr Merryville's the one I'm to talk to.

'You hear me?' he says. 'You hear what I said about Wainwright?'

'I heard you.'

'He been bothering you?'

'He's always in school. I see him every day, nearly.'

He presses a finger to my lips. 'He tries to talk to you, make sure you keep that shut.'

I hear the front door slam. I like being home on my own. He won't be back for hours. I check the paper bag on the mantelpiece next to Nan's photograph. He hasn't left a penny for Mum. She'll go mad. Maybe she'll go to Eileen's house and take me with her this time. I think about Eileen's house and just me and Mum together. I hope he spends the lot. Once Mum gets angry, though, it's like she's been saving it all up in her head. She shouts and screams at him until he loses his temper as well.

And then he'll hit her again like he has done a couple of times now, since Nan moved. He doesn't say sorry. He lights two cigarettes at once and gives one to her, sits up at the table to eat his tea with us. I feel like shaking her, screaming at her, can't you see what he's doing? He's no good. Instead, I say nothing because I'm just a kid and what do I know?

15

'If anyone asks, you're fourteen. And for fuck's sake, don't drop anything.'

I've got a Saturday job, opposite Mum's stall in St Michael's Market. I collect empty plates at Jimmy's Café.

Everybody takes two sugars in their tea and plenty of brown sauce on their bacon. The last Saturday girl got the sack for dropping things. 'A bag of nerves, she was,' Jimmy the owner tells me. 'So, be careful. Don't mess up.' He shouts across the café to a woman. 'Edna, this is the new girl, Robyn, so be nice.'

I look across at Edna; watch the slow way she looks me up and down. Edna has hair the colour of tomato sauce. It is pinned up high on top of her head. Her face is wide around the cheeks and when she talks her small mouth looks like it's sinking. Jimmy asks me if I can write, hands me a little pad and a pencil so that I can take down the orders. He lifts a yellow overall off a hook behind the counter. 'Here, might be a bit big, but it'll do. Oh, and you get to choose your dinner for free.'

Jimmy lifts the flap open on a little glass box. Slides chocolate éclairs, custard pies and ring doughnuts inside. Music plays on the radio, there's the smell of bacon frying, and me, in the middle of a world with nothing but grown-ups that aren't Mum or Dad. I look around the café and feel a lovely flutter in my belly. This is all mine.

As soon as a plate is empty I clear it away, to where Edna waits behind the counter. I'm not allowed behind the counter. If my cloth needs rinsing, I hand it to Edna. Only Jimmy is allowed to use the till. I watch him spread his fingers wide across the buttons; the price pops up in a window at the top. Two white tickets with numbers printed in black ink. 'That's just seven and a half pence,' he says to a lady. He counts out the change in his own hand before he gives it to her.

Jimmy says the customer is always right, which means we can't mess up. Edna rolls her eyes. I watch, and if somebody gives him a note, a pound, five or a ten, he sits it on a little shelf above the drawer. After he's given the change, he watches the customer walk away. Then he puts it inside the till. Above his head there's a handwritten sign on the wall. NO MISTAKES CAN BE RECTIFIED AFTER YOU LEAVE. Edna isn't allowed to use the till. If Jimmy goes to the toilet and somebody gets up to pay, Edna smiles at them and says, 'Won't be a minute.'

I've never heard the name Edna before. When we get quiet, I use my pencil and pad to jumble up the letters of her name to see if there's a better one hidden inside. In Edna I find: nead, dane, ande, dean and aden. I like dean best, but that's a boy's name, like Dean Martin the singer.

Edna cracks eggs into a massive black frying pan, chews on a stick of Juicy Fruit. Blows out big bubbles and says *shit 'n' hell* when fat splats at her skin, thickens two pieces of toast in Stork. It doesn't sink in. She picks up my pad. 'What you writing?'

I snatch it back. 'Nothing.'

'Take this to table five,' she says. 'Don't let Jimmy see you doing nothing. If you can't find anything that needs doing, get the brush out and pretend.'

I feel like I've been here for hours, then I see Mum at the counter. 'All right, Jimmy, lad, can she take her break with me?'

He nods.

We walk away and Mum lights a cigarette. 'Don't wait to be told, Robyn, standing there like gormless Gail. Look around, see what needs doing and do it. Once they have to start telling you, it's all over.'

By the time I get back to Jimmy's Café, I'm feeling like I've already messed up. The frying pan lies face down on the draining board. Two pans of scouse bubble on the back oven rings. Six jars of beetroot stand to attention next to a basket full of crusty cobs. The steam from the pans makes Edna's mascara streak down her face. She shoves pies and pasties into a glass-fronted oven, brushes bits of pastry off her hands. Unwraps a fresh stick of chewy and folds it into her mouth, slowly sharpening her tongue.

She sees me watching through the glass. 'Clear and wipe table five then take table eight's order.' As she speaks, drops of spit fall onto the pasties and pies and I know what I won't be eating for dinner.

Smelly red ashtrays with TETLEY written on the sides sit in the middle of every table. I lift one up and it slurps away from the plastic tablecloth. I wipe it clean and take table eight's order. 'One bacon butty and a cup of tea please, love.' He's got hardly any teeth and wears thick glasses. He hands me the coins and I give them to Jimmy. Edna has a bowl of bacon with a plate on top already cooked. I give her the order and she takes a new tub of Stork out of the fridge. It's rock hard. She tries to spread it across the bread but the bread curls up in the middle. When she takes the knife away, the bread has a hole in it.

Edna tries again but the same thing happens. She squirts brown sauce over the bread anyway and cuts it in half. 'Here,' she says to me. 'Take this over to Mr Magoo.'

The man lifts the bacon butty to his mouth, and it falls to bits. Pieces of bacon drop down onto the plate. He looks over at Edna. Stands up, makes his way to the counter and shoves the plate at her. 'I can't eat this,' he says. 'It's fallen apart.'

'Saves you the problem of chewing then,' Edna says.

'I'm not here to be insulted.' The man walks away, bumps his leg on a chair. 'I'll take my custom where it's appreciated.'

Edna tips his tea away down the sink and watches him leave, blows him a tiny goodbye bubble. It bursts on her lips. She looks at his plate then at me. 'Clear that away.'

I hand her the plate and she grabs my wrist. 'Say nothing, or I'll cut your water off.'

She doesn't have to scare me. I'd never say a word.

'You hear me?'

I nod.

Then she goes and says it again. 'I mean it. Say nothing. Or I'll cut your water off.'

Like I need telling twice, like I don't know how to pretend I see nothing at all. Nothing at all gets bigger, as big as a mountain. Until that's the only thing you can see. Edna makes sure she sees cluttered tables before I do, stands on her tiptoes and shouts across at me. 'Table two needs clearing soon as.' Cracks her chewy. I wish it would stick her lips together.

I get to sit down at an empty table for my dinner. I choose scouse with beetroot and a crusty cob with butter. Jimmy dishes it up for me and brings it to my table.

While I eat I watch Dad in Mum's queue. He buys two ounces of salted peanuts, pockets the change. When he turns to leave he looks straight through me; he doesn't even wave. I carry on eating, act like it doesn't matter. Mum looks across at me, throws me a smile. I look away, carry on eating like I haven't seen.

I don't want to clear tables. I want a go at using the spatula, at sliding it under the white of an egg and lowering it onto a plate. I want a go at stabbing sausages with a fork; stand over them while they change, from a sickly pink colour to a rich golden brown, the smoky smell of them cooking. I want to feel hot fat on my skin and say *shit'n hell*. I want to stir beans with a wooden spoon, roll the spoon around in the pan until it changes to orange. I want to make things change. Once the heat's turned up, everything changes.

Jimmy has the reddest face and reddest nose I've ever seen, like his body is cooking his face. The purple and red cracks across his cheeks make him look like a volcano about to erupt. Jimmy twiddles with the dial on the radio. He shouts, '*Come on you reds.*' Edna rolls her eyes, says she's going to the toilet. Looks back at me and shouts, 'Floor.'

I finish wiping the tables, get out the brush. The backs of my legs are hurting, my hands are red and blotchy from the soapy cloth and my shoes pinch. The man with no teeth is back at the counter talking to Jimmy. 'I'm not paying for something I didn't eat,' he's saying. 'And that puffed-up cow insulted me.'

Jimmy looks at me. 'What puffed-up cow?'

'Not her, the one cracking chewy. Bread falling apart it was, disgusting. Nobody would eat that.'

Jimmy points to the sign above his till, reads it to the man. NO MISTAKES CAN BE RECTIFIED AFTER YOU LEAVE.

'Sorry, mate, nothing I can do after you've left.'

The man throws Jimmy a filthy look, walks away.

Edna comes back from the toilet, reeking of perfume. 'For Christ's sake, Edna,' Jimmy says. 'You smell like poison.'

'You smell like shit. Hear me complainin'?'

Jimmy picks up a dishcloth and swipes it at her. He laughs a big belly laugh that makes me decide to like him. Jimmy explains about the man coming back, and how he wasn't pleased with his bacon butty. 'Robyn dropped it,' Edna whispers. 'I saw her, clumsy sod, but pretended I never, to give her a chance, like.'

16

Mum and Dad are in the pub. They won't be long, Mum said. 'I'll fetch you curry and chips back as a treat.' Outside, it's staying lighter for longer. We've had a week of April showers, fat drops of rain that soaked everything. But now the weather's dry there's a new smell in the air that makes my skin fizz, makes everything feel wrong and swollen on the inside. I open the front door even though I'm not supposed to. I climb up the landing wall a bit and stretch out my fingers towards the washing line. I can almost reach it now.

I hear my name being called. Bernie is in our square riding a bike. It has a white basket on the front. He looks up and sees me. 'Look what somebody threw away.'

I laugh. 'That's a woman's bike.'

'So? A bike's a bike. Want a takey?'

'Can't.'

'Want me to come up?'

I shake my head.

He rides off.

I strum a tune with my fingers on the warm wall. It tickles.

Before long my palms are chalky white. Mrs Naylor is at the chute. My palms are tingling and I wipe them down my dark blue dress.

'Look at the state,' Mrs Naylor says to me. I look where she's looking. My dress is covered in chalk. 'If your father could see you, he'd give you a crack.'

I toss my head away, look over the landing. Bernie is back in the square without the bike. In no time he stands next to me on the landing and I shiver.

'Cold?' he asks.

I nod.

'Coming out?'

Mrs Naylor is looking. I stoop so Bernie's face hides mine. 'Can't, got to wait for my mum and dad to get back.'

'Where are they?'

Mrs Naylor leans her head to the side like she's playing peek-a-boo.

'On a message,' I whisper.

Bernie nods at the open door. He whispers back.

'They'll be ages.'

Mrs Naylor is next to Bernie. 'A proper little street girl, aren't you? Talking to lads in broad daylight at your age, you'll be sorry. I suppose it's only to be expected with the likes of you lot.' She walks away.

'Nosy old cow,' Bernie says. 'Let's come in?'

'I'm not allowed . . .'

'Go on, they won't know. Five minutes?'

I check over the landing. There's no sign of them.

'Come on then.'

Inside the flat he sits in Dad's chair. 'Got anything to drink?'

'Water?'

'Water it is.' He rests his arms on the wooden arms of the chair, strums his fingers and smiles.

I smile back. 'What are you like?'

'Just fetch me my water, woman, or there's no wages for you this week.'

We laugh together.

I'm back in the living room with Bernie's water. Bernie's not in the chair. He's at the fire.

'What are you doing?'

'You're cold. You said so. I'm lighting you a fire.'

'No. Dad'll go mad.'

'He'll be made up. Nice and warm for when they get back.'

'No, Bernie. He'll go mad.'

He piles coal from the bucket on top of the newspaper, takes his matches out of the back pocket in his jeans and looks up at me. 'You can tell them you built it if you like. They'll be made up with you.'

'Stop it, Bernie. Drink your water and go.' I hold out the pint glass.

'Put it on that little table, woman.' He smiles.

I don't smile back.

He's got a match lit, wafts it against a balled up piece of news-paper. It catches light, blue and yellow flames curling towards the black coal. Bernie blows out the match, throws it onto the fire. A warm smoky smell fills the room. Bernie edges his palms towards the growing flames. Without taking his eyes from the fire he says, 'Come and get a warm.'

I crouch down next to him, tip water from the glass all over the flames. The fire hisses before it dies. I stand over him. 'Get out, you stupid bastard,' I scream.

Bernie jumps up. 'Ooo! Robyn's got a cob on. What's wrong?' He spies Dad's all-dolled-up box by the chair.

'What's this?'

'Get out.'

'Aw, c'mon, I was only . . .'

I grab the shoebox.

Bernie follows me outside, watches me toss the box down the chute. 'Now beat it,' I shout.

'Fine, won't stay where I'm not wanted.' He walks away.

I slam the front door shut.

I was scared then. Scared enough to think about punching Bernie in the face; scared enough to want to rip his hair out. He didn't listen, didn't stop when I told him to, didn't care that he was upsetting me. Once the fire was lit he didn't think. I saw his eyes like he'd seen an angel.

It did look brilliant. The way it started to glow and spread. Colours lit up colours; real, alive, flames dancing cheek to cheek, changing, changing shape. The crackly sound of fire burning and the warmth on your hands, knees, face. Bernie made that fire, made it live, like making a whole world. I wasn't scared of the fire; I was scared I wouldn't want him to put it out. I only wanted to sit with him in the living room. To be able to say to somebody like Angela that I'd invited a mate to mine. I've never invited anyone here because of Dad. I've had it now when he gets in.

Mum and Dad go into the living room first and I can hear his shouts. He's at my room door stinking of ale.

'You been at that fire?'

'I was cold.'

He pulls on my bad ear. 'Then put a fucking coat on.'

I cry out.

'Next time I catch you doing anything like that, I'll fucking kill you.'

Mum coughs in the lobby. He lets go of my ear before she sees.

'Don't go near that again, Robyn,' Mum says. 'That could've got out of control in no time. You hear me?'

I nod, turn my face to the wall so they'll leave. I'll never let Bernie in again, ever.

Next day I see Bernie; he's in the big square with Johnny and Ged. He acts like what happened never happened.

'All right?'

'Fine,' I say.

Johnny is sitting in the cart. He remembers me. Squishy fingers reach out. I crouch down, let him hold my finger. He curls his whole hand around it and holds on tight. I look into his eyes. Six little blinks to my one.

'He likes you,' Bernie says.

I stare up at Bernie. Suck in my cheeks, bite them inside my mouth.

Ged looks at Bernie then back at me.

A gang of kids from another square run past playing ball tick and the ball rolls away towards Ged's feet. He picks it up and throws it back to them.

'Sorry, Robyn,' Bernie says.

'Piss off.'

'Aw c'mon, don't be like that. It was shitty what I did, I know.'

I think about how much he doesn't know.

'I'll never do it again.'

'You'll never get in again.'

'I've got money. Wanna come round to Dolly's?'

'What for?'

'I'll treat you. You can take your pick once we get there. Then we can go to the park.'

I pick Johnny up and swing him through my legs.

Bernie smiles at me. I don't smile back.

Ged comes over, takes Johnny in his arms. 'Let's get him home.'

'You take him. I'll be there in a minute, going on a message, just me and Robyn. Aren't we?'

I say nothing. I'm going to make him wait.

'She your girlfriend now, Bernie?'

Bernie looks at me. 'If she wants.'

'I don't want.'

'Suit yourself. Bet you a penny I know what you'll choose in Dolly's.'

'Bet you don't.'

'I'll whisper it to Ged.' He says something in Ged's ear. 'Go on; tell him what you'll choose.'

'You think I'm soft? Whatever I say, he'll say you said the same.'

'I won't, honest.'

Ged holds Johnny on his hip. Ged looks too big for short trousers, grey socks baggy around his ankles. It matters to Ged that Bernie wins.

Bernie moves in close. 'She's too smart for us, Ged lad. But maybe, just maybe, she's ticklish?'

'No.'

'Bet you are.'

Ged grins at me. I grin back.

'Am not, Bernie, get away.'

He wriggles his fingers up in front of my face. 'We'll soon find out, won't we, Ged?'

I take a step back. 'Stop it, Bernie, now.'

He takes two steps forward and pushes his fingers closer towards me, touches my sides. Ged laughs.

'All right, all right, I'll come, but I don't want anything, not off you anyway. I've got my own money.'

When we get to Dolly's shop I buy a Flake. Bernie gets a bag of jelly babies, stuffs the bag deep in his pocket.

Back at Sylvia's, Johnny runs up and down the landing without a nappy, sucking on a green jelly baby, slobber all over his bib. He walks in his new shoes like he's had them for ever. Bernie picks him up, sits on the step with Johnny on his lap. He pees all over Bernie as if he's promised to wash away the lobby smell and replace it with his own sweet pee smell. Bernie goes in to get changed.

Johnny spies a stood-on jelly baby on the landing, stoops and picks it up. He goes to put it in his mouth but Ged grabs it off him, walks along the landing to the chute. This sets Johnny off screaming, mouth wide open, green frilly line down the middle of his tongue.

Bernie is back on the landing. 'C'mon, let's go the park.'

We sit on two swings together in the playground. A couple of big lads walk over and tell us to move. They are bigger than Bernie, so I jump off. Bernie stays on, pushes himself higher and higher. One of them grabs his shoe, his bare foot, pulls him off the swing. With his other foot Bernie kicks him in the face. The lad goes down, holds his nose through gaps in his fingers, says, 'Fuckin' bastard.' Bernie jumps off the swing, punches the other lad in the face. The three of them take turns, fists working on each other's faces. *Boof* for you, *boof* for him, *boof boof* for me. I look around but nobody seems to have noticed this knock-down-stand-up fight. *Boof* for you, *boof* for him, *boof boof* for me.

A couple of kids walk over to take a closer look. They edge past and take the being-fought-for swings. The three fighters move away, towards the grass. *Boof* for you, *boof* for him, *boof boof* for me. It gets bad for Bernie, taking two sets of punches. I start to scream. 'Stop, stop it now, he's bleeding.' The two big lads run

130

off. I watch them both run to the gates towards Tommy Whites. They stop. Turn around and push two fingers up at Bernie.

Bernie doesn't see; he is breathing fast, blood dripping from his eye. He lies down on the grass and starts to laugh, spit and snot all over his face, red sticky out ears. 'That was brilliant,' he says. His clothes are splattered with blood.

'No, that was stupid, taking on two of them. You could've got battered.'

He stands. Tucks his shirt back inside his trousers.

'Yeah, but I didn't, did I?'

I look at him now, and think about how he is with Johnny; when he swings him backwards and forwards between his legs, carries him close and kisses him. I think it's mad how fast people change. One minute gentle, give you the world; kill you stone dead the next. Bernie's not scared of anything or anyone. That's what I like about him. He reminds me of Jack, and how he must have felt after a boxing match. He must have been brave, Jack, to get into a ring knowing that he could have got his head punched in.

When we get back Bernie whistles his way along the landing. Ged grins at him and says, 'You'll have two black eyes tomorrow.'

Sylvia has Johnny in her arms.

'He's bleeding,' I say.

She laughs. 'A real lad, our Bernie. Real lads get into scrapes. A bit of blood's nothing to worry about.'

He walks inside the lobby. Sylvia lowers the baby towards his big brother's face. Johnny plays Bernie's bloody mouth and eyes with his fingers. I can see this means more to them than collecting rubbish for coins. But I am too stupid to know what.

17

Early next morning Nellie, Nan's friend, is in bits at the door. 'It's Chris, come quick, Babs, he's . . .' Nellie's words fall away, like ash on a dying fag.

Mum grabs her coat, stuffs fags and matches in the pockets. She turns to me. 'Won't be a minute, there's cornflakes in the cupboard.'

The milk's turned. It's thick and lumpy. The smell from the bottle flips my stomach and I vomit in the sink. After a while, I get dressed and sit on the step, a horrible taste in my mouth. Nellie and Chris live on our landing in the end flat. Her front door opens. Nellie is out on the landing, sobbing. Mum has an arm around her.

Nellie comes back to ours, sits in Dad's chair. 'Sweet tea, it's good for shock,' Mum says. 'Sorry it's black.'

Nellie's hands shake when she picks up the cup. 'I'll have to get word to our Mary.'

Mum tells her she'll sort it in a minute. Dad is up. He walks into the living room in his vest. 'It's Chris,' Mum says. 'He's dead.' Nellie starts to howl all over again. Dad doesn't get dressed. He goes back to bed, says he feels sick. I get Nellie some toilet roll. 'Robyn, run to Dolly's for milk,' Mum says. I take the coins and leg it to Dolly's.

Over the next couple of days neighbours walk in and out of Nellie's flat without knocking. Nellie wears a black dress, which makes her face glow white, like a ghost. On the last day, they bring sand-wiches, pies and little jellies with cream on the top. They come in twos and threes when it's dark, like shadows from a washing line. They kiss and hug Nellie hello and goodbye, shake their heads as they walk away. 'He was a gentleman,' they say. 'Salt of the earth.'

Today they took Chris down the stairs in a coffin. They put him in the back of a long, dark car and drove off. He was buried in Anfield cemetery next to his father and mother. When they get back from the pub, Mum and Nan go to Nellie's for most of the night. Dad's stayed in bed for two days; his stomach's been bad. I watch from the landing.

Nellie walks a few of them to the stairs. I'm looking over the landing. When they've gone she takes my arm.

'You know, Robyn, Chris thought the world of you, said he saw Granddad Jack in your eyes. Made of strong stuff that one, he'd say.' My body shakes. I don't know what to say to her.

When it gets cold I go inside and sit on the settee. I leave the front door unlocked. Mum comes in with a few people from Nellie's. They bring bottles of beer and leftover pies. Dad gets up when he hears the noise, takes the top off a bottle of beer with his teeth. His face is pale. Mum offers him a sausage roll. He pushes her hand away.

From her pocket, Mum takes a jelly with the cream squashed flat. I get a spoon and eat while they open more bottles. Mum sits on the settee next to a woman with yellow-white hair. The woman touches my hair. 'She's dark like her dad, isn't she, Babs?' Mum looks at me with cider eyes, looks across the room at Dad, red lipstick on her teeth. 'She's nothing like him, apart from them both being bastards.'

I scrape my spoon around the paper cup, then when there's nothing left I carry on scraping with a sideways spoon, down each thin narrow pleat. The cup starts to lose its roundness; bits of it stick out in points and I scrape it clean until tiny holes start to form, until it looks nothing like it did to begin with. Mum and the woman hold bottles of cider by the neck. Mum pats the place next to her for me to sit. She leans her head on the woman's shoulder, looks over at Dad. 'Listen,' she whispers to the woman. 'I've got something to tell you.'

I listen.

She drops her bottle to the floor and throws up.

Inside my room I open the window, push my head outside, away from the stink. I can hear them talk and laugh and sing along to the records. I've just checked on Mum. She's asleep on top of the bed wearing her clothes. I've pulled off her shoes and covered her up. Back in my own room I keep my head out of the window. I can feel damp from the night air on my face.

It's nearly light when I hear the final 'see yer', the final click of the front door latch. I get into bed and drift off. In my dream I am on the landing. I see Chris come out of his flat, tap, tapping the side of his nose, telling me I'm strong like Granddad Jack. I turn away from him; rub the skin on my finger against the wall until I get to the bone. The bones stick out ugly and white. I go back to the wall and rub until there's nothing left but a pile of white powder on the landing floor.

After Chris's funeral we don't see much of Nellie. I see her a few times when she leans over the landing at night, looking up at the stars. I wonder if she's checking that Chris has thrown the rest of his fags away for good. I look where she looks and see him standing inside a crowd shouting over at Granddad Jack, 'That's it. Give him a taste of Thor's hammer.'

Mr Thorpe sits at his desk reading rules from a piece of paper. It's May already and everybody's off to Colomendy today. They get to choose partners. Halfway through the morning, Mr Thorpe says *Jesus tonight* when Gavin Rossiter throws rolled-up bits of paper at Anthony Greenbank. He opens the classroom door and tells the class to run it off on the playground. He asks me to stay behind. When the rest of the class has left Mr Thorpe takes off his glasses, sits on his desk, hands under his legs. 'I've arranged for you to go in with Miss Fennel while we're away, Robyn. I told her you'll be a great help to her with the little ones. I'll be expecting a full report when I get back. Don't let me down.'

For the next half an hour the talk is of partners. Angela's sneaking loads of black jacks and fruit salads because Dolly sent a load round to her mum. All of the girls want to be her partner. She makes an on-the-way-there list, and an on-the-way-back list, of people who are allowed to play with the vanity case on the bus. They ignore me, which makes me feel better. By the time their bus arrives, I can't wait to see the back of them. I go out onto the playground to join Miss Fennel. At the gate Angela shouts, 'Hey, ugly mug, you'll scare the little ones sick.'

Miss Fennel teaches five-year-olds. They sit on the carpet for register and need help with coat buttons, name tags, hooks and milk, which they spill all over the tables. They twiddle hair and stare at me, nudge each other and giggle. Miss Fennel has asked me to get the straws and milk ready for break and I have to tidy the books in the library. A little boy with slicked-down hair comes in late, points at me and says, 'Who are these?' I look at Miss Fennel and smile. She smiles back.

In the morning the children sing the alphabet and do sounds. There's a smell like vinegar in the room. 'Tell me a word that begins with *b*?' Miss Fennel asks.

Hands go up and she chooses a little girl. 'Bernadette?'

'Bottle, b for bottle.'

'Well done. Anybody else?'

Hands go up again and again.

'Find me something in this room that begins with *n*.'

The little boy who came in late stands up. 'I know, Miss Fennel.' He climbs over sticky-out knees and untied tongues to get to the front, scratches his head and puts something in Miss Fennel's hand. Miss Fennel shushes everyone, checks her hand. 'Nits, n for nits,' he says. Miss Fennel jumps up, runs over to the sink turns on the tap. The children laugh. At break there's milk left over. Miss Fennel says I can take one. She checks the library is neat and the milk spills have been wiped, smiles, tells me to go out and play.

On the playground, the little ones crowd around me. They link arms and lock me inside a tight circle. I try to escape but they push their elbows up higher and higher. I laugh and laugh until the tears fall down my face and I can't stop. They move around me and sing. *The farmer's in his den, the farmer's in his den, eeee, aye, the, adio, the farmer's in his den. The farmer wants a wife . . .*

At dinner time I help Blackbeard take the little ones to the canteen. She doesn't ask me why I haven't gone on the trip; she doesn't speak to me at all.

In the afternoon I watch Miss Fennel's reflection in the window. She has long straight hair that flicks out at the end. Miss Fennel sings the afternoon register; every name falls into place. I sit with four kids. They put on old shirts and dip their fingertips in paint pots then print them onto the paper.

The classroom fills with the warmth from the afternoon sun. Miss Fennel stops the class and holds two of the paintings up. 'Look, Class Three, aren't these wonderful?' The children look up and tinkle, 'Yes, Miss Fennel.'

A few minutes before the bell rings, it's story time: Hansel and Gretel. I sit down next to Bernadette in case she's scared. This story gave me nightmares for weeks after I first heard it. 'You okay?' I whisper.

She rolls her eyes. 'Have you seen houses made from sweets?'

'No.'

She shakes her head, makes her hand into a beak. 'The birds would come down and peck, peck, peck them.'

'They'd get fat.'

'Too fat to fly or walk.'

'They'd have to roll.'

'Rock 'n' roll.' She giggles. 'A rock 'n' roll bird, like my mum in the Grafton on Saturday night.'

Mum and Dad didn't go out Saturday night. His stomach got bad again. Mum said he didn't give it time to heal. She said he needs to leave the beer alone for a bit so it clears up properly. He hasn't been near St Michael's Market, Mum says. So he must be sick. I think about the all-dolled-up box down the chute. Maybe he'll be sick for weeks.

The week passes too fast and they're back. Angela got sent home with a rash on the second day. Anthony Greenbank was sick all over his bed. 'I was gonna let him have top bunk as well,' Tommy Taylor says. Back in Mr Thorpe's class it's still collective nouns, times tables and long multiplication. He calls me to his desk. 'Miss Fennel said you were a great help to her, a great help. That's good news.' He stands, pats me on the head and opens a brand new tin of biscuits.

Everybody watches me choose one.

18

In the café it's early. Edna turns on the radio, blows tiny cream bubbles that won't grow, gathers up her cigarettes and lighter, tells Jimmy she's going the toilet. Jimmy spoons two sugars into a cup for the only customer in the place. He sits down opposite the woman and hands her a cup of tea. She has blond hair that falls down in curls to her shoulders. Her skin is almost see-through, scrubbed clean and shiny.

I grab a dishcloth, wipe blobs of hard red and brown sauce off the plastic tablecloths. I tip ashtrays overflowing with cigarette stumps into the bin, slide a brush over the floor. Scoop crumbs, a few chips and cigarette stumps up onto a shovel and bin them. Jimmy talks to the woman in a low voice; I can't hear what he's saying. A swingy trumpet song plays over the radio. Something about *Blueberry Hill*. Jimmy jiggles his shoulders up and down in time with the music. 'Daft sod,' the woman says. Jimmy stands up, opens the glass box on the counter, brings her a chocolate éclair on a plate. Edna is back; she watches them.

'I'll get fat.'

'So?'

She breaks it in two, leans forward and pushes one half between Jimmy's lips. Edna lets out, 'Oh, for Christ's sake,' too loud and there's nowhere for it to go.

Jimmy turns to face the counter. 'What's wrong, Edna?'

'Nothing, dropped something that's all.' She busies herself, lifting packs of bacon and trays of eggs out of the fridge, slaps the streaky bacon down on the counter. Unwraps a fresh stick of Juicy Fruit, drops it on the floor, says *shit 'n' hell* under her breath. 'What are you gawping at?' she says to me. 'Take table five's order.' I turn around and see that we have our next customer. I take out my pad, walk over to the table.

It gets busy so Jimmy goes behind the counter to help Edna. The woman at the table takes a magazine out of her bag and reads.

It's so busy that we don't stop all morning. At one point people are standing outside waiting for a table. I can feel the thick strap on my ski pants twisted inside my shoe. It stabs into the arch of my foot. I walk on my toes around the café to ease the pain. They used to fit, but now, when I walk in them, the elastic waistband rolls too far down. I have to scrunch at the sides of my overall to pull the stirrup back up. Edna said it gets on her nerves. She said if she catches me doing it one more time she'll cut my water off. I want to take them out of my shoes but Mum says they look daft like that.

A few minutes ago they ended up around my ankles. Everyone laughed. Jimmy gave me a large safety pin, told me to go to the toilet and sort myself out. I thought about everyone laughing and how I must have looked, like gormless Gail. I thought about not going back. I thought about Mum on the stall opposite and how she might have seen me mess up. I thought about how easy it would be for me to walk home to Dad in bed sick, or sitting in his chair reading the paper, and that's when I went back to the cafe.

It's past lunchtime and I haven't had a break. Jimmy asks me what I want and sets my plate down opposite his woman. 'Sit down, then,' Jimmy says. 'She won't bite.'

I sit.

'Hello, Robyn, I'm Sue, Jimmy's wife.' She looks at my plate. 'Tuck in, love, before it gets cold.'

Her eyes are a warm grey colour. She pulls a magazine out of her bag, wets her fingers, flicks through the pages. She looks like some of the women on the pages, only better. 'You work hard, Robyn,' she says, without looking up. 'I've been watching.'

I put down my knife and fork.

'Sorry. Me rabbiting on. Eat your dinner.'

Sue carries on flicking through the pages.

When I've finished my dinner I feel better. Jimmy brings me a glass of orange juice and says I've got ten more minutes.

'You like it here?' Sue asks.

I can see a black polo neck, sleeves rolled up past the elbow: Dad, in Mum's queue at the Nut Centre.

'Robyn?'

'Yes, yes I do.'

'Better than being at home?'

'Yes.'

'You have nice eyes, Robyn, nice bright eyes.'

My face burns.

'Jimmy loves this place. He works like a dog here.'

I watch Dad move to the front. Mum turns to the scales with a scoop full of peanuts.

'Stop looking so serious. For a young girl you need to laugh more. You seen this?'

Sue shows me a picture of a woman in her magazine. She is dressed in a white blouse and blue jeans.

'You'd look smart in this outfit. And her hair, the feather cut. You'd suit that style, it'd make you look older, more with it.'

Edna shouts *shit 'n' hell* louder than usual. I look over at her, she's running her hand under the tap.

'Edna giving you a bad time?'

'No,' I lie.

I watch Mum hand him the bag.

Sue closes the magazine. 'Maybe she's giving herself a bad time, depends how you choose to look at it.'

I don't understand.

Dad takes the change from Mum's hand, pushes it into his pocket. I think about Dad's all-dolled-up box and how he doesn't know it's lying in a bin at the bottom of the chute.

'Edna lost her little lad. He choked on a sweet. She blames herself.'

'Oh, I didn't know.' And I think about Sylvia, and how sad she'd be if that happened to Johnny.

'She hates everybody right now. Edna needs somebody to blame for how bad things are for her. It matters to Jimmy that you know about Edna and why Jimmy lets her get her own way. It helps, I think, to know?'

'Yes,' I say. 'It does.'

I finish my drink and take out my pad. It gets quiet in the afternoon. Jimmy sits with Sue. I've never seen a person look at someone the way he looks at her. Seeing it makes me feel warm inside, like a little bit of that feeling has accidentally sprinkled onto me. I hope I find somebody (a boyfriend or a husband I haven't met yet), somebody who will look at me that way. I feel pleased I've found myself something to look for when I'm older, something that will make me a chooser.

Edna gets in close to me. 'What's runaround Sue been saying?'

'Nothing.'

'She say anything about me?'

'No.'

'Ask anything about me?'

'No.'

'You berra not be lying.'

'I'm not.'

'Clear table nine now. Don't mess up.'

The last thing I want is to mess up. I have a dishcloth I'm in charge of, tables to clean, a floor to brush and I have Sue who thinks I have nice eyes.

I worry about things before they happen. Sometimes I worry and things never happen. This worry does happen. And it happens fast. After work, Mum says we're not going home because it's her birthday tomorrow, so we're getting the bus to my nan's flat.

Nan opens the door, not surprised to see Mum and me standing there. 'Long time no see,' Mum says. She sits down on Nan's settee and looks around the living room. Nan sits in her straight-backed chair by the radio.

'I can guess what you want,' she says.

'Who says I want anything?'

'There's a drop of lemonade, Robyn, in the kitchen if you want some.'

I get up and pour myself half a glass of lemonade. Nan buys it in for her port. It must have been there a while; without the fizz it tastes like sugar and water. From the living room I hear Mum's voice. 'Don't bite my head off.' More words from Mum that I can't make out and Nan says, 'Oh, is that right?' I root around in Nan's kitchen drawers. The stirrup pain is worse now, but Mum says I've got to keep them in because they look a disgrace hanging out. I find a pair of scissors, roll off my leggings and cut the tab in half. I'll tell Mum they ripped. I put them back on. The tabs flap either side of my ankles like ears. I put the scissors back in the drawer on top of a pink envelope with *Babs* written on it.

Nan shouts. 'Don't start this malarkey with me, coming in here on your high horse. You should be ashamed of yourself, supporting a lazy good-for-nothing like him. He should be shot.'

'You don't have to say I disappoint you. I can hear the sting in your voice.'

'You're not disappointing me, you're disappointing yourself. Giving money over, paying him, for what? It's backwards . . .'

'You'd rather I stayed on the shelf, damaged goods.'

'You're on a shelf, not the one you jumped off, but a shelf all the same. You just couldn't wait, could you? The problem was Jack spoiled you. You got everything you wanted at the click of a finger and it's done you no good.'

'Nothing I ever did was any good. Picking at the way I did my hair, when I see the way you are with Robyn . . . I only did my hair so you'd say I looked nice. You didn't have the time. My dad always made time for me.'

'Robyn needs to know the truth about her dad.'

'What's that got to do with anything? I'll tell her, when she's old enough.'

I can hear the shish of a match being struck. Smell Mum's smoke drift into the kitchen. Mum turns on Nan.

'You've got a cheek. What about your own daughter? It's once a year a birthday, you tight cow.'

I move closer to the door.

'And rearing a child's for life. I told you that when you chose to keep her, told you what it'd be like for a bastard.'

I sit down on a chair in Nan's kitchen. Mum had a choice about whether or not to keep me. Mum chose to keep me even though I was born a bastard. I remember she told that woman in the flat I was a bastard just before she threw up. I thought it was just a swear word, but it's more than that. It must be. When I was born, they saw me and saw that I was a bastard. They saw something about me that every bastard has.

Nan has a mirror on her windowsill. I look carefully at my face. Two eyes, a nose and a mouth, all in the right place. A few freckles on my nose, dark hair, lots of people have dark hair, a pink tongue. I'm tall for my age, but so are plenty of people. I take off my shoes and socks and look at my toes. My second toe is much longer than my first. Am I different because of my toes? Bastards have freaky toes. I didn't know you could give babies away just because of the size of their second toes. Nan said it means I'm going to be a ballet dancer; she must've said that so I wouldn't find out what it really means.

'You'd have been happy to let me stay on my own; a reject on a shelf. And Robyn would have had a dog's life from the other kids, skitting her. Yes, you can call him a lazy good-for-nothing, but at least he didn't run away once he found out I had a kid.'

'That man only wanted a bit of time to think things over, but no, that was too much for you, wasn't it?'

'A bit of time? When it really mattered, he didn't wanna know. He made his choice and I had to act fast. I had to put Robyn first. No other fucker did. They weren't exactly queuing up to marry me. I was lucky to get him. If it was up to you I'd never have married. You just wanted me to live with you, be on my own like you, look after you, you jealous cow. Wear a keeper's ring. Have every nosy fucker in Tommy Whites feel sorry for me because I couldn't keep a man. Well, I showed you, showed the lot of you. You wouldn't understand.'

'I know what it's like to be on your own. When Jack was away in the army . . .'

'That's different. My dad *had* to leave.'

'I don't care what you say; he's no man, taking a kid's deposit for a school trip.'

'How do you know about that?'

'Never mind how I know, but I know you're not happy.'

'I'm happy enough now you've left. Robyn, get in here, now,' Mum shouts.

Nan shouts back at her. 'Liar, you're not happy. I'd rather have a thief than a liar. Any woman with half a brain would leave.'

'I won't give up and run away, not without trying.'

I walk in from the kitchen.

Mum stands. 'We're going. And if I ever find out you've been down here, I'll kill you, understand? You had no right.'

Nan stands up. 'No, *he* had no right,' she says, pointing her stick at Mum, 'and you letting him. Get out. It wouldn't bother me if I never set eyes on you again.'

We leave. Mum looks back, sees Nan on the step, shouts at her. 'Nice mother you are, not even a fucking birthday card, you tight cow.'

Nan is in the street shouting after us. 'Robyn, you're welcome down here any time, love. Any time at all.'

I have to run to keep up, stirrups flapping up and down like wings at my ankles. 'What the fuck have you done to them?' Mum says when she sees them.

'They're all the go, them, Babs,' I want to say, but don't. We walk home without saying another word. Mum lights one cigarette after the other, stabs me with her sideways glances. I don't care.

She can bounce me off every lamp post on Scotland Road if she likes. She could have given me away, but she never. That's all that matters now.

Mum buys a bag of chips and a loaf. We get back home, but Dad isn't in. Mum checks the mantelpiece for money; it's empty. I go to the toilet. When I get back in the room Mum has Nan's picture outside the gilt frame, cuts it in half with the scissors. 'I'll show her.' I hear the front door slam and I know she's gone to throw it down the chute.

Mum dishes up the chips with two slices of thin bread and margarine. We eat at the table with a knife and fork. Top the chips with a blob of Daddies brown sauce. We're halfway through when the front door slams. Mum's face lights up. It's Dad, drunk. Not wobbly can't-stand-up drunk; just drunk. He sits in his chair. 'Want some chips?' Mum says.

No answer.

Mum looks at me. Eyes tell me to leave the room.

I stay where I am. Pretend I haven't seen.

He sits in his chair, strums the wooden arms with LOVE HATE fingers, dark eyes on Mum. 'Where's my fucking box gone from under the sink?'

Mum shakes her head. 'Don't ask me.'

'What about her?' he asks Mum, nodding at me.

'Robyn, you know anything about the box?'

'No.'

He stands up.

Mum puts down her bread.

He walks towards her.

Mum stands, picks up the knife from her plate.

He grabs her wrist, twists it hard; bangs it again and again against the table.

I jump up from my seat and run at him.

I punch him in the mouth, feel his teeth scrape my knuckles. I scream at him to leave her alone. He gets me in the face with his elbow. My eyes fill with water. I can't see properly. He forces Mum to the floor by the hair. She still has hold of the knife. Mum is screaming at him, 'I'll kill you, you bastard.' I jump on his back, pound my fist into his neck. He pushes me off. I fall back against the table, grab hold of the cloth. Everything falls to the floor. I get back up but he's got the knife. I step towards him. He points the knife too close to my face. 'Try it, you little bastard,' he says, 'I'll slice right through you.' Mum is back up. She twists his face in her fingers. He bites her hand, she screams; he knees her in the stomach; she falls to the floor and that's when he kicks her in the face. Blood seeps from her nose, mouth. Seeing the blood is what makes him stop. He throws the knife on the floor and runs out of the room, slams the front door shut.

I help her up. There's blood all over her clothes. She's still bleeding from her nose. It won't stop. Dots of red all over the brown lino, they splat out around the edges like tiny explosions. She holds her stomach and cries out with the pain. I run to the bathroom, wet a towel; she dabs away the blood. 'Get my fags, girl,' she says. 'And put the latch on the front door and the bolt. That bastard's not getting back in.'

I lock and bolt the front door. Give Mum her fags and matches. Her hands shake. I take the matches off her, strike one and light her cigarette. 'You all right, Mum?'

She nods.

I pick the mess up from the floor. Take everything out into the kitchen. I spread the tablecloth back over the table. I don't cover the holes. Some of them have torn so bad they've become part of another hole, a much bigger one that's difficult to cover.

Through it I can see dark wood. It looks like a dirty pool of water inside the white of the cloth. It looks like something that shouldn't be seen.

'Leave that, Robyn, go to bed,' Mum says. 'Everything's going to be all right.'

I slide the knife that Dad dropped under my pillow. I open the bedroom window and stick my head outside, feel sweat cool on my skin, take in a deep breath and blink away the tears I don't want to come. I feel them burn hot down my face. When it gets cold I close the window, unhook all of the coats in the hall, lie on top of the bed and cover myself up. In the dark, shadows play tricks by the window. I think I see Chris, tap, tapping the side of his nose. *Come on now, Robyn. It's all right, you're made of strong stuff, strong, like Granddad Jack.* And I wish my dad could have died instead of Chris.

19

'He fell on his arse outside the Stanley last night,' Nellie says. 'A couple of the lads tried to help him up, but he was swinging punches at them. In the end they stopped trying.'

Mum touches her face, squints her eyes with the pain.

'You need to get the Bobbies involved, Babs, in case he tries it again. The likes of him will try it again. Next time, you might not be so lucky.'

Mum nods. 'I'll sort it.' She opens her fags and lights one, leans her head back on the settee and blows the smoke high; it touches the ceiling.

'It looks bad,' Nellie says.

'I'll put make-up on now. It'll be fine.'

'A bucket of panstick wouldn't hide that lot.'

Nellie's right. Mum's eyes, cheeks and one side of her lip are swollen. Nellie fusses around in the kitchen making Mum a cup of tea. She comes back into the living room. 'Mark my words, by the time that kettle boils, the whole of Tommy Whites will know.'

'Let them know, nosy fuckers. I'll announce it on the landing so there's no need for talk.'

Nellie goes back into the kitchen.

Mum turns to me. 'We'll find our own place, just me and you. A little flat somewhere, maybe in the South end, where he won't find us.'

I nod. Everything is going to be all right.

Nellie comes in the living room with the hot tea. She takes something from her pinny pocket. 'Here, Babs, take this couple of quid and go out for the day. New Brighton's nice on a Sunday.'

'Ahh, thanks, love. You sure?' Mum says. 'At least somebody's being nice to me on my birthday.'

Nellie smiles at me. 'Get yourself washed and dressed, Robyn. You and your mum are going out.'

Nellie nods at Mum. 'Give yourself time to think.'

Mum takes me to New Brighton on the ferry. We have to queue for ages to get on board. Mum walks slow, rubs her side, her belly, catches her breath. People are all dressed up; babies gleam inside blue prams, some with Silver Cross written on the side. The wind out on the river whips up hair, skirts have to be kept down with both hands. A man holds down a flat cap, tries to light his cigarette against the wind. He ends up sliding a door across and going inside a room with benches.

With her make-up spread on too thick, Mum's skin looks like a smudged chalk drawing hung on the wall in Miss Fennel's class. Two women pushing prams nudge each other, give Mum sideways glances, crinkle their noses and say *ahh*. I look away, hope Mum doesn't see or she'll go for them.

We walk along the front. The sun makes the top of the water sparkle. I'd like to cut out a piece of it, make a twinkly tablecloth to cover the dark holes.

Men with yellow and red buckets and spades at their feet hold up pinwheels, which spin and whirr in the wind. I can smell onions and fish and chips and it makes me hungry. Mum is quiet. She smokes more and more fags, asks me if I want something to eat. We queue for curry and chips. Mum takes out another fag while I eat, flicks ash to the ground everywhere we walk, like a trail for somebody to follow. She picks one or two chips out of my tray, dips them in the curry and blows on them before she eases them in to the good side of her mouth.

'Take another,' I say.

She shakes her head, takes out her fags.

She pays for me to go on the bumper cars and the carousel. I watch Mum sit on a bench and smoke. A couple walk by holding hands and Mum's head goes down so I can't see her eyes. On the way back to the ferry she buys me an ice cream with raspberry sauce. It drips down the inside of my wrist like blood. I lick it away before Mum sees. On the ferry home she catches a woman arm in arm with a man staring over at her. 'Want a fucking picture?' Mum says. We glare at them until they look away.

After school the next day Mum is waiting at the gate. She has two Kwik Save carrier bags full of clothes. 'I've found somewhere for us to stay,' she says. 'Come on, I'll show you.'

She takes me on the number 25 bus. When we get off we walk for ages. There are no flats like Tommy Whites here, just tall houses with massive windows and doors. Some of the windows have no net curtains, so you can see right in. I have already seen a man through one of the windows, sitting at a piano.

There are lots and lots of trees, rising up out of the concrete in a line along the streets, as well as front gardens. Around here, even on the streets, it smells different, like Stanley Park.

After a while Mum stops at a house. I put my fingers on the tall metal gate and it feels rough; there is dark orange stuff inside the twists. Mum puts the carrier bags down, lights a cigarette. For a long time we just stand at the gate. Mum picks the bags up again and pushes open the gate.

The front door looks like a gigantic bar of chocolate. It has a gold knocker and a gold knob on the middle. The woman who opens the door has a baby in her arms. She takes us through a huge hallway with black and white tiles on the floor. Some of the tiles have cracks in them and edges missing. If I'd been born in a house like this I'd never go out.

The staircase is directly opposite us; it's like something out of a film on the telly. She leads us to the kitchen where there's an oblong table made of wood. Light wood. The table's in the middle of the room; you can walk all the way around it. We sit down. The lady puts the baby in a pram and fills the kettle. She turns to me and smiles.

'You must be Robyn?'

I nod.

'I'm Carmel.'

She pours me a glass of lemonade, puts three jaffa cakes on a plate. Gives Mum a cup of tea. 'There you go. I'll show you your room in a minute. We're full to bursting, but there's one small room, at the back of the house.' Carmel leaves the kitchen.

Carmel doesn't talk like us. Mum says she came here from London to get away from a man. Mum says you can tell from the way she talks she was born with money, and people like her can't survive in the real world. And if the whole world was full of the likes of her it would be a scary place and to top it all off her name sounds like a fucking sweet. When Carmel comes back into the kitchen I wonder what it must be like to be born in London with loads of money and not have to live in the real world.

Women with babies come in and out of the kitchen all the time. Stand a bottle of milk inside a pan of boiling water. Test it on a wrist or a tongue before nudging the teat between a baby's gums. Little kids run in and out of the kitchen, sneak a biscuit from the tin, take a sly look at me and Mum while they're at it, walk away giggling.

We follow Carmel up three flights of stairs to our room, last door on the left. It has a high ceiling not even Dad could reach and a big window with no curtains on it. I walk over and look out. I can see more trees and grass and people walking dogs and pushing prams. I try to lift open the window to stick my head out. It won't move. Then I see the nails. The window is nailed shut. I look around at Carmel. She's showing Mum the bathroom. It's outside our room on the landing. I hear Carmel tell Mum, 'You have to share it with everybody on this floor.' She shows her a small cupboard where we can put our clothes. Then she leaves us alone.

We sit on two single beds opposite each other. 'This is just temporary,' Mum says. 'We'll get a place of our own faster if we stay here.'

She takes out her fags, strikes the match then goes over to the window. She tries to open it. 'It's nailed,' I say.

Mum shakes her head. 'It's not us that should be locked away in a fucking hostel, it should be that bastard.' She finishes her fag, taps it out in the ashtray. 'It's a fucking man's world all right.'

I lie on my bed and think about how it is a man's world. A man can take money from you, beat you, stay out all night, call you names, say he'll stab you, walk the streets without pushing a pram, look at you with soft eyes, sing to you, slow dance you, pin you against a wall by the neck until your face nearly bursts, kick you in the face, run away from your blood to the pub.

*

We get up early next morning. Every seat around the kitchen table is full. Kids sit elbow to elbow, eating breakfast. Carmel is at the oven cooking eggs and bacon. There's a kid about my age buttering toast: thick brown hair all over the place, a green T-shirt and faded blue jeans.

Carmel sees us in the doorway. 'Ah, morning, Babs, Robyn, help yourself to toast.'

Mum looks around the table. 'We're not hungry.' She turns away. 'See you later.'

Carmel turns back to the oven.

'Babs, is that you, love?'

Mum turns back around. It's the lady from Greaty Market. The one who looked shattered, with the twins and two other kids either side of the pram. I don't recognize her at first. She has no front teeth and her hair is cut short now. She wears rosary beads around her neck.

'Margy? What the fuck happened to you?'

Margy stands, puts a twin boy in the pram next to the other one. She gives Mum a sideways nod to follow her into the hall. Mum takes her fags out, hands one to Margy. 'Get yourself some toast, Robyn, sit in Margy's place, won't be a minute.' They step outside. Carmel gives me a plate with fried eggs, bacon and two slices of toast. The girl who was helping Carmel sits down opposite me.

'I'm Lizzie,' she says. 'Who are you?'

'Robyn.'

'Just you and your mum?'

'Yes, you?'

'Just me.'

'Where's your mum?'

'Who knows? We came together five days ago. She left, hasn't come back.'

'Your dad?'

'Left us years ago.'

I look up at Carmel.

Carmel rubs Lizzie's shoulders. 'She'll be back soon. You wait.'

'When she sobers up,' Lizzie says.

Mum is back in the kitchen with Margy. I finish my breakfast and she takes me on the number 25 bus to school. 'We'll have to find you a new school,' Mum says. 'This one's too far now.' Mum tells me a neighbour told Margy that her husband was in the pub with another woman. Margy went around and saw them together. She went for the woman with a glass. Margy's husband dragged her home by the hair and kicked out her teeth. I feel sorry for Margy.

I like Mum telling me things, grown-up things. It makes me feel like somebody. Mum lights a cigarette. 'Men,' she says. 'Bastards, all of them, fucking bastards. Especially that drunken bastard I married.'

20

I sit on the front step with Lizzie. The gates are locked. The rain stopped an hour ago and the little ones have got the toys out. There's a circle of grass in the front garden, over by the fence, with a tree in the middle. A concrete path takes up the rest of the space. We're in charge Carmel said, me and Lizzie. Mum is in Margy's room, having a little chat.

'Any news?'

'No. She hasn't turned up. They want to put me into care,' Lizzie says.

'Care?'

'In a big house in Formby called St Theresa's.'

'Like this place?'

'No. No parents, just kids. I went to visit.'

'Do you still have to go to school?'

'You get taught stuff there, go to a class.'

'Do you have your own room?'

'Dorms, ten girls in each, the younger ones are together in a different dorm.'

Two of the kids are fighting over a bike, legs sprawled half on half off. I wriggle the little bike up high away from them. 'Share it. Ten minutes for you, then ten for you,' I say.

'That's not fair,' the smallest lad says, milk teeth wet with crying.

'It is,' the other one says. I give him first go.

'You're good with kids,' Lizzie says. 'They get on my nerves. I've got a brother, well a step-brother. Mum's first boyfriend. His name's Michael. He lives with his dad, Mike.'

'Can't Mike take you?'

'My social worker asked. He's with a new woman now. She said no chance. She's already taken on one, that's enough. What about you and your mum, what's happening?'

'Mum said we'll get a place away from Dad faster if we stay here.'

'Did he do that to her face?'

'Where's Formby?' I say, not wanting to answer.

'Dunno. I went in my social worker's car. On the way to Southport she said. Why?'

'I was just wondering.'

'You planning to visit?'

'I'll visit, if you want.'

'That's up to you.'

'Anyway, your mum could still turn up. There's time.'

The lad who said it wasn't fair is back at the bike. I stand up.

'I'll go and ask Carmel for the proper address, if you like. Get her to write it down.'

'Okay.' I pick the little lad up off the bike. The other lad grabs the handlebars and sits down. 'Want a swing?' I say. He nods. I press his back into my belly, swing him through my legs. *What's the time, Mr Wolf? One o'clock, two o'clock*. He giggles. The lad on the bike watches. 'That's not fair,' he says.

Lizzie is back outside. 'You giving out free sweets or what?'

I look down and see a queue. They all talk at once. *I want a swing. So do I. Me next.*

'Come on, Lizzie; give us a hand with this lot.'

And she does. We swing them, one at a time between our legs until our backs ache, around and around in circles until we fall down dizzy on the bit of grass. We take an arm and a leg each and give them shake the beds. Lizzie's cheeks are red. 'I can't remember the last time I felt this great,' she says.

At the dinner table Lizzie sits down next to me. Carmel's made egg and chips with baked beans. There's a mountain of bread buttered in the middle of the table. We make chip butties, dip bread into the runny egg yolk. It tastes delicious. Carmel tells us to leave some room, there's cake to shift yet. Before bed, Lizzie gives me the address of St Theresa's in Formby. I fold the piece of paper up and put it in my pocket. 'I'll visit.'

'That's up to you,' she says.

In Jimmy's Café Edna's got the radio turned up loud. She says it makes the day go faster listening to music. I love the songs. Learn words by heart for when they play them again in the early afternoon. Sing along in my head to 'Waterloo'.

Edna still moans and screams at me but I just nod and hum along with the radio. Now I know she's angry with herself and it's not about me, I play little games with her like hide and seek. If I see a table that needs clearing, I save it for her to catch. Let her say, 'Table five, Robyn,' see her shake her head at Jimmy. Jimmy looks across at me and grins. I might even let them pile up if we're busy; give her a whole list of tables to scream about.

Mum is serving people on her stall. It's been a month now since we've seen him, but Mum says he's bound to turn up sooner or later. She says she's gonna tell him straight, she wants nothing to do with him.

Saturday is mad in St Michael's Market. People jammed together shoulder to shoulder, at Jimmy's Café it's non-stop food, and he loves it. It's late in the afternoon before I get a break today. People saying how warm the weather's getting now. The heat brings people out, Jimmy says. The till's full three times over. Jimmy puts the notes into a blue cloth bag, hides it in the bread bin.

I sit at a table, eating a cheese sandwich when I see him in Mum's queue. Black polo neck jumper, sleeves rolled up past the elbows. I put down my sandwich and watch. Mum doesn't see him at first. When she does she looks like something has been flung in her face. He holds his hand out towards her. She doesn't move, doesn't speak.

He reaches over the counter and presses something into her hand. There's nobody behind him in the queue. She can tell him to fuck off if she likes. Tell him all men are bastards. Choose not to live in a man's world. Start screaming out loud how he tried to kill us both. Scream out loud that he still can. She turns, picks up the scoop, fills it with peanuts and takes it to the scales. I push the plate away, my face and ears feel hot. She hands him the white paper bag and turns to the till. Counts the notes out into his hand: *That's one pound, and four ones make five. Thank you.*

When we finish work, he's outside on the street. He walks with us to the bus stop and waits, pops peanuts into his mouth from the white paper bag. I look at Mum and think if she looks at me I'll scream at her, *what the fuck are you doing?* But she looks away. We're at the wrong bus stop, I want to say, this bus will take us back to Tommy Whites. The bus is full and I have to sit at the back away from them. I watch him talk and talk at her all the way back to the flat, saying stuff into her ear. Her face stays straight ahead.

Once we're inside I go to my room, open the window and stick my head out. My throat is hot and the tears come fast and I can't stop them. I wipe them away but they just keep coming. I can hear them talk in the living room. That's all it is, talk. Mum isn't shouting or throwing stuff at him. She talks, and all I can do is wait.

When it's dark, Mum comes into my room. 'Robyn, we're just going around the Stanley for the last hour. You can watch the new telly if you like. Your dad got us it off a man in the pub. The picture on it's a bit fuzzy, better than nothing though. I'll bring curry and chips in later.'

Her words suck the air out of me. *She chose to keep me.* Why keep what you want just to throw it away? She sits down on my bed. 'Robyn, you know your dad had a bad time when he was a kid. His mum put him in a home and he got battered there every day by the adults. He's sick, love, needs help. He's said sorry and he's going to try harder and I believe him. When I think of the way Margy's been treated, left with all of them kids on her own. At least he hasn't gone off and left us. I'm giving him another chance.'

I hear the click of the latch then push my head out of the window. I hate this flat; the tiny kitchen with no space to turn around. The three-sided table pressed tight against the wall, and the tablecloth full of holes.

I hate how she tricked me with all that talk about men, and how they're no good. And about how we were going to get a place of our own. All lies. And now, she's gone out for a drink with a man who can kill us both any time he chooses. I hate how people blame the wrong somebody for how bad things have been for them. But right now, I hate her for not wanting better. I wonder what the next thing to make him snap will be? Somebody closes the door too loud? Somebody puts his slippers in the wrong place in the living room? Somebody peels potatoes the wrong shape for roasting? Nellie said next time Mum might not be so lucky. I think she's right. I check under my pillow, the knife's still there. Knowing it's there makes me feel safe.

I don't have to change schools, Mum says, as it's my last couple of weeks at Our Lady's. All of the teachers are nice to us. Even Blackbeard, the dinner lady, lines us up without a poke. They say we're off to big school soon and it's going to be a very different story. Heads get patted more, we get smiled at more and in the dinner centre our plates are filled up more. Mr Thorpe puts the telly on for an hour for us in the morning while he teaches Gavin to count without using his fingers. When Gavin eventually does it, Mr Thorpe leaves the room to fetch Mr Merryville. Gavin gets to choose a treat from Mr Merryville's box. Mr Thorpe has a grin on his face which lasts all day.

I'm going to St Josephine's all girls' school on Westminster Road. So are most of the girls from Our Lady's. The boys are going to the English Martyrs, an all boys' school, which is across the road from us. Anthony Greenbank is going to a different school. His mum and dad are teachers.

Nitty Nora pays us one last visit. If we need a letter, we line up in the hall. Most of us do. Mum takes me to a clinic up on Everton Road, says she's fed up using lotions that don't work. 'You're a carrier,' she says, 'so the lotions that work on everybody else won't work on you.' She says carriers attract nits then give the dirty bastards to everyone. Colette Crace said when you're asleep, if there's enough of them, they plait your hair and drag you down to the river Mersey so you'll drown.

I sit on a wooden chair and lean forward while the lady in the white coat washes my hair. Mum sits on a seat by the door. 'She's walking alive,' the woman says, rubbing my hair with a towel. 'Her hair's thick. Is it okay if I cut it first?' Mum nods at her. She covers my shoulders with the towel, takes a pair of scissors out of the drawer. She click, clicks the back first, clumps of thick dark hair all over the floor.

I close my eyes. Feel cold shakes of lotion seep into my scalp. The terrible painty smell takes my breath away. She catches the top of my ear with a scrape of the steel comb. I moan. She holds my head in her hands. 'Keep still.' The tinkle of a steel comb on the bowl, loads of dark nits float dead on the top of the water. White gloved fingers pull the rest off the comb. Rub them into a piece of newspaper spread out on the table. 'Got you,' she says, like they knew all along they needed to hide.

On the newspaper I can see lots of dark little creatures walking over each other, some bigger than others. I shiver to think they've been living in my hair and I didn't know. 'How come they're still alive?' I ask.

'They're called survivors. The ones the lotion didn't get.' She takes a bottle of lotion and sprinkles it on top of them until they stop moving. 'Dead survivors now.' She laughs.

She carries on dragging the comb across my scalp. 'I'll be here till next week with this lot,' she says, looking at Mum. 'Walking alive she is. I've never seen anything this bad.'

Mum lights a fag, shakes her head.

When we get back to the flat my head throbs. I go to my room and get into bed, Dad's face at the door. 'Putting your mother through that, don't let it get that bad again, or next time I'll take you myself, and they can shave the fucking lot off.'

Maybe I should have been given away. Anything's got to be better than this.

Next morning, before he gets up, Mum takes me on a bus to a place that looks like a warehouse. 'You'll be off to big school before you know it,' she says. 'We need to get you a coat.'

We climb an endless flight of metal stairs that lead to a huge room with tiny square windows. Long bare bulbs spread out across the ceiling. Mum hands the lady behind the counter a letter and she leans over the counter to look at my feet. High shelves stacked with clothes and boxes are behind her. She returns with three shoe boxes and two coats draped over her arms.

'Six or seven?' she says, looking at my feet.

'Six,' I say.

She opens a box. White tissue paper covers the shoes. They smell like paint. She peels the paper back to reveal a brown pair of lace-ups. I have to try them on. They feel a bit tight across my toes.

'Have a walk on the paper in them,' she says.

When I walk around on the brown paper, the shoes don't crease across the front. They seem to push my feet backwards. I think the shoes feel ugly and wrong.

'How are they?' the lady says.

I nod.

'Good. Take them off.'

But they're not good, these shoes that won't bend. The laces are stiff; they make a loop that won't soften into a knot.

Mum kneels down, feels through the shoe to my big toe.

'Give her the seven,' she tells the lady. 'Her toes are right on the edge.'

I try the seven on. My feet slip in and out of them as I walk.

'They're better,' Mum says. 'Try the coat on next.'

The black duffel coat has no lining inside. I look in the mirror, turn to the side. The hood is lined with thin red tartan, that's the only part that stops me looking like a coal man. If I undid the buttons and let it fall back, it could stand behind me on its own. The hem falls just above my knee, scratching against my skin as I walk.

'Give her the next size up,' Mum says. 'She's got all summer to grow yet.'

I try a coat on the next size up. The lady fastens it up to my neck and it feels scratchy. I pull my body away. 'Straighten the face,' Mum says. 'Beggars can't be choosers.' The hem falls below my knee and the sleeves cover my knuckles. I look up at the lady, who looks away.

'Right, that's it, we're done.' Mum walks over to the counter where the lady stamps her letter.

Outside, I'm carrying the shoes and coat wrapped up in brown paper when I see Angela getting on the bus with her mum. She carries big bags with Blacklers written on the side. Angela is not a beggar. Angela is a chooser. What if beggars could be choosers? I'd choose to be somebody everyone else wants to be, instead of somebody I don't even want to be myself.

21

'Look how wonky the fringe is. It's a living disgrace. She's butchered you, that's what she's done. You'll be a laughing stock in that new school.'

Nan opens her purse. 'There's a new hairdresser's opened on Great Homer Street. All the young ones go there; I've seen them, when I queue up for my pension. Here, take this.' She hands me a five pound note. 'Go down there, see what they can do. Wear one of my rain hoods if you like, to hide it. And don't forget my change, that's a five pound note.' She takes a clear plastic hood out of her bag. It has two white pieces of ribbon either side. Nan ties it in a knot under my chin, pulls it forward with a swish to cover the wonky fringe. 'Tell them you want it shaped,' she says. Outside, once I am around the corner, I untie the hood and push it in my pocket.

In the hairdresser's I sit on a leather seat and wait. Both sides of the room are covered with mirrors, a black leather seat opposite each one. Three hairdressers are busy cutting hair, one lady stands behind a desk. 'Can I help you?'

'Can I have my hair shaped?'

She smiles. 'Okay, won't be long.' She hands me a magazine. 'See if there's anything in there you like.'

I do see something I like, on the first page. It's the same style as the one Sue showed me. The girl behind the desk is back.

'What's that called?' I ask.

'The feather cut.'

'Thanks.'

The towel around my neck is soft and fluffy. The shampoo smells like fruit salads, the girl's fingers glide across my scalp and make me smile.

I have the magazine on my knee open on the picture of the feather cut. Another lady slips a rubber cape across my shoulders. She smiles when she sees the picture. 'Feather cut?'

I nod.

'You'll suit that,' she says, combing my hair back. 'I'd kill to have hair this thick.' And away she goes. Not much hair on the floor, tiny ends, nothing more. The blast of a hairdryer, a flick through her fingers and I'm done. Here I am. It looks like the picture, the fringe is a little shorter but there's no mistaking it, the feather cut. I can't wait to show Nan.

'Like it?' the lady says, looking at me.

I nod.

'Told you,' she says.

When I get back, Nan is sitting outside her block on the wall. I hand her her change. 'That's better,' she says. 'It's a proper shape now, shows off your face.'

I'm sitting on the Southport train on my way to visit Lizzie. It's the middle of August. I can't believe we're halfway through the summer holidays already. It's early in the morning, the sun is shining and I've got a carrier bag full of drinks and sweets so we can have a picnic. Nan gave me some money and told me where to get the train. I told her Lizzie was in my school and she was in a home because her mum ran away. Mum's not speaking to Nan and Nan wants nothing to do with my mum. I don't want Nan to know I met Lizzie in a hostel, in case it causes any more trouble. I get off the train in Formby. The man in the ticket office tells me St Theresa's is only a few minutes' walk down the lane.

It's a huge place, bigger than the hostel. I have to push a bell next to a pair of tall metal gates. A lady looks at me through the black curly metal. 'Can I help you?' she says.

'I'm Lizzie's friend. Can I see her?'

'Are you on your own?'

'Yes.'

'I'm not supposed to let you in without an adult. But Lizzie hasn't had a visit yet, apart from her social worker.' She unlocks the gate. 'What's in the bag?'

'Drinks and sweets.'

She takes the bag and tips it out onto the grass. Kneels down, puts each item back inside the bag. 'Follow me,' she says. Once we are in the hallway, she asks me to empty out my pockets. 'I'll have to search you, before we go any further.' She taps my arms, tummy, back, legs, socks. 'Slip your shoes off,' she says. Once that's all done, she smiles. 'I'll tell Lizzie she's got a visitor.'

Lizzie stands on the other side of the room. The lady closes the door on her way out. Lizzie leans back against the door. 'What do you want?' she says.

'I said I'd visit.' I hold up the bag. 'I've brought sweets.'

'Big deal,' she says. 'Any fags?'

I shake my head and think about how I could have taken a couple of fags from Mum's box if I'd have known. 'I thought we could have a picnic.'

Lizzie bursts out laughing. 'A picnic?'

I want to go back to the train station. My idea to visit Lizzie, a girl I spent a few days with in a hostel, a girl I don't really know, seems wrong. I want the lady to come back in the room so that I can ask her to let me out. I stand on the other side of the room from Lizzie and I don't know what to do. So I say, 'Remember that day, me and you in the front with all the little ones, giving them swings and . . .'

'A girl got stabbed in here last week.' Lizzie's voice is cold. 'She was my mate. And you turn up wanting to go for a picnic.' She laughs. 'Don't you think that's funny?'

I don't speak.

'I said, don't you think that's funny?'

'No. It's not funny. Is your mate okay?'

Lizzie knocks on the wrong side of the door and the lady opens it. 'This visit's over,' she says. 'Take me back to my dorm.'

My eyes start to fill. I don't want to leave. Not like this. I hold out the bag to Lizzie. 'Keep them for your mate then, for when she's better.'

Lizzie leaves the room. I feel like she might have done when her mum left her in the hostel and never came back. The lady shows me and my bag the way out. I wonder how things would have turned out if I had brought fags. They must be important to Lizzie, especially after what happened to her mate. I dump the sweets in the first bin I see, get back on the train and go home.

A couple of weeks later I go back. I've got a packet of Mum's fags with four left inside. The same lady comes to the gate. 'I've come to see Lizzie,' I say.

'She's not here any more. Her mum came.'

'When?'

'Yesterday. Sorry about that, love. Have you come far?'

'It's okay. Only a few stops on the train. Thanks anyway.'

I walk back to the train station and sit down on a bench. I watch a passenger drag her luggage onto the platform like it's the most important thing in the world. I wonder about her high-heeled shoes and that little gap between the platform and the train; a pointy heel could easily slip down there and get stuck. That would change how she saw everything. That would become more important than the luggage. I think about Lizzie, and how she might have sat on this bench next to her mother, waiting for the train. I wonder how long her mum will stay with her.

Except for Saturdays, I spend the last couple of weeks in August going to Stanley Park with Bernie. We play on the swings, play hide and seek or just sit on a bench and talk. Sometimes we bring Johnny and Ged with us. One day, Sylvia gives us a pound note and an old bed sheet. We buy loads of sweets, cans of Coke and crisps. We get to the park early in the morning, spread the sheet out on the grass under a massive tree, and have a picnic. In the afternoon, Johnny falls asleep in his pram. Out of the whole summer, that day was my favourite, because even when it got dark we never went home. We went home when we felt like.

22

September is here. I'm in Bernie's square. Mum and Dad are still in bed. I've got my new uniform on ready to walk down St Domingo Road with Bernie, like we've arranged. I shout his name up to the landing. He opens the front door. 'Come up,' he shouts. 'I'm not dressed yet. It's only seven o'clock.'

I haven't slept all night, haven't bothered to look at the clock this morning; I saw daylight and got up. I sit on his step and wait. Johnny comes down the lobby in just his vest. I pick him up, bounce him up and down in my arms. He giggles, clenches his knuckles, stuffs them inside his mouth, slobbers all over his vest. Bernie dresses him in the hall, wakes up Ged. When they are all ready he shouts down the lobby to Sylvia, 'Taking the kids out, Mum, for a walk.'

'All right, lad,' she shouts back. 'Don't go far.'

We sit at the bottom of Bernie's block. Johnny is in the pram. 'What do you wanna do?' Bernie says.

I shrug.

Ged yawns, rubs the sleep out of his eyes. 'Dunno.'

A man with black hair and a black beard walks towards us. He wears a donkey jacket, a blue cloth bag flung over his shoulder. 'All right, lads,' he says. 'I've brought you something.' He grabs Johnny out of the pram, throws him up in the air and catches him. 'Look at the size of you,' he says, rubbing his nose against Johnny's nose.

Johnny's face crumples; he holds out his arms to Bernie. The man puts him back in the pram, opens his bag. He pulls out a huge truck and gives it to Johnny, a leather football for Ged and a pair of red boxing gloves for Bernie. He gives us all a penny from his pocket, fluffs up Johnny's hair. 'See you in a minute,' he says, then climbs the stairs two at a time. Ged takes Johnny's penny off him in case he swallows it.

Ged looks at Bernie. 'Who's that?'

'That's our dad,' Bernie says. 'Home from sea.'

'Liar,' Ged says.

'Am not,' Bernie says, tossing up his penny and catching it. 'Race you to Dolly's.'

We run the pram around to Dolly's shop to buy sweets. When we get there Dolly has a For Sale sign up. She tells the woman in front of us she's moving to Jersey, as soon as she gets a buyer, to live with her sister.

'Where'll we get our sweets from then?' Ged says.

The school hall is huge, and packed and scary. It smells of old sweets. Somebody puts a record on the record player and we all stand. A lady with blue hair walks down the centre of the hall, eyes straight ahead. She looks like the Queen, lilac dress and coat to match. The wooden floor is even shinier than her black patent leather shoes and bag. 'Good morning,' she says. She even talks like the Queen. 'For the benefit of our new pupils, my name is Mrs Bullock. You may sit.' We sit. She stands for the whole assembly in the same position. She tells us to count from the front row of chairs to find the number of our row. 'Look either side of you and behind you because every morning you will sit in the same place for assembly.' I have already counted, row six, eight seats in. The girl in front of me turns her face around to look at me. She has high, sticky-out bunches and sticky-out nostrils to match. She tosses her face away from me. Her back parting is wonky.

Mrs Bullock stands on a stage, red velvet curtains either side of her. All of the teachers dotted around the hall are women. When she has finished talking, somebody puts the record on again and she steps down from the stage and walks back down the centre of the hall, eyes straight ahead like she's in a trance. Once Mrs Bullock has gone, the music is switched off. The girls on the front row lead out. I follow them towards the door. A teacher stands in front of us, says we have to follow her.

From our classroom on the ground floor, we can see the playground. Our teacher is called Mrs O'Connor. 'I'm your form teacher and your English teacher,' she tells us. She has short feathery hair, soft brown eyes and wears a bottle green cardigan draped around her shoulders. She sits down, flicks her slingbacks off under her desk. Takes the register, looks up as she reads, trying to match the face to the name. 'Bear with me,' she says.

I look around the room. Plenty of faces I don't know, some I do. Trisha Fisher is in my class and so is Angela, the girl from the hall with the wonky parting, and Tina Egan from my old school. When the register is finished a bell rings and Mrs O'Connor stands.

'After play, make your way back to this room; you're staying with me all day. Tomorrow you'll begin school properly with a timetable.'

I don't know what a timetable is.

On the playground behind a wall big girls smoke one cigarette between them. One, two, three pulls each and pass it on. 'For fuck's sake, Mandy, you've soaked the tip. I'm first on at lunch.' Mandy has a big chest with a badge pinned to it that says MONITOR. She has the feather cut. She catches me watching. 'Piss off, you. You'll get us caught.'

I watch the teacher patrol the playground, but she doesn't go near the wall. She stops and talks to the little kids, points the way to here and there. She doesn't look at the wall, not once. Our classroom window opens and two girls sell drinks and sweets out of it. There's a long queue and the bell goes before everyone is served.

Back inside the classroom, Mrs O'Connor hands us a book each: *Anne of Green Gables*. We spend the rest of the morning reading aloud around the room, one paragraph each. Mrs O'Connor listens to us all read and writes things down in a big book. Sometimes she stops a reader and says, speak up, or slow down, but most of the time she writes.

Next day we are given a timetable. It has names, times and classroom numbers on it. Mrs O'Connor explains how, if we get lost, we are to ask a monitor to show us the way. You can easily spot them, she says. They wear a badge that says monitor. 'Watch how the monitors behave, and you can't go wrong.' Mrs O'Connor leads us to our first maths lesson with Mrs Much. 'Don't want you being late for that,' she says.

Mrs Much has red hair and cat glasses. She's the deputy head, she tells us, and homework is compulsory in her class. She fires times tables questions at us; a squeeze on the shoulder means it's your turn to answer. As the weeks go by the questions get harder and so do the squeezes.

Mrs Jones teaches RE. She's a big woman with thick ankles and a thin smile. We sit in alphabetical order, which means I always end up sitting next to sticky-out bunches and nostrils, Rose Mooney. Mrs Jones tells us to copy passages from books into our exercise books. Rose Mooney rolls the pages of her exercise book around her pencil. 'I'm going to be a hairdresser when I leave school like our Rita,' she whispers. 'What are you going to be?'

I carry on copying the story of Lazarus and say nothing.

'Where did you get that feather cut done?'

'Great Homer Street.'

'Our Rita says it's too dear there. You should go to her shop next time; it's dead cheap.'

Mrs Jones looks up. 'Something wrong, Mooney?'

I carry on copying and Rose finds a new page to roll her pencil around. 'Big bones Jones, our Rita calls her; locked our Rita in that cupboard once for talking.'

I look over at the brown cupboard door near the window.

'She found big bones Jones's lunch box in there and scoffed it.'

'She never.'

She dabs the tip of her finger on her tongue, crosses her heart.

'Honest to God,' she says. 'Cheese and pickle sandwich on brown bread, an apple, a KitKat and a bottle of lemonade.'

'What did Mrs Jones say?'

'Sent her to Bullock for the cane; six of the best she got. Big bones Jones had to go the chippy.'

'Rose Mooney, one more peep out of you and you can stand outside for the rest of the morning.'

Rose cocks her head down to the side, pretends to write in her exercise book. 'She hates me,' she says, hardly moving her lips. 'She knows Rita's my sister.'

On the playground I walk around with Rose. We watch the girls smoke behind the wall. I queue up for a carton of orange juice while Rose talks about hairdressing and things her Rita told her about the teachers. Mrs Much once hit her Rita over the head with a text book and called her a dunce. Her mum came up to the school and dragged Mrs Much out of the classroom and gave her a good kicking in the corridor. She didn't pick on Rita again after that. 'Mrs O'Connor's the best,' Rose says. 'Our Rita says she's kind and we're lucky to have her.'

Rita is right. English is my favourite lesson. Not just because Mrs O'Connor is kind to all of us. We get to read books and stories and poems. On Friday, Mrs O'Connor says that we can take *Anne of Green Gables* home with us to read if we promise to bring it back on Monday in one piece. She asks those who want to take it home to show hands. Half of the class show hands and Mrs O'Connor smiles. 'That's great,' she says. 'If you don't bring it back on Monday though, you have to pay for it.'

On Sunday morning while Mum and Dad are still asleep, I race down to my nan's with *Anne of Green Gables*. 'What's it about?' Nan asks.

'I'll tell you a bit about it in an hour when I know more,' I say, curling up on the settee with my book.

When she's in her flat, Nan listens to the news on her radio on the hour of every hour.

'We've read some of it around the class, but I'll start again from the beginning because some of the girls who read out loud stumbled over words and mumbled them so it didn't make sense. The main character is a twelve-year-old girl, Anne-Shirley. She is an orphan sent to work on a farm for a brother and sister, Matthew and Marilla. They asked for a boy, but the orphanage sent a girl by mistake.'

'They're not going to send the poor beggar back, are they?' Nan says.

'Dunno.'

Nan goes into the kitchen to put the kettle on. 'They want shooting if they do.' She waves her hand at me. 'You read on and find out.'

After an hour, Nan points at the clock. 'Well?' she says.

'They're going to give her a chance. Marilla didn't want her but Matthew said it's only fair to give her a chance.'

'He's a smart man.'

'She's got to stay out of trouble and help them around the farm.'

'That's not hard. Do you think she can?'

I shrug.

'Well, read on and find out,' she says.

Every time I read a chapter I have to tell Nan what's happened. When it's time for me to go, Nan says I'm to bring the book back on Sunday, so she can find out what happens next.

'It's better than the bloody news. The news has done nothing but depress me lately.'

The following Sunday, from St George's church, I run down the grass hill until I reach Netherfield Road. The sideways rain pelts through my duffel coat giving off a horrible nail-varnish smell. My socks and shoes are soaked. I pull up my hood but it falls back down, too big for my head. My ears sting with the cold. I take *Anne of Green Gables* out of my pocket and slip it inside the coat. I cross the road, run down another grass hill until I reach Great Homer Street. It's Sunday. There's no market today. It looks bigger when the stalls are here.

I walk up to Scotland Road. The sign above the Throstle's Nest pub creaks over my head. I walk up to Limekiln Lane, across the caged tarmac where the lads play football. Her front door is open. Nan sits in her straight-backed chair by the radio. I sit down on the settee. I'm soaked through. She gets me a towel, hangs my coat up in the bathroom.

She's back in the living room. 'I've been thinking, if you read it out loud, then I won't have to wait to find things out. I could find things out when you do.'

I don't want to share it, have it taken over. Nan shuffles back in her chair, pats her hair into shape, eases the hem of her pinny down.

'Sorry, love,' she says. 'I'm ready now.' Gives me the nod to begin. I open the book and start to read. I take her through fields, schools, classrooms, bedrooms, markets and ministries, forwards, backwards, up and down stairs, into stables. She sits and listens and laughs and sighs. I watch her listen to the words, let my eyes read on a little faster, find out something new seconds before she does, and wonder how she'll react, even guess how she'll react, watch how she takes the news and, bit by bit, I begin to enjoy it.

When each character speaks I give them their own special voice; deep and kind for Matthew, sharp and brisk for Marilla, bright and funny for Anne. These characters take over my mind and I can see and hear them live and breathe in the room. It's as if they are living next door and we get to see right inside their lives, without ever having to reveal anything about ourselves.

Every couple of chapters Nan rushes around the kitchen and makes tea, brings out a box of Family Favourites, says wait, so she can settle herself back into the chair before a new chapter begins. Sometimes, she asks me to go back and read chapters all over again. Especially the ones that describe the countryside. 'Makes me feel like I've been on a day out,' she says.

When it's time for me to go I close the book. Nan's eyes are glittery. 'One more chapter?'

'Can't, I've got school tomorrow. Next Sunday?'

Nan nods. 'Next Sunday.'

When I get to the front door I can hear Nan's voice.

'She's a real livewire that Anne-Shirley, isn't she?'

23

BLACK LACE-UP SHOES, SIZE 9

1 BOX OF FAIRY SNOW

1 JAR OF COFFEE

1 BOTTLE OF LOXENE SHAMPOO

ROBINSONS LEMON & LIME JUICE

'Do me a favour?' Sylvia hands me a shopping list. 'Big Bernie's not going back to sea. He misses me and the kids too much. We're down to our last few bob.' She opens her purse, gives me three pence. 'Buy yourself a Curly Wurly or something.' She roots in her purse again, gives me an extra two pence for my bus fare. 'See what you can do. He needs shoes to go looking for work, eight and a half, even if there's no nines.' She hands me a blue shopping bag; the handles are attached with gold rings. It makes me think of Mr Wainwright's pen. It costs one pence there on the bus to County Road and one pence back. 'You'll have to be quick. The shops close in an hour.'

I look up St Domingo Road but there's no bus in sight. I start to walk, look back when I reach the next stop to check for a bus. There's no sign of one so I run all the way, bet myself I can get there before it. By the time I get to County Road, no bus has passed me. Inside Timpson's shoe shop it's busy. The shoes are in boxes stacked up against the wall. Every box has the shoe size printed on the front. I look for size nine. Open a box and look inside: brown slip-on shoes. I take the note out of my duffel coat pocket and check: *black lace-up*. I lift up lids on loads of size nine boxes before I find a pair of black lace-up shoes.

I take a walk around the shop. Pretend to look at a pair of shoes for myself. I try one on, walk about in it. Check to see what the staff are doing. Two ladies and one man, all serving. My heart starts to flip in my chest. I unzip the bag. Look around to see who still needs serving. A lady holding a little girl's hand waits by the handbag rail. One of the staff is behind the counter taking money. I have to be quick while they're all busy. I slip my own shoe back on.

I lift the lid, reach inside and grab the first one. My back to everyone, bag against my belly, I drop the shoe inside. I can feel my face burn, breath stuck in my throat. A quick look behind: all clear. I slip the second shoe into the bag and close the lid on the box. Bag zipped, my eyes fix on the door. The walk from the boxes to the door seems to take for ever.

Outside, I breathe out. Walk fast steps towards the super-market, pull the list out. It takes me ages, but I get everything. I can't stand still at the bus stop, can't stop looking behind. I leg it back all the way along County Road and Walton Road. By the time I reach the bottom of St Domingo Road I'm breathless. The number 25 bus pulls up behind me. I put out my hand, the bus stops and I step on board. 'One stop, please,' I say.

The driver laughs. 'I could spit further. Go on, get on.' He doesn't take my money. Nellie is sitting on the front seat. I sit next to her, push the penny back into my pocket.

'Your face'll get you the parish,' she says. 'Where've you been?'

'On a message for Sylvia, Bernie's mum.'

She looks at the blue bag on the floor. 'Well, I don't know who Sylvia is, but I do know you're a good girl, Robyn,' she says. 'Your mum's lucky to have you.' She taps my knee, taps my sins away.

I look at the bag on the floor. No, I'm not a good girl, I think. I'm a thief, a rotten sly bastard thief.

Sylvia is taking washing in off the line. Her face brightens when she sees me. 'How did you do?' she says. I open the bag and show her. 'Soap powder, shampoo, juice, coffee and the shoes?' She lifts one out. 'You got the shoes.' She gives me a hug. 'You clever, clever girl.'

'Is Bernie in?'

'No, love, his dad's taken him to join a boxing club.'

I was looking forward to going to the park with Bernie. I've knocked up a couple of times now and he's always out boxing.

'Ahh, look at that face, it's not the end of the world. He'll be back soon. Call back in a couple of hours.'

I remember the bus fare; hold out the coins to Sylvia.

'Keep that, Robyn. You've saved me a fortune.'

I go back to my square. There's a gang of girls sitting on the bottom of our block having a sly smoke. I recognize one of them, Mandy, the monitor from my school. Mum stands on the landing with Nellie. I go inside and get a drink of water. Dad's not in. Me and Mum have cheese sandwiches and lemonade, watch television for a bit. I can't be bothered now knocking back for Bernie; he'll probably be out anyway. After a couple of hours Mum tells me it's time for bed. I cover myself up with the blanket, hear the front door open. 'Won't be a minute, Robyn,' Mum says. 'Just running to the offy for a bottle of cider and some fags.'

I listen for ages but Mum doesn't come back in. I get up, go out onto the landing. Mum is there chatting and smoking with Mandy and her mob. Mum turns around. 'You all right, Robyn? I'll be in now, love.'

'Oh, I know her,' Mandy says. 'She's one of the new kids in our school.'

'She's my daughter, Robyn. Keep an eye on her for me.'

Mandy smiles at me. 'I will.' I smile back, then go inside to bed and fall fast asleep.

Next day on the playground, I walk around with Rose. From behind the wall, Mandy sees me, calls me over. Rose looks behind us, then back at me. 'Do you know her?'

'Robyn,' Mandy shouts. 'Over here.'

The way Rose looks at me makes me feel like I'm somebody important. We walk over. They are just about to light up. 'Her mum's brilliant,' Mandy says. 'Dead funny, isn't she?'

I stand next to Mandy and think about how we look the same with our feather cuts.

'Keep dixie for us, Robyn, you and your mate. We'll let you have last drag on it.' Mrs O'Connor is on playground duty. She's right over on the other side of the yard; steam rises from a blue cup in her hand.

'It's all clear,' I say.

They huddle into a circle, one, two, three pulls and pass. The fag burns down fast, it's nearly down to the brown tip by the time they pass it to me. 'Here,' Mandy says. 'Take the last pull.' She clamps it between my fingers. I put it to my lips; the tip is soggy. I push my breath out. The end lights up. 'You're not taking it back. Taking it back is what matters.'

One of the other girls holds out her hand. 'Give it here. She's wasting it.'

Mandy knocks her hand away. 'Let her have another go.' She looks at me. 'Suck it back right down your throat,' she says. 'Go on, it's easy.' Everybody gathers around me to watch. It's right down to the brown tip now. I put it to my lips, breathe it back hard. My lip burns. The smoke takes my breath away. I cough and choke, hold the cigarette away from me, eyes watering. Somebody takes it from my hand. When I stop coughing, I see Mrs O'Connor throw the tip to the floor and stamp on it.

Her face is in Mandy's face. 'What do you think you're doing?' She looks at me and Rose. 'These are first years.'

Mandy's face turns pink.

'Wait for me outside Mrs Bullock's office.' She glares around the broken circle. 'All of you.'

I walk behind Mandy. 'Robyn Mason, Rose Mooney, not you. You go to my room.'

We stand in front of Mrs O'Connor's desk and wait. The taste of smoke in my mouth makes me feel sick. She comes into the room, throws her bag to the floor and leans back on her desk, arms folded. 'What were you thinking of?'

We say nothing.

'You don't have to do the same thing everybody else does, if you know it's wrong.'

'Sorry, Mrs O'Connor,' Rose says.

Mrs O'Connor looks at me. 'And next time?'

'I'll say no.'

'I hope that's true, Robyn, because next time you'll be sent to

Mrs Bullock.' She looks up at the clock on the wall. 'Better get a move on. You're late for class.'

There's no sign of Mandy and her gang on the playground at dinner time. 'They all got six of the best,' Rose says. 'Mandy's had her monitor's badge taken away. None of them are allowed on the playground for a week.'

In English, I can't look at Mrs O'Connor. I feel like I've let her down. When it's my turn to read out loud, I say I need the toilet so I can get out of the room. I've read well past them all anyway. When the class is over Mrs O'Connor tells me to stay behind. 'It's okay to make mistakes, Robyn. That's how we learn. You haven't killed anybody. The only one you've hurt is yourself. No more sulking.'

If I had stayed in bed last night Mandy would never have seen me. I would just be another nobody on the playground she could tell to piss off. It was a mistake to get up and find out what was going on. It was a mistake to go over to the wall and smoke.

On the way home I wonder who taught Lizzie to smoke. I wonder what happened to her. I wonder if she ever thinks about me. The more I think about it all, the more I convince myself I'm probably better off not knowing.

We've had a busy Saturday. Nearly all of the cakes in the glass cabinet have been sold. One chocolate éclair and one jam doughnut left. I think I'll ask Jimmy if I can have the éclair with my lunch. 'Robyn, take table two's order.' Edna is in a good mood. She cracks big bubbles, sings along with every song on the radio. There's another hour before Liverpool kick off, before Jimmy switches the radio station over.

I walk over to table two; he's sitting there, blue denim jacket, blue jeans. He makes his eyes big for me to pretend I don't know him. 'Cup of tea and a jam doughnut,' he says. I can see my hands shake when I write the order, place it on the counter. I try to think why he's here. I can't get him money out of this till. I look over at Mum's stall; she has a queue. Why doesn't he join it?

I take him his tea and cake, look where he's looking. Jimmy counts out the notes from the till. Rolls them inside the blue cloth bag, puts the bag in the bread bin. Dad spoons two sugars in his tea, slow-stirs it. Breaks the cake in half and eats, jam dripping down the sides of his mouth like blood. My neck burns. I tell Jimmy I need the toilet. He nods. 'You all right?'

'Fine,' I say. 'Back in a minute.'

I lock the cubicle, put the toilet seat down and sit. He's going to spoil everything. I try to think what to do. I need to let Jimmy know he's being watched, but how? When I get back to the café Dad's gone. 'Have your break, Robyn, while it's eased off,' Jimmy says. I sit down with a glass of orange juice. 'What are you having to eat?'

'I'm not hungry.'

'Have a cake then.'

'No thanks.'

'Are you feeling okay?'

'I'm fine. Go on then, I'll have a cake.'

I eat half of the éclair so he'll stop asking questions.

In Mum's queue, blue denim jacket, blue jeans. I let out a big breath, pick up the rest of the éclair and eat.

'Got your appetite back?'

I smile. 'I'll have a cheese sandwich, if that's okay.'

'One cheese sandwich coming up.'

After work, he's waiting for us outside. Mum goes into a sweet shop to buy fags. I wait outside with Dad. 'Fat Jimmy,' he says, 'he keep that cash there all day?'

'No,' I lie. 'Some man tried to take it once. Jimmy cracked his skull open with a hammer, blood everywhere. An ambulance had to come.'

Dad looks me in the eye. 'How do you know?'

'I've seen the hammer. He still keeps it under the counter.'

'You could get at it.'

'There's no way. I'm not allowed behind the counter.'

'You're a smart alec. Think of a way.'

Mum and Dad go to the Stanley. They won't be back for ages. I've taken Mum's key off the mantelpiece. I knock at Bernie's to see if he's coming out. Sylvia tells him to go on a message to his Auntie Jackie's. 'Want to come?' Bernie says.

'Where does she live?'

'Ten minutes away. I'll show you.'

'Who is she?'

'Mum's sister.'

We walk up St Domingo Road, behind St George's church, to the top of the grass hill. 'Where about?' I ask.

'See that tower block over there?'

I nod.

'Fourteenth floor, you can see the whole of Liverpool.'

Netherfield Road sits at the bottom of the hill. Cars speed by in both directions. Bernie looks at the hill then back at me. 'Race you down.'

I shake my head. 'What are you like?'

'Wanna race or what?'

'What do you think?'

We leg it towards the bottom, Bernie looks back, sees me beaten, starts to do a funny run. Legs wide, arms curled like an ape. 'Come on, slow coach.'

'I'm scared. There's a road. Slow down so you can stop.'

Bernie stops, toes on the edge of the pavement, arms out, drawing sideways circles in the air. We cross the road and head for the tower block. The lift is tiny and it smells of pee. Bernie sees me crinkle up my nose.

'You'll stick like that,' he says.

'I want to,' I say.

Jackie doesn't look like Sylvia, she looks young. She's tall with dark, little-girl hair that ends down her back. It nearly touches the hem of her short dress. 'Come in, Bernie lad. Let me get you the money.'

I can't stop staring at how high her heels are; she has eyelids topped with blue glitter. Bernie pulls me inside. 'You've got to see this,' he says. In the living room there are two armchairs with wooden handles, a television and a round, glass-top coffee table. The window has no nets or draw curtains. I look out through the glass. From here, everything looks like a toy town. A giant could lift up a car, a tree, a home from here and move it to another part of Liverpool.

'Wow,' I say.

Bernie looks at my face. 'See?'

Jackie hands Bernie a ten pound note. 'Keep that safe for your mum.' Bernie stuffs it inside the front pocket of his jeans.

'What's your name?' Jackie asks.

'Robyn,' I say.

'Love your hair. This your girlfriend, Bernie?'

'No,' I say. 'We're mates.'

I don't like the way she looks at us. Why doesn't Bernie tell her off? I don't want Bernie to think about me that way. Like the teenagers in Stanley Park, all kissy kissy behind the cocky watchman's hut. There's no way I want Bernie as a boyfriend. It would mess things up. I've got enough to think about with other stuff, like my dad. He won't let me do anything. He'd probably murder Bernie if he knocked up for me at our flat. Right now Bernie's a good mate; not somebody I need to worry about.

'I believe you,' Jackie says, in a sly voice.

Bernie turns back to the window.

Jackie checks her watch. 'Come on, Bernie lad, shift yourself,' she says. 'I've got someone coming over any minute. He's taking me dancin'. She takes a bottle of perfume out of her bag, sprays her neck and wrists. 'Hold your wrists out,' she says to me. She sprays them both, puts the bottle back in her bag. 'Tap them together, like this.' She nods at Bernie. 'Drives the men crazy.' Jackie sees us to the door. When she closes it the bang echoes around the block. Bernie presses the button for the lift. The doors open and an older man in a suit steps out. He doesn't look at us. His eyes are on Jackie's door; he straightens his tie before knocking.

'How old is Jackie?' I ask when the lift doors close.

'Dunno, twenty something, why?'

'Just wondered.'

When I get home there's nobody in. I put the key back on the mantelpiece, watch a bit of telly, check I've got *Anne of Green Gables* in my pocket for tomorrow. I'm in bed when I hear them come in. I can't stop thinking about Jackie, living up in the clouds just ten minutes away. I imagine her out in a fancy place, dancing. I want to go back and visit, try on her shoes and her make-up. I lift my wrists up to my face, press them to my nose.

I wonder what I'll wear when I first go dancing. I want blond hair like Doris Day's. A nipped-in, belted waist and pointy shoes with kitten heels under a sky blue dress. The dress will have a matching cloak that I swirl around my shoulders. If I'm seen, I can flip it over my head as a disguise. I'll dance with a man wearing a light grey suit, burgundy tie and a white shirt. We'll go to the dance in a carriage, a gold carriage with six white horses. The dance will be in a palace in London. We'll dance all night under a crystal chandelier. A live band will play; violins and guitars. Outside on the balcony I'll feel his breath on my neck. See his eyes look at me like Jimmy looks at Sue. What would I say when he asked me to marry him?

'Robyn!'

Her voice like a needle in my head. 'You've left the fucking telly on again.'

24

Nan sits in her straight-backed chair, pulls down the hem of her pinny. I open the book and begin reading. Anne has been invited to a picnic. Marilla's amethyst brooch has gone missing and Anne was the last one seen with it. Marilla says Anne isn't going to the picnic unless she confesses to taking the brooch.

'Has she taken it?' Nan says.

'No, she doesn't know anything about it.'

Nan shakes her head. 'Tell Anne to fetch the police.'

I can't help laughing. 'The story's already been written, Nan.'

'I know that. I mean, the police would get to the truth.'

I read on. Anne confesses to taking the brooch. She tells Marilla she lost it, so that she can go to the picnic. Nan shakes her head. 'She won't let her go. She's got no chance now. I'd rather have a thief than a liar.'

Nan's right. Marilla tells Anne she's to miss the picnic as a punishment. Just before the picnic begins, Marilla finds the brooch dangling from a loose thread on her shawl.

'I bet she gets to go now,' Nan says.

I read on. Nan's right again. She loves the happy ending. I turn the next page; even though the chapter has ended I pretend to read on. Something about Nan knowing what's going to happen before I read annoys me.

I lie, tell her how Marilla only thought she'd found the brooch. When she looked closer, it was a worthless glass one she'd won in a raffle. The amethyst brooch is still missing. This new piece of information throws Nan. She picks her bag up off the floor, opens and closes the catch over and over. 'Where did Anne see the brooch last?' Nan says.

'In Marilla's room.'

'Then she needs to get in that room and search it. It can't be far. Is there a window open in the room?'

'Why?' I say.

'Just flip back through the chapter and check.'

I pretend to find a sentence that says the window was open. My lies feel like the opposite of lies.

'Got it,' Nan says, shaking her head. 'I don't know why I didn't think of it before.'

'Think of what?' I say.

'Magpies, they're known for stealing from open windows. Shiny things. Marilla's brooch is in a magpie's nest.'

I open the book back up. Pretend to read on. This is fun. I tell Nan that Marilla found the amethyst brooch after all, dangling from a thread on her other shawl. 'Stupid woman,' Nan says. 'Needs to get at the truth before she goes accusing people of stealing.'

I feel bad and want to laugh out loud at the same time. You can tell by the look on her face, the truth isn't what she wants; she wants to be right. Like when Nan told me about my toes. She told me a long second toe means I am going to be a ballet

192

dancer. That's not true. She told Mum she was right about what things would be like for a bastard. I realize that the truth isn't as important as getting things right.

I close the book. A thousand times since I heard Nan tell my mum about me being a bastard I've wanted to say:

'Nan, what's a bastard?'

The book is closed on my knee. Anne-Shirley says things as they pop into her head. I like that about her. I've never done that. I think too much about things. If I was Anne-Shirley, just for a minute, I'd say out loud, 'Nan, what's a bastard?'

Nan stares at me. Asks me to give her a minute, leaves the room. I feel like I've found a new side of me, a side that is something like Anne-Shirley. I hear the toilet flush. Nan sits back in her chair.

'That's not for me to say, love. Ask your mother.'

'I wanna know, Nan. I know it's something important, tell me the truth.'

'Let me know what happens to Anne-Shirley in that next bit . . .'

'Nan?'

'Ask your mother.'

'I'm asking you. Please, Nan?'

'You can't breathe a word.'

'I won't.'

She tells me my dad is not really my dad, but somebody my mum met on the rebound. My real dad, she says, was a gentleman. He was in the army when he found out about me, she says. When he got out of the army, he came back to marry my mum, not straight away cos he needed time to think. It wasn't long before he found out she'd already married somebody else. He knocked at the door. I was three months old. But it was too late. Before he left he asked Nan for my name. To tell the truth, Nan says, I felt sorry for the lad.

I toss the book to the floor as if it had suddenly burst into flames in my hands, and I run from the room. I feel like I've been punched hard from the inside.

After a while, Nan taps on the bathroom door.

'Robyn, love, open the door. I thought you had an idea he wasn't your dad. I thought they might have told you something. I'm sorry, love.'

Snot and tears cover my face. I wipe it all away with toilet paper. Go back into the living room, sit down on the settee. Nan brings in tea and biscuits, puts them on the table by the back window. 'Come and sit over here.'

She puts her hand over mine. 'All right?'

I say nothing.

'To answer your question, do you still want me to?'

I nod.

'If a child is born without a dad, I mean, if the woman's not married, or the dad buggers off, or if it's a mistake, like they didn't mean to have a baby, then the child's called a – well, some people use the word . . .'

'Bastard?' I say.

Sunday, while I read the words from *Anne of Green Gables*, my eyes catch Nan's. And we carry on another story that's already been written. The story of how my mum didn't know that the man she was really meant to marry would come back.

In our flat, I watch Mum light her cigarette off the cigarette of the man she pretends is my dad. And I think about how it began almost from the time I was born, the telling of lies that feel like the opposite of lies.

25

Saturday. It's gone eight. I wake Mum up. Tell her we've over-slept for work. She tells me I don't have a job any more. She got the sack. The boss told her since she started working on the stall, his takings have been down. Mum goes into the kitchen, puts the kettle on. 'And he told Jimmy everything, so that's that.' She takes out a fag from her pocket, taps it on the top of her hand.

'They can fuck off, all of them,' Mum says. 'I won't set foot in that market ever again, even if they start giving the stuff away.' She points the fag at me. 'And you're not to either.' She puts the fag to her lips and lights it. 'His takings have been down since I started?' The kitchen fills with smoke. 'Cheeky bastard, they're all robbing him blind. Four of us work on that stall. He hasn't got rid of anyone else, though. It's me that's taken all the shit.'

I get washed and dressed, eat a bowl of cornflakes. When I've finished, Mum gives me a piece of paper. *Three jars of coffee. Four tins of salmon, boneless.* Hands me the bag with the handles frayed down to the white wire and money for a packet of malted milk biscuits. 'Do I have to?'

'I'll find another job soon.'

I scrunch the list up in front of her face; drop the bag on the floor. 'I don't want to.'

'Look, if he gets up and there's no money he'll be a fucking nightmare all day.'

I think about what he did to Mum's face before. 'Why are you with him?'

Mum turns away, looks out of the kitchen window.

'Mum?'

She doesn't turn around when she speaks. 'Will you do it or won't you?'

'I'll do it this time.'

'Thanks, love.'

I pick the bag back up.

I walk away, slam the front door hard. Back to this and all because of that lazy good-for-nothing. He spoils everything. If he'd get himself a job then he'd have his own money for ale. I don't mind getting stuff for Sylvia, that's different because I know it's important; she asks me to get stuff she needs. When they sell this stuff, the money will be spent in the betting shop and the Stanley, then get pissed up the wall. I won't do this again. I'm never doing this again.

'Maybe there are jobs on Greaty,' I say to Mum when I get back.

'Doubt it.'

I tell Mum I'm taking a walk down the grass hill to Netherfield Road, and on to Great Homer Street. Mum nods at me. 'Stay away from that old bastard's flat,' she says. 'Don't want her knowing my business.'

It feels wrong being in the market when I should be in Jimmy's Café. At least I never went near his till, so I can't get the blame for taking any of his money. 'Any jobs, mate?' I say at least fifty times. I even try the smelly fish stall. They're nice to me. Shake their heads and say, *sorry, love*. Mum's right. Most of them already have kids serving.

The market is packed. Outside the chippy, men eat from trays with plastic forks holding it all away from their red and white scarves. I follow them along Great Homer Street towards Anfield. I stand close to them outside Liverpool's football ground and look for my real dad. Nan told me he was a red-hot Liverpool supporter when she knew him. He had a season ticket and went to the match with his brother. He had dark hair like mine and he wore glasses. Nan said he was a gentleman. Maybe he looks like John Steed out of *The Avengers?* I smile. Nobody in the queue wears a bowler hat.

On stalls smaller than the market ones, men sell scarves and rattles and badges. Kids queue up with rattles that they shake until my head feels like it's going to split in two. It smells like the market, hot dogs and onions, pink candyfloss on a stick. I can't stop thinking about my dad. Bit by bit, I have put together a picture of him in my head. And now I see his face everywhere. It changes all the time. Any dark-haired man with glasses that passes me could be him. I stand by the gate and wait. Hope he will see something of himself in my face, something that will help him remember me.

Nan said he always brought her two bottles of Guinness when he came to take my mum out on a date. He would laugh and joke with her, even ask her to follow them to the Stanley with Nellie for the last hour. 'You don't get many like him,' Nan said. 'I opened the front door to your real dad when he came back to marry your mother. I shouted down the lobby for her to come to the door. She screamed when she saw him. Screamed again when he asked to marry her. Then that lazy good-for-nothing appeared from the living room and told him to get lost because you were his kid now. He'd done it all legal. There was a fist fight outside on the landing. But in the end, there was nothing he could do. He didn't even get to see you. Somebody told me he moved away after that, to Speke.'

A man walks towards me with a kid. He looks like my dad. Dark hair and glasses, a kid's hand in his hand. I've thought about that, a new family he might have made. Nan said looking for him now would be like looking for trouble. She told me to forget all about him and wait. But that's all I ever do, wait for things to happen to me. I want to make something happen for a change. You never know, Nan said, he might get in touch with you. But I could tell from her voice she didn't mean it. She knew what I knew. He'd given up on me and Mum, and found somebody else. *You don't get many like him.*

I'd written down a few questions on a piece of paper in Mrs O'Connor's class, in case he was with a kid when I saw him. I had to think about the questions, make them sound ordinary, write them so nobody but us two would know what they really meant:

1. Did you know a woman called Babs?
2. Do you remember May Crown from Tommy Whites?
3. Were you ever in the army?
4. Do you know a girl called Robyn?

But by the time I get the piece of paper out of my pocket the man with the kid has already walked past me.

If my real dad had met my mum after he got out of the army, none of this would have happened the way it did. Everything is about time and where you are inside time. There is a right time and a wrong time. They met at the wrong time and that adds up to making a mistake. That mistake is me. If they had met at the right time I would be the opposite of a mistake. I would be in that queue with a rattle clamped inside my fist, my other hand in my dad's hand. I would tell my real dad all about Jimmy and the café and how he listens to the match on the radio. My mum would be speaking to Nan. They would be in Greaty Market right now, getting a few bits. And that lazy good-for-nothing would have met somebody else, somebody that isn't my mum.

There's a roar from the crowd inside the ground. The match has started. I sit down on the pavement and watch the police officers ride by on their horses. The floor is full of litter: half-empty chip wrappers, trays with forks in, empty cans, cigarette stumps, pools of spit with green blobs in the middle. Women with full carrier bags of shopping sidestep heaps of horse shit. There are bins full with stuff nobody wants any more. I feel stupid. This whole idea of coming to Anfield is stupid. How could he know me? He didn't even have a baby picture of me in his head. Everything is wrong. I tear up my careful questions into little bits and throw them away with the rest of the rubbish.

I could go and see Jimmy. To ask him if I could still have a job. If Mum found out, she'd go mad. Jimmy will be tuning the radio to listen to the game right now. Edna will roll her eyes when she comes back from the toilet. It will have eased off, the rush. Edna will fill the mop bucket; glide the sweet flowery smell across the floor. One or two cakes will be left sitting in the glass cabinet, maybe a chocolate éclair and a jam doughnut. She'll check the tables and shout my name to clear the one left behind on purpose. Jimmy will catch my eye and send me a smile.

I think of my dad somewhere inside that massive crowd enjoying the game with his new kids. I think of Jimmy's sign above the till in his café: NO MISTAKES CAN BE RECTIFIED AFTER YOU LEAVE.

*

We walk around the playground. Rose wraps her scarf across her mouth. The air stinks of smoke from the fireworks and bonfires that were lit last night. I wasn't allowed out. Mum and Dad had no money to go to the pub. I could see the bonfire in the big square from my bedroom window. Gangs of kids had been collecting for weeks; a settee, chairs, stained mattresses, doors without handles. I watched the low heap grow into a high tower. A crowd stood around it, watched the flames stretch up towards the sky. Bernie was there; I could make out his shape in the crowd. Ged beside him, Johnny in front sitting in the pram waving a sparkler. In the dark, the flames lit up the square orange.

Mandy got her monitor badge taken off her, but they are allowed back on the playground. They sit on steps where the teacher on duty can keep an eye on them. Nobody is allowed to go behind the wall. The punishment will be six of the best.

It's cold. Rose keeps her hands inside her pockets. 'Want to come to a disco on Friday?' she asks.

'A disco?'

'You know, dancing.'

'Where?'

'Walton Youth Centre.'

'Where's that?'

'You know Timpson's shoe shop, on County Road?'

My face turns red. 'Yes.'

'Just across the road from there.'

'Okay. Who's going?'

'Me, you, our Rita, Anne, Paula and Linda, our Rita's mates.'

'What time?'

'Seven, on Friday; it's fifty pence. You live in Tommy Whites, don't you? We'll knock up about half six. What number is it?'

'Erm, I think I'm in my nan's Friday. Why don't I meet you at the disco?'

'Oh, okay then.'

I never speak about home like the other kids do. They talk about holidays they're going on to Butlin's, or in a caravan, things they laugh at on telly with Mum or Dad, the new bedside lamp and table in the bedroom. I nod as if I know. In this school I want to keep them thinking I'm like them. If I don't talk about it, I can keep my home life invisible. The way to stop them knowing about me is to listen and nod and say *I know*.

26

It's dark inside. The music is loud and the dance floor is full of girls dancing and twirling to the rhythm. Rose waves at me from across the hall. She grabs my wrist, pulls me over to meet her Rita. 'All right, Robyn,' Rita says. Rita looks like a mum in lipstick and high heels. She sits on a low stool next to the man who plays the records. He has a spiky beard growing on his chin. I can smell shampoo and soap.

'Come on, let's go,' Rose says. She pulls me onto the dance floor. We are the only two dancing. It's not long before two other girls get up. I watch what Rose does and copy her. Red, blue, green and orange lights flash across the walls. The music is so loud I can feel it like thumps trapped inside my chest. Rose looks great. She wears blue jeans with a green checked shirt. Her hair is loose to her shoulders, bouncy fringe. I sing along to every song that comes on.

'How do you know all the words?' Rose shouts.

'From where I worked,' I shout back, but I don't think she hears. Rose points over to a boy standing by a wall.

'The boys don't get up until the end for the slowys.'

Skinny boys stand like smudges against the wall; some tap their feet along to the beat. Others point at a girl and snigger.

'What time does it end?'

'Nine. It's worth staying, though, especially if the talent's good.'

'Talent?'

'The boys.'

I can't stay until the end. Dad said I've got to be home for eight.

Rose is close to my ear. 'Don't look, but see that lad in the blue jumper, he's staring holes through you.'

I turn and look for the jumper. 'Bet he gets you up for a slowy at the end.' She grins.

It takes fifteen minutes to get home. I have to leave at a quarter to eight the latest. I don't know what to say to Rose. She's got my wrist. 'Come on, let's get a drink.' In another room, there's a man behind a hatch selling crisps and drinks. Rose squeezes coins out of her jeans pocket. She slaps them on the counter. 'An orange cup drink and a packet of cheese and onion please, mate.' She turns to me. 'Want anything?'

I shake my head. There's a big clock up on the wall. It's only twenty past seven, I've got loads of time. A woman wearing white bib-and-brace jeans asks the man for a mop. 'Somebody's been sick in the toilets,' she says.

We go back to the dance floor. The sound of the music is fantastic. More people fill the floor, the room gets warmer and warmer. Rose's fringe is stuck to her face. The room stinks of sweat and bleach. When a song ends we start to walk off the dance floor. Another begins and Rose pulls me back on again. 'I love this one,' she says. Finally, I get her to come with me for a drink. I glance up at the clock. Ten to eight. Clutching my stomach, I turn to Rose. 'I feel sick,' I say.

'You can't go yet. The slowys haven't been on.'

I start to walk away. 'I said I feel sick and, anyway, the talent's crap.'

Outside the air is cold and I can see my breath ahead of me. I leg it to the number 25 bus stop, looking back every few seconds. There's no sign of it. I feel for the penny in my pocket in case it comes. At the bottom of St Domingo Road I take a rest at the bus stop. It's well gone eight by now. I'll get killed when I get in. They'll never let me out again. Behind me there's no sign of a bus. I walk as fast as I can up the hill. Get to our front door and knock. There's no answer. I knock louder. 'They went out, couple of hours ago,' Mrs Naylor shouts from further along the landing. I slide down against the wall, the step cold on my bum, get my breath back and wait.

A few minutes later they're back from the pub. 'I've been waiting here for ages,' I lie.

Mrs Naylor's behind them, she nods a head towards me. 'She's only just arrived.'

I stare at Mrs Naylor, eyes big.

'What?' Dad says.

'She's lying.'

Dad narrows his eyes at me.

The air tastes like paper in my mouth.

Mum lights a cigarette, walks over to Mrs Naylor, blows smoke in her face. 'You shut the fuck up.'

Mrs Naylor backs away, heads towards her own front door. Mum follows after her. I hear the front door slam shut. Mum kicks the door, bang bang bang, opens Mrs Naylor's letterbox and shouts through it. 'You want to mind your own business.'

Mum's standing on our step. Mrs Naylor comes back out, shouts over at us. 'And she's a big hit with the lads.'

Dad's face turns white. 'The what?'

'She's had that queer heel in from the back square, and his brother and the lads I haven't seen. There's no way I'd allow a granddaughter of mine to walk the streets with lads.' She looks at Dad. 'Not doing a very good job with her, are you?'

Mum says, 'What's it to you? You're not keeping her.'

Dad shouts at Mrs Naylor. 'No, I'm the only gobshite doing that. Cheeky bastard.'

Mum's face is in Mrs Naylor's face. She makes her voice small. 'You're not likely to know any granddaughter of yours, seeing as your only son wants fuck all to do with you. In fact, you wouldn't recognize her even if she was standing under that big fat nose.'

Inside, I go straight to my room. He follows me, pushes his face into mine. 'Don't open the door, I said.' His lips move but his teeth are clamped shut.

'I didn't.'

'Liar. You're a fucking whore. Sneaky little cow.'

'Naylor's the liar. Robyn's only eleven, for fuck's sake . . .'

'Since day one I took her on, and now she repays you with *whoring.*'

'Go to bed, have a lie down.'

'Shut up, shut up, shut the fuck up. Thinking I wouldn't find out, people looking at me like I've done something wrong, getting that shit thrown in my face.'

Mum grabs his arm to get him away from me. 'Nobody's lookin' at you.'

'Me, left with somebody else's shit.'

'C'mon, I've got a bottle of beer in the kitchen. C'mon.'

Mum's face looks pinched. She pulls him out of my room. I can hear them arguing in the other room. Dad saying I'm more trouble than I'm worth. My body flops down onto the bed. Curled up in a ball, I wrap the pillow around my ears to drown out the noise.

The tears run down my face, make dark spots on the candy-striped sheets. I try hard to think of a safe place I could go to before it's too late. I can tell by the way he looked at me, by the way he spoke, that if Mum wasn't here, he'd have murdered me tonight. No more messing about. I have to get out of here. I need to be the one in charge of me.

On Monday in school Rose tells me the boy with the blue jumper got her up for a slowy. She tells me how he must have been staring at her all along and not me.

'To be honest,' I say, 'I couldn't care less.'

Angela and two other girls walk over to us. They all wear pink lipstick and blue mascara. Angela has a pad and a pen in her hand. 'I'm collecting,' she says, 'for Mrs O'Connor's Christmas present.' She shows me and Rose a list of names, some have ticks next to them. She taps a finger at my name. 'You get a tick every time you pay and you get to sign the card.'

Rose hands Angela coins from her pocket. 'I've got my snack money. Take that towards it.'

Angela drops it into a purse, puts a tick next to Rose's name. She turns to me. 'I'll bring something tomorrow,' I say.

'Make sure you do, ugly.'

Angela and her two friends walk away giggling.

'Bitch,' Rose says too loud.

I burst out laughing.

Rose grins, shouts even louder. 'Smarmy little bitch.'

Angela turns around, with the other two girls, walks back to where we stand. She puts her face in mine. 'What did you just say?'

I look at Rose then back to Angela. 'Bitch,' I say. 'Smarmy little bitch.'

Rose giggles.

Angela hands her pad and pen to one of the girls. She turns back to me, rolls up her sleeves. 'Don't get me started you, you ugly robbing little cow.'

Hit them before they hit you, Nan says.

I ball my hands into fists. Feel the crack of her jaw on my knuckles. She goes down moaning. One of the other girls punches me hard near my eye. Rose is all over her like a bear, drags her hair down to the floor. The other girl with the pad clears off across the playground. Two teachers drag all four of us down to Mrs Bullock's office. 'This is a school for girls,' one of them yells. 'First-year girls, behaving like a gang of football hooligans.'

While we are waiting Rose says, 'How come she called you a robbing cow?'

I feel like somebody has lifted up my skirt and stared at my knickers. 'Dunno,' I say. 'I found a pencil in our old school and she said it belonged to her.'

'Tight cow,' Rose says out of the corner of her mouth.

Mrs Bullock tells us to line up next to each other. She takes the cane out of her desk, uses it to push up under our hands until all eight of them are on the same level. Steam rises from a cup on the desk, a thin smudge of red around the rim.

I'd forgotten how much that first sting hurts and the slow burning sensation that follows, finally the tingling numbness. None of us cries. We have to stand and listen to her rant on and on. I hear none of it. All I can think about is thick green spit spreading across lips, and getting my hands under a cold tap.

It's three weeks before Christmas, a Saturday morning, when I find Angela sitting on the bottom of our block. At first I go to walk right past her. 'Robyn,' she says. 'Can I talk to you for a minute?'

I walk across our square away from her. She runs after me. 'Please, Robyn, I need a favour.' We walk down St Domingo Road together. 'It's the money, for Mrs O'Connor, I've lost it.'

'Liar; you mean you've spent it.'

'I have not. Well, I just borrowed a bit for make-up and stuff. I was putting it back but then I borrowed another bit and . . .'

'You've spent the lot?'

'About thirty-five pence left.'

'Out of how much?'

'About two.'

'Pounds?'

She nods. I walk down St Domingo Road. She catches up. I walk my fastest. She keeps up with me. 'Please, Robyn.' She takes a handful of coins out of her pocket. 'You can have what I've got left. I'll get expelled,' she says. 'You know what Bullock's like.'

'So?'

'Could you get her something worth about two pounds?'

'So you want me, an ugly robbing little cow, to rob something for you?'

'I still have the vanity case.'

I stop. 'What?'

'You can play with the vanity case.'

I can't help it. I laugh in her face.

'Have the vanity case. You can keep it.'

I laugh louder.

She looks away. 'It doesn't matter. It was a stupid idea.' She walks away, back up St Domingo Road. I think about the time I went to visit Lizzie in Formby, and that horrible empty feeling in my stomach.

'Angela,' I shout. 'Okay, I'll do it as long as you come with me.'

It's Saturday, so town is busy. We find a large shop that has four floors. 'What do you want for her?' I ask.

'I'm not sure.' She takes out a list. 'When she went to the cupboard to get me a new exercise book, I checked inside her cardigan. I wrote it down, she's a size fourteen. I made a list of ideas: bag, cardigan, pyjamas, purse. What do you think?'

We browse through rails for ages. Nothing seems right until we find the nightwear. 'Feel this,' Angela says. I run my fingers across the fabric. It feels the way chocolate éclairs taste. A long nightdress with thin straps, a nightgown over it to match.

'That's silk,' a voice says behind us. 'Beautiful, isn't it?'

The lady is beautiful. Dark hair built up on top of her head like it's waiting for a tiara. 'If you're looking for a gift for your mum, chocolates might be more affordable.' She walks away.

'She'd love that,' I say.

Angela looks at the price tags. 'Jesus, have you seen this?'

I unfasten my coat. Look behind me. The lady is talking to a customer on the other side of the store. I take the hanger off the rail, roll them both around it and stuff the lot inside my duffel coat. Angela collapses on the floor laughing. Her hand cups the middle of her skirt.

I fasten up my coat. 'Angela, get up,' I say, looking across the shop. I sound like a teacher. Her face is purple and there's a dark patch in the middle of her skirt. 'I've peed,' she says.

'I don't care.' I start to walk away. 'Get up now, or you'll get us caught.'

Angela stands. 'I'm sorry but when you . . .' Her face grows dark.

'Are you all right?' The lady is behind me. I can feel the nightgown slip down too low inside my coat. I make my eyes big at Angela so she'll walk away.

'Oh, you poor thing,' the lady says, looking at Angela's skirt. 'Of all places for that to start; give me a minute, I've got a packet in my bag.' She walks away.

I don't know what she's talking about, but I do know I've got to get out. I make my way down the stairs; take them three at a time. At the bottom I look back, Angela is behind me. She's taken off her jacket and is tying it around her waist. Once we are outside I see the 17C bus and start to run. Angela's face is bright red; she can't stop laughing. She runs with her legs wide open; drops of pee dribble down the inside of her leg, yellow stains on the top of her white socks. We laugh all the way home on the bus. A lady shouts across at us, 'Are you two wearing mohair knickers?' This sets us off laughing even louder.

27

The next day, I can see Nan watching for me from her window. Hear her voice when I'm in the hall. 'Hurry up, Robyn, you're late. I'm going out tonight, believe it or not, with a man.'

'Who?'

'He'll be in the Throstles Nest at eight o'clock and his name's Eddie.'

I sit down in my place on the settee, *Anne of Green Gables* in my pocket. Nan brings in a box of day-old cakes from Sayers. She puts the box under my nose. 'You get first choice, putting yourself out for an old codger like me.'

I take an egg custard. 'You're not that old, Nan, you've got a date.'

'It's not a date,' she says, taking a cake from the box. 'It's a meeting that's all, with loads of other people around.' She takes the empty box into the kitchen.

I take out the book, the sun comes out and lights up a half–moon shape on one side of the page.

'I might not go yet,' Nan says. 'If I do, I'll be the talk of the wash house.' In front of the mirror she pats her hair into place and winks. 'I suppose I could go around the block one more time before I die.'

'You're not going to die, Nan.'

'Not yet, I hope. But I will some day.'

'But you're not really, really old. Are you?'

Nan doesn't say anything. Just looks at me and I know it's a question without a word answer.

When I've finished reading, Nan can't sit still. She fusses over crumbs, washes through a tea towel in the sink and stays in the toilet for ages. When she finally sits down I say, 'Can you remember anything else about my dad?'

She shakes her head. 'There's nothing more to tell.'

I get up to leave. 'Are you sure, Nan? Please tell me, I promise I won't ask again.'

'Oh Robyn, you should know, you're old enough. Promise me you'll let what I tell you lie.'

I sit back down. 'I promise,' I say.

She crosses herself. 'On Granddad Jack's life?'

I cross myself. 'On Granddad Jack's life.'

'I know his name.'

I lean forward. 'But you said you couldn't remember.'

'I lied. It's Robert, but everyone called him Bob.'

'Bob what?'

'Bob Naylor.'

For a minute I say nothing. My belly drops like a stone too far down. My mind races through all of the horrible thoughts I've had about Mrs Naylor. And how she says I've got the divil in me. And I think maybe she means a different Naylor from miles and miles away. But then I look up at Nan's face and see that it's hopeless trying to pretend.

'Robyn?' Nan says.

'Does she know about me?'

'I don't think so. And you promised . . .'

'I know. But Mrs Naylor's . . .'

'But Bob wasn't like her. He was more like his dad, gentle and just nice.'

I don't know what to say.

'He's married now, love. I asked around. You need to know he's got a couple of kids, a boy and a girl. So you see, unless he comes looking for you, it could cause him a whole lot of bother. But you have a right to know about him. And I'm glad I told you, love. It's best you know.'

I start to cry. Loads of salty tears drench my lips.

Nan gets up and puts her arm around me. 'I'm so sorry. But it's best you know.' She takes a hanky from her pinny pocket and hands it to me. 'And I'm not meeting my maker holding onto a secret like that.'

I dab my face. 'What use is knowing if I can't change anything?' I ask. 'Does he ever come and see his mum?'

'As far as I know, Bob fell out with her years ago. She treated her husband like dirt; he was so unhappy, he drank himself into an early grave. Bob couldn't bear that. Everything Gwyn Naylor ever loved she crushed.'

I know so much about my dad now. I know his name, I know his mother, I know he has a wife and kids and I know he's my dad. I know all of this and it all means nothing. Knowing it makes me feel useless.

I imagine he waits at the bottom of the block for me on my birthday. It's Saturday; he wants to make it a special surprise. He holds my hand in the queue while we wait to go in. My first time at the game. I fling the rattle above my head and shout, *Come on the reds*.

In my dreams we're in the football match queue and his real wife and kids turn up. They pull my hand out of his and say, Who are you? When I tell them he's my dad they flip and chase me away. They scream after me to leave him alone. I shout back at them, I don't need him anyway, I don't need anybody. I can look after myself.

28

I meet Bernie after school by the phone box, like we'd agreed. He's inside, school shirt hanging from his side trouser pocket, black handset in his hand, talking importantly to nobody in particular. He rubs a finger inside the coin return slot but it's empty. 'Who was that?' I say when he steps outside.

'Nobody. I just like to dial.'

'You're mad.'

I don't see much of him any more. He boxes or trains nearly every night. His dad takes him to a club in Toxteth, like Jack's dad took him to a barn in Crosby.

While we walk, I let my feet fall in time with his. I feel safe. We walk through Stanley Park; most of the branches are bare. Bernie's shoulders have grown wide, but he seems to have stopped growing up; he only reaches my shoulder.

'I'm not boxing tonight,' he says. 'Want me to knock up at yours?'

'I'm going to my nan's later,' I lie.

Every Friday, at the disco with Rose, I have to say I've got pains so I can leave. I don't mean it. I have to be in. When I'm older, I want to say the things other people say and mean it.

The grass is damp, so we sit on a bench. I take off my shoes and socks, see the daisy pattern printed on my leg. 'My toes are all scrunched up in these socks,' I say.

'They stink of classrooms and school dinners.'

Bernie looks at my feet.

'Stop looking at my toes.'

'Why?'

'They're horrible, everyone says. Too long and too thin.' Bernie laughs.

'What are you laughing at?'

'Look at the size of that second toe, it looks like a ciggy.' He laughs again, grabs hold of my toe and wriggles it. 'This little ciggy went to market . . .'

I snatch my foot away. 'Very funny, Bernie.'

After a while, I feel drops of rain on my nose and face. Bernie says, 'The sky's turned black, let's go.' I ball up my socks, stuff them inside my coat pocket, put my shoes back on. We head towards the gate that leads to Tommy Whites. Bernie tells me he's starving, runs towards his square, shouts back at me, laughing, 'Wee, wee, wee, wee, all the way home.'

I don't know the front step has been painted until it's too late.

He sits in his chair. Mum's not in. He stands up when he sees me, HATE fingers point to the floor.

The words wriggle from his mouth like disturbed worms. 'Look what you did, you stupid lanky bitch.'

For a moment I am confused. Then I see them, black footprints that trail behind me like a confession. 'I didn't know,' I say.

He twists my foot up behind my back. The tip of my shoe touches the nape of my neck. I cry out with the pain at the top of my leg. It feels like he's tearing me in half. He grabs the back of my hair, pushes my face down hard into a footprint. I can taste the paint in my mouth. I spit.

'All afternoon it took me to paint that while you've been sitting on your arse in school. Wait until your mother sees the lino.'

At my ear his breath reeks of beer and smoke. 'Go running to her, crying like a baby, and she'll get the same.' He jerks my leg up higher and I scream louder. 'I could kill you right now,' he says. 'But that would be too easy. I'm going to make you wait until I'm ready.' His hands are around my throat. 'When I'm ready, I'm gonna squeeze every last drop of life out of you.'

He lets go of me. I collapse to the floor. Crawl away from him towards the table. He comes after me, tears off my shoes. 'You won't need these where you're going.'

I grab onto the tablecloth. He rips a sheet of newspaper in half, places them either side of the mantelpiece, arranges my shoes on top. They sit like twin trophies won for two different events, waiting for Mum to come home. Event number one: not only did she stand in the black paint on purpose. Event number two: she proceeded to traipse the black paint all over the lino.

Fuck you and your lino.

In my bed I don't cry. I close my eyes and see a man with golden hair. He looks like Chris. He smiles at me and I get a warm feeling in my belly. He says, 'Strong, now, like Granddad Jack.' I say this over and over to myself and it makes me feel safe.

A while later I hear a knock at the door. Dad answers it. I get up and look through a crack in my door. It's Bernie asking for me. Dad pushes a finger at Bernie, pokes his kind face. Tells him to piss off away from the step.

I feel under my pillow for the knife, at the same time scared of what my hands might do with it.

The front door slams. He's in my room. 'That dwarfy bastard's just knocked. You stay away from him, I'm warning you. If he knocks here again I'll launch him over the fucking landing.'

The way he looks at me I can see he is not my father. I jump up, knife behind my back. 'If you lay a finger on Bernie, I'll knife you. I'll knife you while you sleep, you bastard. You won't even hear me coming.' The sound of my voice shocks me. The knife in my hand shocks me. Him closing the door and walking away without saying a word shocks me. What shocks me most is knowing I will have to kill him before he kills me. Once I make up my mind to do it I won't stop until he's dead.

My body can't stop shaking. I want to smash his head against the wall and scream at him: 'I'll see Bernie whenever I want. He's my mate, he's nothing to do with you. You're not my dad and you can't tell me what to do.' But I promised Nan, and he knows where she lives. I know I won't be able to keep that promise much longer. I know I'll blurt it out and he'll kill Nan for telling me the truth. I think about running away. Tell nobody where I am. I can't go to my nan's. That's the first place they'll look. I could go back to the hostel, ask Carmel for Lizzie's address. Nobody would find me there. But Lizzie wouldn't want me hanging around her.

I could write on the back of my English book for Mrs O'Connor to find. *My dad plans to kill me. Not with a knife, or a push under a bus, not even with poison. He plans to strangle me with his bare hands.* Maybe she'd invite me to live with her; then again, maybe not.

In the bathroom I look into the mirror. Black smeared lips, red marks on my neck. I bend over the sink to get a wash. The back of my head throbs, there's a dull pain at the top of my leg. I feel as light as a wafer. A voice in my head says over and over again,

Leave this place. I stay awake all night thinking. It feels wrong to leave Mum, but if I stay I know something bad will happen. I'm not his child. He doesn't care about me. He's got nothing to lose if he kills me and I've got nothing to lose if I kill him. It's not about right or wrong, it's about what I believe. I believe if I stay he'll kill me or make me kill him. I'm tired of living in a place where every moment is guarded. There's nothing left for me to do but leave.

29

Next morning while it's still dark, I get dressed. I gather my clothes together, stuff them in two carrier bags, put on my coat and shoes. Outside, I sit on the step. Dab a finger onto my tongue. Draw a smiley face on a tile without needing any new spit. I dab the finger back onto my tongue. I shudder. It makes me think of the back of a skirt sucked too high up chocolate brown tights. I spit the taste out and it splatters onto the landing.

Walking down the steps in the darkness I look up at the oval light shades on the brick walls, bulbs still lit. I follow them down the steps; trace my shadow on the wall with a finger. I feel lighter in a good way like I am stepping away from a terrible accident. The air smells different and it tastes different when I swallow it. Once I reach the bottom of the block I run and run and run. Take in gulps of this new air until it fills me up, fills me right up to the top.

I run all the way down St Domingo Road towards my school. A bus stops right by me so I get on it. I ride around on buses all day to keep warm; see kids walking to school in their uniforms like it's an easy thing to do. I watch them walk towards what I used to have. At night I sleep on the stairs of a block next door to Nan's. It's cold on the stone steps and the light above me stays on all night, making my head ache. I can feel pain at the top of my leg, a bruise I think. I poke it with my finger. From the other side of the doors I can hear televisions, coughs and sneezes and later, much later, the whimpers and screeches I think come from nightmares.

I can't sleep. Every creak or bang of a door makes me think they've found me. I pretend I don't have anybody in the world. I have left everything behind. I need to forget I was ever in Tommy Whites. I don't need anybody's help. I can take care of myself.

One night, I crouch down where the bins are kept because I think I hear Mum's voice calling me. All I want is to wake up in the morning and go to sleep at night without feeling this scared.

I see Chris, tap, tapping the side of his nose. He's covered in light, like an angel or a ghost. If he could give me one wish I'd go back in time. Make sure I was there before it all began, before she decided to marry. Show Mum something else.

Chris disappears too soon and I try to get him back, but it's no use. This is silly. I have to look forward not back. Where can I go? How long have I been away from Tommy Whites? My mind's not working straight.

I fasten my duffel coat over my face to keep out the smells, hide inside the hood of my coat. There are red itchy lumps all over my legs. At night I scratch them and they've started to bleed. My throat aches. The only place I don't shiver is on a bus. Sometimes I steal a bottle of milk off a cart outside Nan's block, drink it down in three goes. It fills up my belly with cold. One morning, my legs walk back towards Tommy Whites.

Bernie is running down St Domingo Road. 'Want to bunk off school today?' I ask.

He smiles. 'Let's walk down to the park.'

While we walk I let my feet fall in time with his. I feel safe. We sit on a cold bench. I look down at my dirty nails. Hide them under my legs.

'Can you smell anything on me?' I ask.

Bernie doesn't answer. 'What's in the bags?'

'Clothes. I've left home.'

'Why?'

I think about what he said about throwing Bernie over the landing. 'Fed up living there, that's all.'

'Have you had a row?'

'Yes, with my dad.'

'Where will you stay?'

'Don't know. Don't care.'

'I know somewhere.'

'Where?'

'Our Jackie's.'

'Will she let me stay?'

'She might.'

'We can't tell her I've run away.'

'No.'

We sit quiet for a few minutes. Bernie bounces his knee up and down. Takes off his tie and stuffs it inside his pocket, unfastens his top button. 'I hate school,' he says. 'I'm going away to sea when I leave, like my dad. He's told me I can. I'm gonna see the other side of the world, Australia.' He takes a photograph from his pocket. Three men in white shorts and no shirts sit on a wall, faces scrunched up in the sun. 'Bet you can't find my dad,' he says.

I take a look and point to the man in the middle.

He nods. 'That was taken in Sydney, Australia. My dad says some parts of Australia haven't been found yet.'

'That's mad,' I say. 'If they haven't been found then how do they know about them?'

'Dunno. What are you gonna do when you leave school?'

'Dunno,' I say, thinking about Mrs O'Connor's class. I want to say how much I love school and wish I was there right now. They are probably reading another book.

We sit for a while without speaking, then Bernie jumps up. 'I know,' he says, 'we'll say your mum has to go into hospital and there's nobody to look after you, because all of your family live in Australia.'

I shrug. 'Okay.' Not believing for a minute that Jackie'll say yes.

'And I'll say my mum sent us down to ask because we've got no room. Jackie'll do anything for my mum.'

'Won't she check up?'

'Nah. It'll be fine.'

'If she lets me stay, promise you won't tell anybody where I am?'

'Not even your mum?'

'No. Tell nobody, Bernie. Promise?'

'Okay.'

Even if Jackie says no, this is the best thing anyone's done for me in ages. Tears fill up my eyes. I lean over and kiss Bernie on the cheek. 'Thanks,' I say. 'Thanks loads.'

'No worries,' he says, then goes all red and grins.

What I'd really like a go at with Bernie right now is holding hands. I look down at my dirty nails again and curl them away inside my palms.

We walk past the swings where Bernie fought those two lads. I remember his face all bloody when we got back and think about Sylvia and the way seeing Bernie was a fighter made her happy. In my mind I can see Sylvia before Bernie's dad came home, locking the windows and doors when it got dark. Checking in on her kids in the middle of the night when she heard a bang, or a cry, or the creak of a floorboard. And I understand why Sylvia loved what Bernie did that day, loved him right then more than anything else in the world.

Jackie is going out on a date. She shows me around, tells me I should use the place like it's my own. She opens a cupboard in the bathroom. 'Palmolive or Lux?' she says. I smell them both through the packaging. 'Palmolive,' I say. She hands me the block.

When Jackie goes out, I take a bath. The water ends up brown. There's a thick black ring around the bath that I have to scrub with Vim. I wash my hair in the sink, iron my clean clothes. Bernie has gone home. I push two chairs together and fall asleep. When I wake up the chairs have parted and I'm on the floor. I try to go back to sleep but I can't get comfortable. The blanket doesn't keep me warm. I get up, look out of the window, press my nose against my arm and smell soap. Jackie gave me cream to put on my legs and they've stopped itching. She told me there's only one rule in her flat. She has going-out dates and staying-in dates and when she has a staying-in date I can't come out of the living room. And I said all right.

It's dark. Below me car headlights rush by. There's nobody about. Somewhere out there I have a brother and a sister I've never met, might not ever meet. I wonder if they know about me. What their names are. My finger squeaks an R across the pane of glass, then again in the opposite direction where it can be seen from the outside.

I play out the scene in my head for the hundredth time, the scene where I get to meet them all and they invite me to live with them. My dad tells me how it had all been a big mistake, how I'd been born just a little bit too soon and ended up in the wrong place with the wrong dad, how it was all right now, how everything was going to be all right now.

I shudder with the cold, lift the cushions off the chairs and lay them down on the floor in the airing cupboard. I get the blanket, close the cupboard doors over and try to get some sleep. Every thud of every front door closing echoes around the block like thunder. The lift creaks up and down and when it stops the two doors rumble open. I get up, open the front door. The air in the block is dry and thick and smelly. There's nobody around. When Nan first moved from her house to Tommy Whites she said it was like somebody had put her away on a shelf and forgot about her and she knew what a jar of lemon curd felt like. At least in Tommy Whites you can stand on the landing and see people in the square, meet them as you cross on the stairs or the landing. You could die here and nobody would miss you.

I can hear the hum from Jackie's small fridge in the kitchen. I get up, stand in a puddle that sits at its edge. My feet are wet and cold so I get another pair of socks from a carrier bag, look out of the window again and see a plane blink across the sky. Back in the cupboard I trace stains on the walls with my fingers, look down at the lines on my palms where Carol saw the planes, lots and lots of planes. Only for me taking the vanity case, we would've been friends. In my mind I can see Angela's mum talking to Carol's mum, calling at me over the landing, *robbing little cow*. I blink away the hot tears inside my eyes. I don't care about any of them. I have this now. A place to sleep where nobody wants to harm me, or call me names.

Next morning I get up, wash my hands and face, wait for Jackie to get up. I open all of the windows. Walk around in bare feet. My soles can feel the warmth from a patch of sunlight that slants in through the window. The sun lights up patterns in the floorboards.

Layers and layers moulded into circles with bits sticking out. Soft bits, that don't hurt. The broken arm on a chair that lifts up like revealing a secret, slot it back down as if it never happened. No clock on the fireplace, no clock in the kitchen. Her living room is empty of cupboards filled with junk. Everything is so simple here, two chairs, a telly, a table and a record player. No holy pictures on the wall, no mats on the floor. In the bathroom I fix the cream fluffy towels back to the way they were before I used them.

These days my worries come in packs, like cigarettes. I worry about Jackie finding out about my lies and asking me to leave. I like it here. I don't want to leave, don't want Mum or Dad to find me. It's late afternoon before I see her. She opens the living-room door in her underwear. 'Shit,' she says when she sees me. 'I forgot about you.' She comes back in the room wearing a man's baggy shirt. She looks around the flat. 'Hey, you like all of the windows open like I do,' she says. 'And you've tidied around. That's great. Shouldn't you be in school or something?'

'What day is it?' I ask.

'Dunno, Friday?'

I shrug.

'Shit, no it's Saturday.'

I hear hurried voices from the bedroom. The toilet flushes. Jackie says bye to somebody, the front door closes.

'I've got to go and see Dave.'

'Who is Dave?'

'My dad.'

After she gets back, Jackie doesn't speak for ages. She unties her shoes, steps out of them and walks into the kitchen. She makes us spaghetti on toast. We eat it on our lap in front of the telly; Jackie sits with one foot tucked under her leg.

'Dave's sick,' she says when we've finished. 'Won't let me get a doctor. He says they killed Mum, botched up her operation.' Tears fall down Jackie's face. I don't know what to do.

I take our plates out into the kitchen, think of Nan and her bad leg. Fill the bowl with soapy water and let them soak.

'How come your mum's in hospital?'

I hate lying to her. 'An operation, I think.'

'Your dad?'

'Dead.'

'No aunties or uncles?'

I shake my head. That bit's true.

'Isn't life crap?'

I don't answer. 'I'll wash the dishes.'

'There's only two plates and a pan. Let them soak until tomorrow. Sorry it's just spaghetti, I'm hopeless at cooking.'

'I can cook,' I say.

'Really?'

'I worked in a café in St Michael's. I know how to make sausage on toast, bacon, eggs, a pan of scouse.'

'Dave loves scouse.'

'Have you got a big pan?'

'No.'

'Get the stuff and I'll make a pan for all of us. We can take some to Dave next time.'

'Okay. Crusty bread and butter?'

'Crusty bread and butter. And beetroot?'

She goes into the kitchen, comes back with an empty envelope and a pen. 'Write a list,' she says.

Over the next couple of days I look through the gap in the living-room door. I see Jackie let in a bald man wearing blue jeans too tight for him, a man with bushy red hair and brown lace-up shoes. A younger man, with a slicked up collar and cream trousers. I think about what would happen if they all turned up together. What would they say and which one would Jackie choose that night?

One night, after we have had our tea, I ask her if she loves them.

'Who?'

'Your dates.'

'Dave thought he loved my mum more than his own life. She put up with him. He was propped up against a bar most nights, went with women behind her back. He was lucky she didn't kill him. And Sylvia, left with the kids while Bernie ran away to sea. All I've seen is what's not love. I made up my mind years ago. I want no part of that. It doesn't mean a thing.'

That night Jackie wakes me up. She wanders around the flat, lifting up the chairs, rooting in the kitchen drawers, tips everything to the floor. She is looking for something. I feel around the wall for a light switch, follow her into the bathroom. She flings the dirty washing out of the basket onto the floor. 'What are you looking for?' I ask.

She doesn't answer. I watch her in her underwear filling the dark places in the flat with her search. In the end I take her hand and lead her back towards the bedroom. I don't want her to see the mess in the morning so I pick everything up; put it back where it's meant to be. Next day she remembers nothing except that she woke up in bed when it was still dark, and she was shivering, her cheeks wet with tears. I want to put my arms around her, but don't.

30

Outside school I watch him smoke. It's early for him to be up. He can't have had any money to go out last night. I'm behind a wall in the shadows where he can't see me, next to St Josephine's church. When the last kid has gone in, the bell rings but he doesn't move. I can see the final stragglers leg it through the gate. If he doesn't move soon Mr McGann will lock the gates. I feel like making a run for it away from here, just keeping going until I run out of pavement. He throws his cigarette to the floor, and with the sole of his shoe squashes it dead.

It's the last day of school before we break up for Christmas. Angela said she would give the present to Mrs O'Connor on the last day and I want to see her face when she opens it. I've got *Anne of Green Gables* in my pocket to hand in. When I look back over the road, he's gone. I give it a few more minutes to be sure before I walk through the gate.

I go all the way around the back of the school; stoop down on my knees when I come to a window so no teachers will see me. Inside the classroom the register has already been called. 'Morning, Robyn,' Mrs O'Connor says. 'You feeling better now?'

'Yes, miss,' I say.

'Your mum's been up to tell Mrs Bullock. Good to see you back. Measles, wasn't it?'

'Yes, miss.'

I can see a carrier bag at Angela's feet. At first play we get all of the girls from our class into the toilets. We take out the silky nightdress and show them it. There's loads of ooooos and ahh-hhs then somebody spots the price tag. Angela winks over at me. 'Me and Robyn had to put the rest to it because we didn't have enough,' she says.

After play, Angela gives Mrs O'Connor the present and she says, 'Oh my God.' She scans the room. Her eyes rest on every single one of us in turn. When they stop on me I think she's going to shout and say stuff about the difference between right and wrong, but she doesn't. She stands, presses the straps of the nightdress against her shoulders, shakes her head. 'You've got to be joking.' Turns it inside out and reads the label. She shakes her head again.

Somebody shouts, 'Try it on, miss.' She wriggles it on over her clothes and laughs. Wraps the gown around herself and gives us a twirl. It makes me smile.

'Do you like it, miss?' Rose asks.

'Unbelievable,' she says and shakes her head again.

Outside, after dinner, I sit on the floor in a corner of the playground with Rose. She is saying something about a Christmas disco in the youth club. Angela looks across at me from the other side of the playground and smiles. I smile back. 'Over here,' she shouts. I tell Rose I won't be a minute. Angela stands beside two girls; she whispers something to them and just before I get there they all roar laughing. Angela turns to me, 'I was telling Tracy and Kate how much of a laugh we had. You're a great robber. They want to come next time. It must be brilliant to go out and be able to take anything you want.'

I stare at her like I am trying to turn her into pressed powder. Push my thumb against the tip of my middle finger, watch her mouth move but hear no sounds. That's still all I am, a robber. It's just a game to her, a penny peep show for everybody to take a look at. Soon the whole school will know, more people with lists asking me for favours. Some people like to take things away from you and watch as you disappear.

I got the present because I wanted Angela to be my friend. To change the way she thought about me. To be like everybody else, but I had done it the wrong way. I made myself different again. I push my face right into her face. 'Fuck off, pissy arse,' I say and walk away.

Rose waits for me at the gate. 'Coming to the Christmas disco at the youthy?'

'When?'

'Friday. I'll meet you there at seven?'

I think about Jackie and how she might not mind if I stay at the disco till the end. 'Okay.'

Bernie waits for me by the phone box. 'Your mum's been in every square asking about you. She says she's been walking the streets day and night searching.'

'You didn't . . .'

'I didn't say a word, but Nellie told her she saw you on a bus once doing a message for my mum. She knocked at our door and Mum spoke to her and they both started crying. Everyone thinks something bad's happened to you.'

'I can't let them find me, Bernie.'

'Your mum's gonna go to the police soon. She's only put it off cos your dad's wanted for not paying fines. My mum thinks there's more to it than fines; she says if any of her kids went missing she'd go to the police straight away. I've got a feeling my mum's gonna go and tell the pigs about you being missing. You've got to tell our Jackie the truth.'

'She'll kick me out.'

'Why don't you go back home?'

'No. I'm never going back.'

'Tell our Jackie the truth before she talks to Mum.'

'I'll tell her.'

'When?'

'I'll tell her tonight.'

Jackie calls me into the kitchen. Shows me what she's bought. 'I got it all,' she says, like a big kid. 'Dave will be made up, can't wait to see his face.' She stops talking and looks at me. 'What's wrong, Robyn?' Her face is close to mine. 'Is it your mum?'

I shake my head, tell her everything. About my mum and how she's not really in hospital and how I've run away from home, and how I'm a filthy rotten liar. I start to cry then because I'm scared she'll make me go back to Tommy Whites. 'Let's go and sit down,' she says. In the living room, Jackie pulls her chair close to mine. My hands are shaking and I'm crying like a baby.

'What are you frightened of, Robyn?'

I can't speak.

'Are you scared to go home?'

It's like Jackie is reading my mind. I nod.

'Why?'

I don't answer.

'You've run away before?'

I shake my head.

'I'll make us a drink and then I want you to tell me what's happened, okay?'

While she's in the kitchen I try to find the words in my head that don't sound stupid. My dad beats me up. Stupid. He's going to kill me. Stupid. I can't find a way that doesn't make it all sound stupid. In my head it sounds too mad, like I'm making it all up. Jackie hands me a cup. I put it on the floor by my chair then Jackie sits down.

'Once,' she says, 'when I was little, I'd gone shopping with my mum. We had bags and bags of food and the bus in front of us was about to pull away. Mum told me to run on ahead and stop it. When I got on the bus, the driver let me on but closed the doors and pulled away without my mum. I panicked, started shouting and screaming at him. I thought he was trying to kidnap me. I didn't realize he was driving the bus to Mum, not away from her. I felt like a fool but I remember the relief I felt when she got on. Your mum and dad are probably panicking about you. I think whatever you've done, once you're home they'll be made up to see you, the rest won't matter.'

For a moment I believe her. I see them on the step waving at me, not angry but glad to see I'm all right. Then I think about how I feel living here with Jackie. Waking up without being scared, the way she knows nothing about me and what I am. Here, I'm a brand new Robyn with a brand new future and I know leaving Tommy Whites to start again was the right thing to do.

'No, I'm not going back. My dad is going to kill me.'

'Once he sees you . . .'

'He hates me. He wants me dead.'

'We all say stuff in an argument.'

I'm not saying it right. Tears sting my eyes. 'When I'm in Tommy Whites, I feel like I'm trapped on a bus like you were and there's no way off. My face squashed flat against the glass so I don't feel like me any more. The day before I left home, Mum was out. He'd painted the step. I stood in it by accident. He had his hands tight around my neck. Told me how he's waiting to squeeze the life out of me. He really does want to kill me. He hates me. You haven't seen the way he looks at me. I'm scared of him, Jackie. The same scared you felt on the bus.'

Jackie is quiet. We sit for a long time without saying a word. In the end, she calls me into the kitchen and says, 'Come on then, let's get cracking with this pan of scouse.' In the kitchen, I tell her it's easy. She helps me chop everything up and toss it into the pan. Carrots, onion, potatoes, salt, pepper, an OXO then lob in the meat and bring it all to the boil. 'Dave will love this,' she says once it's ready.

Jackie gets dressed up, turns the telly on loud, tells me she has a date in the flat and I'm to stay in the living room. I'm never supposed to see her date. That's the way she likes it. Being with Jackie during the day is better. When I tell her about Rose and the disco she lets me try on her clothes and shoes, gives me a few bits she doesn't wear any more. She shows me how to put make-up on, blue glittery eye shadow, turns her records up loud and shows me how to dance. Over the noise she shouts, 'Ever heard of the Bay City Rollers?'

'No,' I shout back.

We let the sounds twist us, bend and shake and whirl us all over the flat. Barefoot, Jackie clicks her ringed fingers around in circles. We laugh, hold hands and spin around. The sound of the music fills me like I'm a bubble about to burst, and when the laughter breaks us up we fall backwards into the chairs, eyes sparkling.

Three of Jackie's blouses hang up in her wardrobe. 'Choose your favourite colour,' she says. I choose a sky blue blouse with tiny pink roses on it.

'I think that's going to look great,' she says. 'Friday, I'll use the blue on your eyes.'

That night I can't sleep. It doesn't seem right for me to be this happy. I close the cupboard doors tight, pull the blanket up under my chin and prepare for the worst. The worst being one day I will have to go back to Tommy Whites.

Jackie takes ages doing my make-up and hair; drops me off at the Christmas disco in a taxi and says, 'Knock 'em dead, girl.'

Rose walks right past me. 'You look about fifteen,' she says when she realizes it's me. 'Come and show our Rita.'

The man playing the records jumps down off the stage. 'What's your name?' he says to me.

Rita elbows him. 'Down, boy. It's only Robyn done up like a prozzy.'

I don't know what a prozzy is.

She cocks her head at Rose for us to move.

I stay at the disco until the end. Skinny boys start to peel themselves away from the walls. A lad dressed like a piece of streaky bacon gets me up for a slowy. Scruffy cream and maroon striped jumper. It's not that great, a slowy. We look like a couple of Frankensteins rocking on the spot from side to side. On the way out a lady on the door gives everyone selection boxes of chocolates, which makes me smile.

31

I can smell smoke. At the living-room door I see Mum sitting on the wide brown rubber bands that stretch across Jackie's chair. I feel like running to the lift to get as far away from her as I can. Instead I open the door and say, 'What do you want?' She looks different, thinner, like there's not much of her left.

She smiles. 'I missed you.'

'I didn't miss you,' I want to say. 'Choosing that bastard over me and then leaving me there for him to kill.' But I don't say it. Jackie looks at me and I look away.

'I'm not coming back,' is what I say.

'I was so worried. I had this feeling, though, that you were okay.' She looks at Jackie then back at me. 'I know what he did to you.'

Why don't you go and leave me alone?

'I don't care. I'm not going back.'

'Okay. I've been to see Carmel and she's got our old room ready.'

I don't want to leave here.

'So?'

'So we're not going back to Tommy Whites.'

Why don't you ever ask me what I want?

This is it. There is no *will you come back with me?* There is no *sorry*. There are no decisions left to be made.

'It'll be just like last time when you told me a pack of lies then went back to him.'

'It won't, promise. I've told him it's over.'

'I don't believe you.'

'I know you don't.' She starts crying, takes out her fags. 'Your nan misses you. She wants to see you. I told her the police were out looking for you, so she didn't worry herself sick.'

'You didn't get the police.'

'No. I didn't want the police involved. They would have contacted social services, had you taken away from me. Put into care. I couldn't take that. I did everything I could think of to find you myself first.'

I see Nan at her kitchen window, watching for me to come across the road. Turning on the radio for the news and hearing somebody has been murdered and thinking it was me. I see myself saying: I am sorry. I never meant for you to worry. I am sorry for being so selfish and running away. Sorry that I never sent Bernie to let you know I was all right. I didn't realize they could put me into care. I think about the care home where Lizzie said her mate got stabbed.

Jackie puts a saucer on the arm of Mum's chair.

I start crying. It makes my nose run.

Jackie tries to give me a hug, but I wriggle away. I can't look either of them in the eye.

'I spoke to our Sylvia and she told me how upset your mum was and I told her you were with me. You're a missing person, Robyn,' Jackie says. 'The police will arrest me if they find out you're staying here. I'm so sorry, love.' She talks like I've already left.

I didn't want to leave Jimmy's Café, didn't want to leave Nan, didn't want to leave my mum, don't want to leave Jackie's and

I don't want to leave St Josephine's School. Lately that's all I've been doing: learning how to leave, learning how to walk away when things don't work any more. I think about Robert Naylor and how he learned how to leave that night when he disappeared, when he must have thought I would be better off without him.

I pack my stuff inside two carrier bags, leave the bits Jackie gave me behind in the airing cupboard. Back in the living room I turn to Mum. 'If you take me back to Tommy Whites, I'll knife that bastard. I mean it. Then I'll run away again and you'll never find me.'

Mum says nothing.

'I know he's not my dad. Why didn't you tell me?'

'Who told you?'

'That doesn't matter.'

'I'll make some tea.' Jackie walks into the kitchen and closes the door.

'I was going to tell you in a couple of years.'

'Why didn't you marry my real dad?'

'I thought he didn't want to marry me. He knew I was pregnant with you and he was in the army. I wrote to him, but he didn't reply.'

'Why?'

She shakes her head. 'I don't know. I suppose he got cold feet or something. He asked me to give him a year to think things over.'

'But he came back before that?'

'He came back when it was too late.'

'Why didn't you wait and talk to him before you got married?'

'I would have been left on the shelf, Robyn. That's what everyone expected when he never came back. Nobody wants somebody else's cast-off with a kid on board as well. I saw an opportunity for us and I took it. Sometimes you have to take whatever you can get.'

238

'But you must have liked him.'

'I did. We had a laugh when we went out. I met him in a pub in town by Lime Street, the Legs of Man it was called. We met while he was on leave from the army. He had his own flat on County Road. We'd sit there some nights watching telly. He took me to the pictures, took me dancing. Your nan thought he was great. I thought he was great. It all happened so fast, the pregnancy and everything, and I think he panicked, said he needed some time to think. I don't regret meeting him. When I had you they wanted to take you away somewhere, they said you'd be better off. I told them I was keeping you. I caused murder on that maternity ward, told the bastard nurse that tried to take you from me to fuck off. I don't regret keeping you. I'll never regret keeping you.'

'Does Mrs Naylor know about me?'

She shakes her head. 'I know Bob didn't say a word. When I met him, he told me he had nothing to do with her. And I certainly didn't tell her. She's a nosy cow, though, so who knows?' Mum squashes her fag into the saucer and stands up ready to go. What surprises me is how my mum put up with the way he treated her. I'm still stunned that she didn't find a way to get away from him. When I ask her why she stayed, her answer sounds so simple. Mum said she had nowhere else to go. If she left and he found her she didn't have a doubt in her mind that he'd kill her.

Jackie opens the front door wide. 'You can come and visit me any time, Robyn. I'd like you to.'

I don't answer. Mum takes one of my bags, presses the silver button and we wait for the lift. When it comes I turn around. Jackie smiles at me. I don't smile back. On the way to the bus stop I walk close to the walls, away from Mum. I look up, see Jackie's face at the window, her hand waving me goodbye. I stop. How could

I ignore her? She knows stuff about me. She knows my favourite colour is sky blue and my favourite soap is Palmolive. She knows I like all the windows open, she knows who scares me most in the world. She was even going to take me to see her Dave. I drop my bag to the floor, lift both hands high and wave back.

I wake up in the hostel on Christmas Eve next to my mum. The room feels smaller than I remember. I get up and look out of the window. It's foggy outside. I can hear the thud of footsteps above my head. Kids racing all around the place shouting, the heavy smell of bacon from the kitchen reminds me of Jimmy's Café. Mum is still asleep.

Wearing the clothes she got me in Greaty Market I go back to the window. The fog is lifting. Lines and lines of tall trees behind a low wall. The branches are bare; without leaves to soften them they look dead to me.

Seeing these trees makes me think of the picture of the little boy, in Nan's room, the boy who died wanting to be like everybody else. If I'd have stayed in Tommy Whites with Mum and Dad like kids are supposed to I would have died.

Downstairs I stand next to Carmel at the cooker. It feels warm against my belly. Carmel cracks an egg into the frying pan. She has a white shirt on and silver tinsel tied up in her hair. She looks like the Angel Gabriel. A few little kids I don't know sit around the big table singing, 'Jingle bells, batman smells, Robyn flew away.' Carmel catches my eye and we both laugh. I pick up a fork and push holes into the pink sausages. Carmel says, 'Can you cook?'

'I can cook bacon, sausages, eggs and scouse.'

The doorbell rings.

'Here you go,' she says, handing me the spatula. 'Knock yourself out.'

I stand over the pan, push the sausages about, flick them over onto the other side; a bit of fat spits out of the pan onto the top of my hand and I whisper *shit 'n' hell*. Behind me the kids giggle.

When the kitchen door opens I can see her behind Carmel. Blue-eyed May, stick in her hand, legs half-past five on a clock. I drop everything, throw my arms around her, squeeze her a little bit too hard and she squeezes me back a little bit too hard. 'Let me look at you, Robyn. Still as thin as a straw. I missed you.' She traces her finger across my T-shirt and says, 'Three Blind Mice.' I am amazed. Nan laughs. 'My new friend Eddie is teaching me. You can meet him if you promise not to disappear again.'

32

Mum takes me to Margy's new place. She lives on the first floor. It's like Tommy Whites, but it's called Kent Gardens. With a black marker somebody has changed the K in Kent to a B. The pavements are filled with kids. A few play on tricycles and scooters. Most of the boys are playing football. 'Maybe we can get a place here, near Margy?' Mum says. The stairs stink of sweet disinfectant and piss.

I try to imagine living here with Mum. It looks like Tommy Whites but the heads above landings and the kids playing out don't interest me and I don't interest them. In Tommy Whites every square knows me, knows the feel of my shoes on its tarmac, remembers the patterns my bike tyres made on concrete, the slap of rubber against brick from playing two balls, the sound of my voice shouting up to Bernie's landing. My marks are all over it and its marks are inside my head, my body.

Late afternoon, Margy has the bare light bulb on in the living room. It's a dull, faded white. From under the table she pulls a tucked-away leg out to make the table bigger. 'Sit down. I'll make a pot of tea.'

The place is a mess. Muddy socks pushed inside black pumps, paper bags still unpacked with holes torn out of the sides. Somebody has ripped strips off half of the brown wallpaper, but left the rest untouched. Through the torn parts you can see what was there before and it looks better than what's there now. I can see a gold leaf pattern. The lino has cigarette burns all over it. The fire's not lit and the room feels cold. Mum sits in the straight-backed chair and takes out her cigarettes. Margy brings in the tea and Mum passes her a fag. Margy looks around the room, lets out a breath and says, 'You know, Babs, I can't think where to start.' Her eyes fill with tears.

'You start where that bastard finished,' Mum says. 'You start here, with your kids and your new place.' Mum rests her cigarette on the side of the ashtray. Margy's face is down low, tears plop onto her blue skirt, cigarette unlit between her fingers. I look at Mum and expect to be given the eye to leave but she is staring straight at Margy. She takes the unlit cigarette, lights it off her own and hands it to Margy.

'If it wasn't for my kids I'd go under, Babs. They're the reason I get up every morning.'

'He hasn't been around here, has he?'

'No.'

'Then what is it?'

'He's not handing over a penny. A decent wage he's on in that barber's shop and tips on top.'

'Take the bastard to court. Rita Fairbrother did it when Terry Dyer denied that her Brian was his, made him get tests and everything. He had to pay up when the judge ordered him to.'

'I can't be bothered with it all, Babs; don't want nothing to do with him. I mean, the one he's with now, let's face it, I wouldn't be surprised if she's already got one in the oven.'

'Oh, fuckin' hell.'

'I know. So where would that leave me?'

'He can still pay something to you. You've got four mouths to feed.'

Margy leaves her fag burning in the ashtray, gets up and goes into the kitchen. I can hear the swish of a tap. She comes back into the room, rubs her face with a towel.

'I'd get a job, but there's nobody to mind the kids.'

'What about your mum?'

'Her health's bad. I wouldn't leave the twins with her. She couldn't cope.'

'There must be somebody you could ask. Even a little cleaning job would do for a couple of hours a night.'

'I'd have to pay that somebody, Babs. They wouldn't mind them for nothing.'

'Yes but you'd have more than you have now. Once you get to know the people on your block I'm sure you'll find someone. Don't worry.'

It makes me feel good to hear my mum talk like this. To see her helping somebody else put all the pieces back together again. But there is something so angry about her, like it's trying to burst out of her skin but can't. Whatever it is I'm glad she can keep it back.

Margy gets up and looks out of the window. 'They'll be in soon for their tea. I haven't had time to . . .'

'I saw a chippy on the way up here, right opposite.' Mum takes a pound note out of her purse and hands it to me. 'Run over for us. Get two portions of chips and a loaf. Plenty of salt and vinegar and a bottle of lemo for the kids.'

Margy gives Mum a smile.

When I get to the bottom of the block I bump into Margy's kids. They have a look in their eyes that I have seen in my own and in my mum's. It's called scared. Scared is when a little bit of you falls out and shows itself to the whole world. It makes me feel warm in a strange way to see it in somebody else's eyes. 'You're having chips for tea,' I say, like chips will take all the bad things away. 'And lemonade.'

We stay at Margy's for a couple of hours. I take the kids out on the step with some marbles in a dented tobacco tin. We play for a bit but it gets cold so we go into the bedroom and make a den out of the mattresses on the floor. We pretend the enemy are coming and make sounds like guns. We fight them off with fake swords and high kicks and loud noises. After a while the twins get restless and start to cry for Margy. She says they are tired and Mum says it's about time we got the bus back to the hostel.

'Listen,' Mum says. 'We'll have a night out. We'll go to the pictures or something in a couple of weeks. Maybe nip somewhere nice for a drink after and a little bit of rock 'n' roll?'

Margy shushes one of the twins in her arms. 'Rock 'n' roll, me? I don't think so, Babs.'

'You're coming and that's that.' Mum looks at me. 'Robyn can mind the kids for a couple of hours.'

I say nothing.

There's nobody at the bus stop and the roads are empty. We sit at the front of the bus and look out of the window.

I'd like to go somewhere nice with Mum, maybe to New Brighton or Southport for the day. I get up and sit away from her on a seat by myself. I don't want to mind the stupid kids. I hope we never go to Margy's again.

33

Mum opens her make-up bag, takes out her compact and looks into the mirror. The glass steams up with her breath; she rubs away a smudge with toilet roll, then presses powder onto her face. She wears a black and white flared skirt and a black shirt. Her hair is loose in curls to her shoulders, lips pillar-box red. She steps into her slingbacks, pushes money into a black clutch bag. I follow her downstairs. In the kitchen she tells Carmel we'll be staying out tonight, at Margy's. Outside on the road Mum pulls a taxi and says, 'Kent Gardens, mate,' to the driver.

Mum has a new job in a chippy down the road from the hostel. She works every night except tonight, Saturday. Sometimes she brings pies home and big bags of warm chips. She puts them on the kitchen table and Carmel shares them between the kids. They have started to wait for her on the step, but sometimes when they've been extra busy, she brings nothing. She smells of greasy chips and vinegar. Carmel says the housing have a place for us to look at. Mum says we can go as soon as she gets the keys.

Margy's kids are in bed when we get there. Finger on her lips, she shushes Mum's kitten heels.

Margy turns to me. 'I tired them out for you, love, had them in the park all day. Run themselves right out of puff. You shouldn't hear a peep. Had to sit there all day in me rollers.'

She looks different, younger, in a shiny gold dress and gold high heels. Her hair pinned up on top in waves, creamy peach lips. Margy has new false teeth. 'I got you a magazine.' She goes into the kitchen. 'Here it is. Some teenage girls left it on a bench so I picked it up for you.'

'Thanks.'

'If the twins wake up give them a drink of water and take them back to bed. Lie next to them until they drop off. It won't take long if you stroke dead light on their foreheads in swirls, sends them right off again.'

Mum heads for the door. 'She's not soft, Margy. Come on, it's half eight now. We'll have to skip the flicks.'

'Oh and if anyone knocks, don't open the door.'

Not even for the devil himself.

Margy doesn't have a telly so I read the magazine over and over until my eyes begin to sting. I check in on the kids twice but they're fast asleep.

I must have fallen asleep for a bit because Margy has to shake me. 'Have they been all right for you?' Margy's lips are red, her breath smoky and dry on my face. 'Did they wake up?'

I shake my head.

'God bless them.'

'Where's Mum?'

'In the toilet, been mixing her drinks.'

Mum's voice is breathless from the bathroom. 'Margy . . . a cloth.'

Mum comes into the living room, wobbly-can't-stand-up drunk. One of Margy's kids starts crying. 'Come on, Robyn, I need to get back . . . can't stay here. Feel fucking terrible.'

Margy takes Mum's bag off her, wipes it with a cloth. 'It's late, Babs.' She checks the clock. 'Nearly four. Get your head down here.'

'I'll get a taxi, Robyn's with me . . .'

Margy opens Mum's bag. 'Have you got enough?' She hands it to me. 'See what she's got.'

'One pound something.'

Mum walks the palms of her hands across the living-room door. She grabs the handle with both hands, sways backwards, Margy catches her.

The crying gets louder.

'Wanna go, Robyn,' Mum says.

Margy sees us to the door. 'Sorry, love,' she says.

I link Mum's arm all the way down the stairs. Her breath reeks of sick. It's only a short walk to the main road where we can get a taxi. I tuck her bag under my other arm. She leans her weight on me. By the time we get to the road she can't stand up. I sit her down against a low wall and step out onto the edge of the kerb.

It's cold and under the street lamp the wind peels gaps between Mum's curls, showing her white scalp. Her head has fallen to one side and her eyes are closed. There's no sign of a taxi. I've left my magazine in Margy's.

Mum is fast asleep against the wall. If I can get her up, get her to walk towards town then we'll have more chance of getting a taxi there.

I look down at Mum. There's no way she'd make the walk, she can't even open her eyes. Why did she get that drunk? There's no way I'm ever minding Margy's kids after this. When she wakes up I'll tell her straight. I check the road both ways for a cab. I start to think it might be better if we turn back around, spend the night in Margy's flat. I look up at the landing to see if her light's still on and it is. She must still be up.

I see him step out from the block opposite Margy's.

He walks fast. Black polo neck, blue jeans, blue denim jacket. My heart licks the inside of my throat. I think maybe I am seeing things. I check both sides of the road, say out loud, *Bastard bastard taxi hurry up*. Then I see an orange light speeding towards me. I put out my hand and the taxi driver turns in. Dad's beside me. 'Your nan's been taken to hospital,' he says. 'Nellie knocked tonight.' He looks at Mum sitting on the pavement, eyes still closed. 'Told me to let her know.'

'Where is she?'

'In hospital.'

'What hospital?'

'Dunno. Nellie knows. We'll have to be quick. She says it's bad.'

The taxi driver gets out, helps Dad get Mum into the cab. 'Where to?' he asks.

'Tommy Whites,' Dad says.

I feel sick. 'What's happened to Nan?'

'Nellie said she was crossing the road.' The way he speaks I can tell he hasn't had a drink. The cab pulls away. Mum's head flops all over the place. I rest it on my shoulder and hold it still with my palm. All the way to Nellie's he talks in a low voice to the driver about football. He does not look at me or Mum.

He carries Mum over one shoulder up the stairs. When he turns to take a corner, her shoes scrape across the wall. He stops at 33B.

'I'm not going in there,' I say. 'You said we're going to Nellie's.'

'Can't bring her to Nellie's like this. Get the key out of my pocket and open the door, then get her a drink of water first. Once she straightens herself out, you two can go to Nellie's.'

As soon as the front door opens I can smell paint. The heavy wooden wardrobe from Mum's room is standing in the hall. All of the doors have been painted black so have the skirting boards. I can't believe I'm back in this place where I felt more afraid than I did sleeping in the stairwell. I think about turning around and running to Nellie's, but I don't want to leave Mum on her own with him.

Sometimes when I try to sleep at night it feels like I'm drowning. My head fills up with shadows; I sink lower and lower inside the darkness. It is a weird, floaty feeling. There's no way up that I can see and no part of me feels like searching for it. When I am close to the bottom it gets cold. That's when I turn myself around, kick my legs and push back up again. I wake up feeling lucky. Tonight, I think, I might not be so lucky.

LOVE HATE fingers strum on the wooden arms of the chair. Mum's lying on the settee. I get her a drink of water and put it to her lips. Eyes closed, she pushes my hand away.

'Mum, just take a sip. We've got to go to Nellie's. Something's happened to Nan.'

Dad watches me try to wake her up.

'She won't drink it. I'll go and get Nellie now.'

'It's too late,' he says.

He leaves the room and I can hear the click of the latch, the rumble of the bolt being pushed all the way along. I shake Mum's arm and whisper to her. 'Wake up. Something's wrong with Nan.' I start to shout at her, feel like hitting her hard in the face. 'Mum, for fuck's sake, wake up.'

He is back in the room.

'I'm going to Nellie's,' I say.

'I said it's too late.'

'No, it's not too late,' I say. 'I want to see my nan.'

250

He doesn't answer. He's looking at Mum in a bad way. He folds his arms, sweat shiny on his forehead. He pushes away a strip of dark hair that's come loose from his quiff. He gets down on his knees, crawls across the floor, pinches Mum's mouth together between two fingers. He bares his teeth. 'Dirty little slut, been out dancing, have you?'

Mum swats his arm away with a flimsy wave.

He squeezes tighter. 'Think I don't know what's been going on. Well, I've got people watching and I've been watching.'

'Leave her alone,' I say. His eyes rest on my hand.

'What's in the bag?'

'Nothing.'

'Toss it over.'

I hold onto it.

'Toss it over.' He grips the front of Mum's neck. 'I'll break her neck.'

I slip my hand inside the bag and grab the note, scrunch it into a ball.

'There's money inside. Let her go and you can have it.'

He wraps Mum's hair around his hand, pulls her head backwards. Mum groans.

'Toss the fucking thing over – now!'

Mum opens her eyes.

I throw him the bag. He pulls her off the settee, lets go of her. She falls to the floor. He opens the bag, takes out the coins. Her key to the hostel falls out; lipstick, cigarettes and matches. He picks Mum up again by the hair, pushes the tip of the key under her chin. 'What's this for?' He stabs harder. She lets out another moan.

'Margy's house,' I say. 'Margy gave her that key.'

'Shut the fuck up. Nobody's talking to you.' He walks towards me, holds out his hand. 'Give it.'

'What?'

'Whatever you just took out of the bag, give it.'

'I didn't take . . .'

He's got my arm twisted up my back. I hear a crack and feel liquid drain inside my head. He lets go and my arm won't do as it's told. It hangs there, the wrong shape for anything. He stuffs the note into his pocket. I hold my arm still across my belly, flop down onto the settee.

He drags Mum up off the floor, flings her next to me. She hits the back of her head on the wall and starts lashing out into the air with her hand, cups the back of her head with the other one. For a second she opens her eyes. 'Robyn?' she says.

'It's your fault, all of this,' he says to me. 'I should have never taken on another man's bastard.'

'You're the bastard,' I scream at him. 'You're only here to take her money.'

He grabs my neck. 'I told you to shut up.' He squeezes it hard. I do as I'm told.

Mum's eyes are open. He lets go of me, moves over to her. Mum's head nods up and down, she can't hold it up on her own. 'Why?'

He doesn't answer.

He kneels at the fireplace; balls up pieces of old newspaper, places wood on top and bits of coal. I want to say I'll get Mum a coat from the lobby to cover her up. I want to say, 'Is my nan really hurt in hospital?' Something tells me not to speak, not to say anything at all. To keep him away from me. I look over at Mum, who doesn't really know the trouble we are in yet. I must keep my mouth shut, at least until there are two of us again.

He piles on more newspapers and more wood. Lights himself a cigarette from Mum's box, sits down in his chair. He takes long pulls on the cigarette, a mad thin smile on his face that looks like it could spread to a grin any minute. 'I'll show you,' he says looking at nobody. His words make me shiver. I look down at the black splashes of paint above the skirting boards, feathery edges coming apart like dark clouds. I didn't see this coming. I should've made Mum stay in Margy's. My skinny eleven-year-old mind scrambles for a plan.

I keep thinking about the wardrobe and why, like me and Mum, it isn't in the place it's supposed to be. I remember how often I imagined leaving this place in bed at night, and how good it felt when I finally did. I look at the ugly wallpaper and hear an echo of my screams. They disappear again behind the black paint which is the only thing that holds them back.

Outside I can hear the milkman's cart rattle, the belch of a bus from the front road. A world carrying on without us. My arm is killing me and the light from the bulb above my head stings my eyes. There's no way I'm going to let myself fall asleep. Mum is sleeping it off, but he sits there staring straight ahead, waiting for something to happen.

After what seems like ages my heart still bangs loud in my chest. I want him to fall asleep in that chair. I know how to open the living-room door fast so it won't creak, how to avoid stepping on the long runner mat in the lobby in case it slides and I slip; I know how to shuffle the bolt up and down and along to the end all at the same time so it won't squeak. I see myself running along the landing to Nellie's house to get help for Mum.

His eyes are closed. I watch the rise and fall of his chest, feel my body move forwards. My feet grip the floor. My eyes don't leave his face. I look over at Mum, think about giving her a nudge. What if she makes a noise and wakes him? It's better if I get to

Nellie's on my own. My bum is on the tip of the cushion. I hold my bad arm close to me and stand. The settee creaks. He opens his eyes and looks at me just as I sit back down.

'I need the toilet,' I lie.

He stands up, waits outside the bathroom door. I turn the cold tap on over the sink, just a trickle so it sounds like I'm peeing. He watches me walk back into the living room and sit down. Mum is still asleep. In the distance a yappy dog barks. It is a sharp, annoying sound that I hope will wake Mum up. He lights a cigarette. The smoke floats into his eye. He rubs it with the edge of his finger and sits back down with his eye all bloodshot.

I close my eyes, count the minutes that pass into hours. I can see the view from our bedroom window at Carmel's. The shape of my favourite tree, arm arched above itself like a ballerina, the bar-of-chocolate front door and the small patch of grass in front of the house. Carmel, cooking in the kitchen. It's right there in my mind, so close I step inside, let it cover me, whisper, *Everything's going to be all right.*

Mum's awake. She looks around the room, looks at me as if she is seeing me for the first time. She stands, cups the back of her head. 'Come on, Robyn,' she says. 'We're getting out of here.'

He stands up. 'You're going nowhere,' he says. He slaps her hard in the face.

Mum's eyes are watering. Her face is shiny and red. She sits back down. 'What are you talking about? What do you want, you mad bastard?'

He strikes a match, lights the fire. 'To be rid of you two once and for all.'

Mum starts to laugh a raggedy laugh that makes me feel sick.

'We'll see who has the last laugh,' he says.

I think of Bernie and the way he lit the fire when I didn't want him to. I wish he would knock at our door and punch my dad in the face hard.

Mum stands.

'Mum, sit down,' I say.

He throws more balled up sheets of newspaper onto the fire. Gets behind the settee and pushes us up close to the fire. My legs are just inches away from the flames. 'You two look cold. Can't have you feeling cold now, can we?'

'For fuck's sake . . .'

'You'll both be toasty in a minute.'

'Stop it.'

'Stop what?'

'Let us go.'

'There's only one place you're going.'

He puts his shoes on and his jacket. Takes Mum's fags and matches, slots them into his coat pocket. 'Now you're awake it's your turn to watch me leave you.'

He takes a piece of wood, lights it from the fire, waits for it to gather strength, then sets the nets and the draw curtains on fire. He lights a piece of newspaper, throws it onto his chair. The cushion cover catches fire. I can feel the terrible heat against my cheek. I move away, hold onto Mum. Mum screams and so do I. We scream as loud as we can. 'For fuck's sake,' Mum shouts. Then I know what he's going to do with the wardrobe before he leaves. We'll have to jump out of the back window onto the concrete path. Like he reads my mind, he says, 'Oh yeah, every window is nailed down.'

Mum stands, starts lashing out at him. I scream as loud as I can. He punches her hard in the face. She falls to the floor, but he carries on punching.

We don't hear the thud as the front door falls backwards into the lobby.

Police officers are in the living room. Three of them grab him and rush him to the floor. They handcuff his wrists behind his back, march him out of the flat. Two officers are in the kitchen filling pans up with water to throw onto the fire. One is talking into his radio asking for the fire brigade. Another officer takes off his coat and smothers the flames on the chair dead.

My legs tremble. Mum holds me and I cry out with the pain in my arm. Somebody puts a blanket around me and Mum shouts, 'Get an ambulance.'

'Fucking lunatic,' Mum says to the officers, her face red raw. 'The mad bastard was trying to kill us.'

An officer leads us outside the flat.

'Will you check my nan's all right?' I tell them what he told me, give them her address.

Out on the landing blue lights flash around our square. Margy appears in her gold sparkly dress and her gold shoes. She runs to Mum and hugs her then she hugs me and it hurts. 'I saw him, Babs. I was looking out of the kitchen window to make sure you and Robyn got in a taxi okay and I saw him.'

Margy tells us how she got the kids up and legged it to the police station. It took her ages to convince them something was wrong. She said, because she was still drunk, they thought she was making a mountain out of a molehill. She was told by the sergeant to calm down and stop getting hysterical. They didn't want to interfere in business between man and wife if they didn't feel it necessary. Margy finally convinced them to at least check on us. She knew we lived in Tommy Whites, but she didn't know what number. Margy took the cops to Carmel's to get the right address. Carmel kept the kids with her. 'Thank God you're both okay,' she says.

At the hospital the doctor says, 'Have you been rock and roll dancing, young lady?' I smile and shake my head. My arm is put in a cast they say has to stay on for six weeks. It feels heavy and awkward and I wonder how I'll get to sleep because I sleep on my side. On the way out of the hospital one of the officers is parking his car. 'Your nan's fine, love,' he says. 'Snug as a bug in her bed she was. Gave us a right mouthful; nothing to worry about there.'

When I get to the hostel the kids want to draw pictures and write their names on the cast. A couple of them shout, 'How did you do that?' I don't answer. Carmel walks with me upstairs to bed.

33

Mum isn't the same after that night. She doesn't get dressed and only drinks the cups of tea I bring up to the room. She says she can't stomach the thought of food, smokes one cigarette after another and sleeps the rest of the time. I go to school because I can still write with my good arm, but I can't do PE. I tell the kids in school I fell off a wall. Rose queues up for our snack at the tuck shop; helps me get my coat on at home time. 'You won't get a slowy with that on,' she says. It makes me laugh and I tell her she's slowy mad.

Back at the hostel Mum is still in bed asleep or sitting up with a fag. When she does get up she puts on her nightgown and disappears inside it. Her face is pale and she's thinner than me now. While she sleeps I sit on the chair and look out of the window. The rain slaps against it, tree branches blow this way and that.

Sometimes I light myself a cigarette; watch the red tip glow around the edges. I like to put it to my lips, but the taste makes me feel sick. It gives me something else to think about, instead of the worry that my mum isn't going to get better.

Carmel gets the doctor out. He says it's delayed shock and nervous exhaustion. She needs plenty of rest. 'Look after her,' he says to me before he leaves. 'She needs to ditch the cigarettes.'

'Don't worry,' Carmel says. 'We'll look after her.'

Back upstairs she lies on her back, eyes closed. Her hair greasy on the pillow. Her breath comes in short and shallow and wheezy.

I sit on the edge of the bed. 'You okay?' I ask, whispering into the darkness.

She nods. 'Know fuck all, doctors,' she says. 'Rest, that's all I need.'

Mum doesn't go back to the chippy to work. After school I help Carmel with the little ones and cook with her in the kitchen. She calls me her one-armed bandit. She shows me how to make apple crumble and roast potatoes. Carmel doesn't mention Dad or what happened that night, neither does Mum. Carmel says I'm not to worry about anything because, apart from Nan and Margy, nobody else knows where we are. The air is full of things not spoken. It wears me out, not being able to ask questions.

Carmel keeps checking on Mum. She brings her scrambled eggs and cups of tea. Carmel asks me what her favourite chocolate is and I say Fry's with the white stuff inside. I run to the shop and buy her two bars. Carmel places it on a Christmas paper napkin folded into a triangle. It reminds me of Nan's scarf.

Carmel explains to the people at the council that Mum isn't well. She asks them to hold onto the keys a while longer for us; she even sends a letter off the doctor to prove it. The reply she gets back was they had a waiting list and they had to be fair to everybody.

One Saturday afternoon Margy comes with the kids. I mind them in the front of the house while Margy goes upstairs to see Mum. I play with them; not shake the bed with my arm, but hide and seek. It's getting dark when Margy comes back downstairs with my mum. Mum wears a blue dress with pink roses on it and pink lipstick. She links Margy's arm. I look at her and swallow hard. It's as though something in me is alive again. She takes ages getting down the stairs. Margy walks her into the kitchen; from inside I can hear Carmel squeal.

Margy comes to the hostel every other night. I can see the colour come back in Mum's cheeks. Margy's kids make the front garden into a den. I help them with bits of wood and old cushions, tell them stories I make up.

Carmel shakes her head. 'I'd never make a nurse,' she says. 'Not with patients as stubborn as your mum. She's been down to the council yelling at them to give her a place. So my guess is you should hear something very soon.' Carmel smiles. 'Let's face it, they won't want another visit from her in a hurry.'

Me and Carmel get to talk a lot more. I tell her about Angela and how I stole the vanity case. And about the morning she asked me to get Mrs O'Connor a present. I don't tell her about sleeping in a bin shed, or about my real dad and Mrs Naylor. I want to meet Robert Naylor some day to tell him I don't blame him for the way things turned out. I don't blame him for anything.

After the doctor takes the cast off it looks like my arm has shrunk. It's shrivelled and crinkly and feels cold. It's good to be able to move it without the weight. When we leave the hospital I hold my arm close to me in case I walk by someone or something that I might bump into. I miss the grubby cast that felt like armour.

'I can show you my house,' I say to Carmel, 'when we get it.'

'And you can get the bus here and see me any time you like.'

It all sounds so easy, I wonder if it'll really turn out like that. Maybe it won't and I wouldn't be shocked by that. Back in Tommy Whites there came a moment when I felt okay about dying; it was something I didn't have to choose. I even felt glad to be getting it over with. In that moment I didn't feel scared any more. I felt safe with it. I somehow knew things were going to be okay, whatever happened.

I look at Carmel and say, 'I'd like that.'

34

It's Friday and Mum says I can have the day off school. Outside, the morning is clear. The sky is full of big fuzzy-haired clouds, which remind me of a stage full of clowns. I see a blue car parked outside the hostel. It is a blue I want to hold onto inside my head, a perfect shade of blue that has probably fallen from the sky. I walk with a bounce in my step, excited about what's happening today. I hear the sound of my shoes on concrete. We're getting the keys to our own place today. I breathe in the cold air, let it go again. In my mind I can see an orange balloon loop in and out of trees.

When we get the key I ask Mum if I can hold it. Inside my coat pocket I trace the hilly rise of metal with my thumb, feel the ups and downs, like fast waves on the edge of the Mersey.

Sitting on the bus I imagine the new house, my feet on the step, the sound my knuckles will make on the front door. The sound of somebody else's knock; Nan's maybe, a snazzy little tap made up to match her mood.

When we get there Nan is waiting on the step. I run to her and hug her. She kisses my cheeks. 'It's a straight bus ride from mine to here,' she tells us.

'How's the reading, Nan?'

'Slow, love. Very, very, slow.'

'But you like it?'

'Ah well, I'm trying to. I like you reading better.'

Mum walks on ahead, opens the door and we step inside.

It is a proper house not a flat. Mum says it's called a two-up-two-down. In my bedroom I look out of the window and see a small back yard. Downstairs I open the back door and sniff up. It smells of bleach. In the small living room Nan tells me I can have the furry rug from beside her bed because it keeps slipping on her floor. Me, Nan and Mum walk in and out of rooms and up and down the stairs and Mum says, 'I wonder who had this place before us?'

I don't want to think about who lived here before. I make up my mind to believe this place was built for us and we're the first people ever to live here.

All three of us end up in the living room. Mum's over by the window taking out a cigarette.

'Robyn says you're courting,' Mum says.

'Eddie? He's a laugh. That's all I want now, to be able to laugh. Men are useful for that, for wanting to give a girl a good time.'

Nan looks across the room at Mum, who strikes a match. Nan says, 'Not all of them.'

I know we have left our old life behind, but Mum carries a new sadness with her. She doesn't suit being on her own. She still has me, but I don't think I'll be enough.

Nan says, 'I got the shock of my life when I opened the door to the Bobbies. They told me what had happened. I knew he had a badness in him. But you know I did . . .'

Mum looks at Nan then turns away. 'Here we fucking go,' she says to herself.

Mum lights her cigarette, shakes the match dead. 'You must be in your apple cart with all this,' she says to Nan. 'Go on then, don't keep me waiting too long for the I told you sos, I rush into things, give up on things too easily.'

The silence in the room makes my bones feel heavy, like sleep does. I think about how Lizzie had given up the last time I saw her, rushed into throwing me away.

'I bet you're glad they've put him away,' Nan says.

Mum doesn't answer.

'Eddie saw it in the paper. You're not the first woman he's assaulted.'

Her words are like knives poking away at rotten meat. I don't want these walls to hear them; don't want the stink to follow us here.

Through the window a child's face looks straight at us. He doesn't do anything, just gawps. He must be about six years old, in a grey V-neck jumper over a white shirt, orange hair. One side of the collar hangs behind him, the other too far in front. He tilts his head back, crusty green snot clogs up one of his nostrils.

The three of us stare at him, then stare back at each other, and back at him again. He doesn't do anything except gawp. And the talk about prison and hate rolls away.

Mum shakes her head at him and says, 'Beat it, you.'

He doesn't move, carries on gawping.

'Can he see us?' I ask.

'He can see us all right.' Nan calls him a cheeky so-and-so. There is something about the way his hair is sticking up. It is Mum who starts the laughing. She looks over at me, shakes her head, laughs louder. Nan starts next, then me. We stare back at this little lad and it's like he's made of stone: he doesn't move, or smile, or speak, or do anything but gawp.

'Look at him, not a worry in the world,' Mum says.

If I never had a worry in the world I'd probably worry about that. I wonder if there's a way to let go of them all.

'Lucky sod,' Mum says.

Once the front door is open, I watch the little lad leg it away from the window down the street. I can see the river, feel the breeze on my face. Across the street, people sit on steps and look in our direction. Nan stands on the pavement. Mum's on the step next to me.

'He'll have no visitors while he's in there,' Nan says, 'and nowhere to live once he gets out.'

She looks at Mum. Mum says nothing.

'Babs?'

Mum's looking at the ground.

There's no word answer, not even a look answer.

Nan gives me a hug, tells me to come down to her flat whenever I like, then walks away.

'Where's Nan going?'

'How should I know?'

Mum goes back inside the house to check all the doors are closed. Upstairs, I take another look through my bedroom window. I can see into other yards. Washing lines full of other people's secrets. I lift the window up easily, stoop down and stick my head out. Behind me Mum strikes a match, lights another cigarette. 'You ready?'

'Where are we going?'

'No more questions. Make sure that window's locked.'

There's room in here for a writing desk. Light wood. Carmel says light colours put people in a good mood. I think of the black paint that covers everything inside our old flat. Back in Tommy Whites somebody new will be shown around flat 33B.

Somebody I might never meet who will ask why everything is painted black. Somebody I might never meet will hear our story from a stranger.

I don't want Bernie to hear about it from a stranger. I'd like to tell him myself. I think he'll be made up when he finds out things have worked out okay for me. I'll wait for him by the phone box on Monday. Tell him to let Sylvia know I'm all right, and, at last, we've got a chance of something better, just me and my mum.

Back at the hostel, I sit on Carmel's step, bags between my legs, waiting for Mum to fetch her stuff. I can hear the groan of our taxi's engine beyond the front gate. I show two little lads how to make paper aeroplanes. At first they are excited and keen to have a go. Then they try to copy me but get all muddled up and angry with themselves. I end up doing most of it for them.

When the planes are finished the boys carry them over to the grass. On tiptoes they try to get them to fly over a bush. Knees bent, arms stretched towards the sky, they try again and again but the wind keeps blowing them back to where they started.

Acknowledgements

I would like to thank Alan Mahar, my editor, and Emma Hargrave and everyone at Tindal Street Press. Special thanks to Alicia Stubbersfield, for her insight and encouragement. And to Jim Friel, for his continued support. Thanks to Mike Morris at Writing on the Wall, for all his help. To Madeline and Robyn, and to Paul and everyone involved in the Pulp Idol competition, for their belief in this novel from day one.

Love and thanks to Mary and Bob. To John, Antonia, John, Patrick and Joel, and to James. To Lisa, Shaun and Callum, Jim, Michael and Stephen. To Libby Mackay for being my teacher and my best friend. To so many writers and friends who have been supportive, especially Mandy Redvers-Rowe and Catherine Selby, Jenny Newman and Dave Evans. I owe warm thanks to Dora and Tommy, Mary and Peter, Rita, Joan, Audrey, Doreen, Angie and Dawn. Finally, thanks to the staff at Frankie's for finding me a quiet corner to work in.